THE
BELLINGHAM
BLOODBATH

D0563501

Books by Gregory Harris

THE ARNIFOUR AFFAIR

THE BELLINGHAM BLOODBATH

Published by Kensington Publishing Corporation

THE
BELLINGHAM
BLOODBATH

A Colin Pendragon Mystery

GREGORY HARRIS

KENSINGTON BOOKS
www.kensingtonbooks.com

KENSINGTON BOOKS are published by

Kensington Publishing Corp.
119 West 40th Street
New York, NY 10018

Copyright © 2014 by Gregory Harris

All rights reserved. No part of this book may be reproduced in any form or by any means without the prior written consent of the Publisher, excepting brief quotes used in reviews.

All Kensington titles, imprints, and distributed lines are available at special quantity discounts for bulk purchases for sales promotion, premiums, fund-raising, educational, or institutional use.

Special book excerpts or customized printings can also be created to fit specific needs. For details, write or phone the office of the Kensington Special Sales Manager: Kensington Publishing Corp., 119 West 40th Street, New York, NY 10018. Attn. Special Sales Department. Phone: 1-800-221-2647.

Kensington and the K logo Reg. U.S. Pat. & TM Off.

eISBN-13: 978-0-7582-9270-4
eISBN-10: 0-7582-9270-8
First Kensington Electronic Edition: September 2014

ISBN-13: 978-0-7582-9269-8
ISBN-10: 0-7582-9269-4
First Kensington Trade Paperback Printing: September 2014

10 9 8 7 6 5 4 3 2 1

Printed in the United States of America

For my parents, David and Jane . . .
two extraordinary people

CHAPTER 1

One of Her Majesty's coaches was waiting to whisk us off to Buckingham Palace. We had only just been told about the killing of a captain in Her Majesty's Life Guard and his wife, and were being summoned, presumably, to solve their murders. The sergeant they'd sent for us had made it sound like an ugly business indeed.

I stared across the room with a mixture of dread and morbid curiosity as I watched Colin continue to fiddle with one of his derringers. Surely he meant for us to leave . . . yet there he sat, painstakingly wiping every centimeter of the little gun until I could finally stand it no longer: "What the bloody hell are you doing?"

He looked up at me with an inconceivably guileless expression. "What?"

"Buckingham . . . ?!" I blurted as though speaking to someone quite undone. "The sergeant who came to fetch us is waiting outside . . ."

"I know," he answered simply.

"Well, are we going?"

"The sergeant's a pompous little twit. He can wait."

"He's an officer of Her Majesty's Life Guard—"

"I don't care if he's having it off with the old girl herself; let him wait. Be good to teach him some manners."

"So we're back in school then?" I parried just as a loud and insistent pounding burst up from the door downstairs.

"See what I mean," Colin grumbled.

"I'm sure he's only trying to follow orders. He wasn't sent here to polish the cobbles pacing."

A second pounding, even more determined, brought Colin to his feet. "If he does that again I shall go down there and shove my boot up his orders."

"No doubt Mrs. Behmoth will beat you to it," I said as the sound of her lumbering from the kitchen to the front door drifted up among her curses. I was certain she would roundly upbraid the young sergeant the moment she got the door open, but no such diatribe ensued. Instead I heard the voice of our elderly neighbor curl up the stairs. "It's Mrs. Menlo," I said with little enthusiasm.

"And what is she complaining about now?" He shook his head as he set his derringer onto the mantel. "Is the soldier out front giving her vapors?"

"I should think she's trying to wheedle information out of Mrs. Behmoth. You know how she despises not knowing our business."

"Yes . . ." He snatched up his dumbbells and began curling them over his head. "And I'm sure we could cause her a good deal of apoplexy with some of the things we get up to." He snickered. "For the moment, however, I believe it's time we learned something about this poor captain and his wife. We mustn't show up at the major's office completely unawares."

I stared at the stack of unread newspapers beside the hearth as he continued to train the already-taut muscles of his arms. "Fine," I exhaled. "Let me see what I can find of it."

"Excellent," he muttered, dropping to the floor and busting out a set of push-ups on his dumbbells.

Turning my attentions back to the pile of papers, I was relieved when my search proved brief. Stretched across the morning edition of yesterday's paper was a banner that cried: *QUEEN'S CAPTAIN AND WIFE BUTCHERED IN BLOODBATH*. I read the article aloud while Colin continued his fevered push-ups, and it was only after I finished that he finally sat up, ran a sleeve across his sweating forehead, and asked me to read it again. This time he listened.

"Sometime during the night of Sunday last, Captain Trevor Bellingham, 32, of the Queen's Life Guard, and his wife, Gwendolyn, 29, were brutally murdered in the Finchley Road flat they shared with their young son. Miraculously, the young boy, just past his fifth birthday, was found unharmed in his bedroom. Police had to break the boy's door down, as it had been wedged tight, almost certainly by the murderer, though one source close to the investigation suggested that one of the parents may have secured the door in order to save their son.

"Mrs. Bellingham was reported to have been shot and killed in her bedroom, but Scotland Yard has yet to release the cause of death for Captain Bellingham, stating that the matter was still under investigation." I glanced over to where Colin remained sitting on the floor. "I wonder why the secrecy?"

"We shall have to find out."

"Police did state that there did not appear to be any signs of forced entry, pointing to the possibility that the killer may have been known to Captain and Mrs. Bellingham. Scotland Yard's Inspector Emmett Varcoe"—I read his name enunciating it with mock esteem—*"assures that everything possible is being done to solve this terrible crime against one of the Queen's own men and his young wife. However, the* Times *would like to remind its readership that Inspector Varcoe is the same investigator who*

remains befuddled by the identity of the vicious killer known only as Jack the Ripper."

"It all sounds rather odd," Colin muttered as he stood up and hurried off toward our bedroom, "though a spot-on summation of Varcoe. He should have retired a decade ago."

"That he should . . . ," I agreed as Colin returned with his straw-colored hair slicked back and our coats over his arms.

"Shall we . . . ?"

Twenty minutes later the carriage that had been awaiting us swung around the drive of Buckingham Palace and once again I was struck by how austere and remote it looked. Partially colonnaded in the Federalist style, it appears like neither a true palace nor a home. Sprawling behind its massive bronze and iron fencing with a contingency of guards precisely stationed across its front, it seems very much to be holding itself with the same reserve as our Queen.

I took note of the lone Union Jack on the roof and knew Victoria was not in residence. Her colors would be flying atop Sandringham this time of year, though even if she had been here I knew it would have made little difference. One does not happen upon Her Majesty in the hallways. Nevertheless, it would have been the closest I had ever come to royalty.

The coachman brought us alongside the gates and slowed almost to a stop as they began to swing inward at the behest of our escort, Sergeant McReedy. We were ushered through and driven across the parade grounds to the far side of the building under the watchful eyes of a throng of spectators.

"They must think us special." I chuckled.

"We are," Colin murmured as he surreptitiously squeezed my hand.

"Perhaps so, but they'll still be disappointed when we climb out."

He laughed as I turned to watch the stiff-postured guards

we were clattering past with their blazing red jackets and high bearskin hats. They ignored us as we went by, none so much as moving his eyes to follow our progress. "You can always count on this lot to put us in our place," Colin said.

Before I could answer we came to an abrupt stop and both doors were immediately swept open. Sergeant McReedy dismounted and led us through a side portico and down a hallway of unremarkable design that I decided no royal had ever passed along. Tiny offices lined both sides, providing the only contrast in the otherwise stark space. It was hardly what I had expected until I reminded myself that these were the niches of those who kept the palace functioning; what use did they have for moldings, ormolu, filigree, or even art?

The sergeant stopped at an office near the end of the corridor and barked out, "Colin Pendragon and Ethan Pruitt!"

An alabaster-skinned young man who looked too young to be in the service sat behind a small desk in the anteroom to a much larger office. "Oh . . . ," he said with notable surprise as Colin and I walked in. "Oh . . . ," he repeated as his eyes fell on me before quickly shifting back to Colin. "It's a pleasure to meet you, Mr. Pendragon," he said, holding out his hand. "I'm Major Hampstead's attaché, Corporal Bramwood." His gaze drifted in my direction again and I knew what was coming. "I am terribly sorry . . . ," he said coolly, ". . . but there seems to have been a misunderstanding." He looked back at Colin. "The summons from Major Hampstead was meant for you, Mr. Pendragon, and you alone."

"Ah . . . then there has indeed been a misunderstanding." Colin offered a smile. "I'm afraid I don't work alone, Corporal. You and your major will take us together or you will settle for my regrets."

Corporal Bramwood opened his mouth to say something, but nothing came out. I saw him glance behind me to where

Sergeant McReedy remained in the doorway and then heard the sound of the sergeant moving off. This young man was apparently on his own.

"Have a seat . . . have a seat . . . ," he mumbled quickly. "I shall let Major Hampstead know you are *both* here." He gave an awkward nod before disappearing through the door behind his desk, making sure it latched firmly behind him.

"This lot seems to think they're all ordained by God," Colin muttered as he sat down.

I snickered. "I don't think that young corporal is used to having his major's orders countermanded."

"I was civil about it," Colin blithely protested.

Before I could say anything more the inner door burst open and Corporal Bramwood hurried out with an older man at his heels. "Mr. Pendragon . . . Mr. Pruitt!" he sputtered. "This is Major Hampstead."

The major stepped forward, a tall man somewhere in his late fifties with a generous middle. He wore a thick white mustache and sported huge sideburns that fanned out several inches along his jawline. His deportment suggested he had been a leader most of his life: ramrod straight with a swagger of marked self-assurance. "It is an honor to meet you, gentlemen," he said, and I knew he was also a diplomat.

"It is always a pleasure to meet one of Her Majesty's lifers." Colin smiled.

Major Hampstead snorted a laugh. "I should doubt the son of Her Majesty's emissary to India is so easily impressed. I would say your father has given nearly the whole of his life in service to her."

"He has." Colin flashed a tight grin. "But the life of a diplomat hardly compares to the work of a regimental guard. You mustn't give my father too much credit."

"I doubt that I am," he chortled. "Please come in, gentlemen. Tea, Corporal," he ordered before retreating back to his office and seating himself behind his massive desk.

Corporal Bramwood brought in a tray of tea and biscuits with a speed that conveyed just how much time he spent in that endeavor. The straining seams along the sides of the major's red tunic also attested to that fact. "I appreciate your willingness to come here without the slightest notice," he said. "I'm afraid I have a very difficult matter to discuss. One that requires the utmost discretion."

"You are referring to the murder of that captain and his wife?"

The major winced. "I am. It's an awful business that has been made even more unseemly by the newspapers heralding it the way they've done."

"I'm afraid our countrymen are always keen for a scandal."

"Which is precisely my point." I could see him relax a bit at Colin's pronouncement. "The Queen's Guard simply *cannot* be party to any such scandal. It is inappropriate and unacceptable."

"That may be, but it would appear it is already done."

The major knit his brow. "I would venture otherwise, Mr. Pendragon. I have asked you here because I believe you can do a great deal to help us staunch this damage. You can impact the public record to not only cease the gossip concerning this very private, very regrettable event, but to allow *us* to deal with it ourselves, outside of the public's lecherous purview."

"Us . . . ?"

"The Guard, of course."

"I see," Colin said even as his own brow creased a notch. "You have summoned us here to divert the newsmen while you and your regiment, untrained in such things, attempt to solve these murders?"

"It is the Guard's business and should be handled as such."

"It is the murder of two British subjects, Major Hampstead, one of whom was in service to the Queen. I'm quite certain the public will remain very concerned about it until it is resolved. The inference being, of course, that the very men prescribed with protecting Her Majesty cannot even protect themselves. Trying to steal this behind the public's eye will be quite impossible, Major. Unless, of course, you are trying to hide something . . . ?"

"Hide something . . . ?!" His face creased into a scowl. "I trust you are being facetious, Mr. Pendragon."

"I've been accused of worse," he muttered.

"Let me assure you that my request comes only out of concern for Her Majesty's Guard," the major said in a tone as filled with condescension as assurance. "The first lesson a man learns when he enlists is that it is not about the individual, but the regiment. Every man who serves under Victoria's banner understands that."

"While I'm sure that's true," Colin allowed with a tightening smile as he fished a crown out of his pocket and began effortlessly weaving it between the fingers of his right hand, "I don't see how it is relevant."

"Then you are missing my point," the major sniped. "The Queen's regiment has a prestige to uphold and cannot afford to be mired down in such things. This Bellingham situation is anathema to everything the Guard represents."

Colin instantly palmed the crown. "Do I understand you correctly, Major? Do you presume to speak for the Queen with such rhetoric?"

"Now Mr. Pendragon"—he exhaled deeply before popping a biscuit into his mouth—"you misunderstand me. Captain Bellingham was one of my most trusted leaders and a man I considered a personal friend. No one in this company is more determined to bring the perpetrator of his murder to justice than I. And I had the utmost respect and adoration for his lovely wife. A kind and wonderful woman whose senseless killing demands all the resources at the Guard's disposal. Yet even so, decorum dictates that it *must* be done with discretion. You said yourself that the public will have no faith in our Guard if they perceive that we cannot even fend for ourselves. I'm sure I do not need to remind you that Her Majesty's Life Guard represents the finest of our country's protectors and as such cannot bear so much as a *whiff* of scandal. This matter *will* be solved by this regiment, but we shall do it *outside* of the gaze of the common masses."

"The common masses?" One of Colin's eyebrows arched up. "Does Victoria encourage her Guard to look down on the very people God has granted her the authority to rule?"

"Mr. Pendragon . . . ," he started to say, only to fall silent. The ticking of the small clock on the major's credenza was the only sound to be heard for several seconds until Colin began to coax the coin between his fingers again. I started to wonder if we weren't about to be dismissed, but I had miscalculated the major. Quite suddenly, without the slightest hint that it was coming, he abruptly let out a bellowing laugh. "You are toying with me, Mr. Pendragon. You mean to prod me into a rise and you almost succeeded. But I shall not be so easily dissuaded." He leaned forward. "I'd bet you would like to see the Bellingham flat for yourself. There is much the newspapers have not reported. Much they do not know."

A cool smirk overtook Colin's face. "And now you are toying with me."

"So I am." He leaned back in his chair with a satisfied smile. "You must understand my position, Mr. Pendragon. Anything concerning the Queen's Guard inevitably implicates our sovereign as well. And I'm sure I needn't remind you that Her Majesty is seventy-seven and in failing health."

"That woman is as delicate as a plow horse," he shot back. "And I find it hard to believe she has any but the most passing familiarity concerning the murder of one of her guardsmen with whom she probably never once spoke. I believe you are trying to hide behind her skirts, Major."

"Do you presume to be privy to what goes on in Her Majesty's household?"

"My father transferred John Brown from Victoria's stable to her personal duty after Albert's death, so I would say I know a bit more about Her Majesty's household than you think. What I don't understand is why you want to bring me here to feed nonsense to the press? I don't control those men."

"You underestimate yourself, Mr. Pendragon. They hang on your words like they are spun from gold." A cloying smile clung to his lips. "If you were to release a statement that you had conducted an investigation and determined the case to be closed, say a burglary gone bad, or a case of mistaken identity, why, they would be only too happy to embrace your conclusion and return their attentions to the horses at Ascot and which lady is wearing what. Everyone would be satisfied, which would allow me and my men to handle this case with the delicacy Captain Bellingham and his wife deserve."

"And the perpetrator?"

"I will personally see to it that their murderer receives the full wrath of the law."

Colin sat up and neatly tipped the crown back into his vest pocket. "And what makes you think these murders will be so easily dispatched? Murder is a complex business in the simplest of cases—"

"I said I will take care of it," the major repeated with noticeably greater force. "And I could use your help with Scotland Yard. I've got them circling like schoolyard boys, on top of which the *Times* is calling the Guard's reputation into question, and the public is terrified for their safety. Until we can release a conclusive statement, Mr. Pendragon, this discord will be relentless."

Colin stood up. "I'm sorry, Major. You seem to have gotten the notion that my integrity can be bargained for. If I have earned the respect of the press it is because I do not spin fables, and, in spite of your desire for discretion, cannot see why I should start now. If you would like to hire me to solve this case I will gladly do so, but until you come to your senses I will bid you good day." He turned for the door.

"Mr. Pendragon!" The major sounded perplexed as I got up to follow. *"Mr. Pendragon!"* he howled as we reached the door. "With all due respect to your esteemed integrity, the public wants immediate answers to their fears. They want the world to return to the status quo. They will not tolerate remaining under a veil of anxiety. You can blame the unsolved Ripper murders for that. And *that's* why there are men like you and me. To ensure that our republic gets what it needs. Now I am beseeching you, Mr. Pendragon, to offer the public a reasoned solution to a horrible crime so that they can get on with the mundanity of their lives. Where is the harm in that?"

"If that's what you're after, Major, then I would suggest you get the Yard to be your mouthpiece. Inspector Varcoe is always good for hot air."

"Nobody wants to hear from that blasted lout. You *will* do this for me, Mr. Pendragon. You are the only man with the reputation for it and I *will* insist."

"Insist?" Colin chuckled. "Are you proposing sticking a hand up my bum to move my lips?"

"You will be handsomely compensated. Now how can I convince you to perform this service for the Crown?"

Colin pursed his lips and I could tell he had already thought of something. "There is one way I can conceive . . . ," he said casually, ". . . and it is the *only* way I would consider it. . . ." He let a moment pass to emphasize his determination. "You must announce to the press that you have retained my services to solve the murders of the captain and his wife. . . ."

"Yes . . . ?"

"And then give me the next three days to do so. During those three days you must ensure I have the full cooperation of this regiment as well as access to whomever I want."

"Not Her Majesty or her family."

"I should hardly think that will be necessary."

"And at the end of the three days . . . ?"

"I will deliver the truth of the case to you."

"And if you cannot?"

"I will." He smiled harshly, even as my stomach clutched at the very idea. I couldn't fathom how he had come up with the notion of three days.

Major Hampstead frowned. "Absolute proof, Mr. Pendragon. You must bring me absolute proof of whatever supposition you're championing or I shall have your word that you will face that mob of newsmen and sell them whatever I deem appropriate."

Colin gave no more than an ambivalent nod.

"Three days then." The major glanced back at his clock. "That would be twelve o'clock on Friday." He turned back to us. "I shall give you until seventeen hundred. Plenty of time for the newsmen to make their Saturday morning edition."

"Most generous," Colin muttered.

"*Corporal Bramwood!*"

"Sir?" The young man opened the door so quickly I knew he had to have been hovering nearby.

"Alert the newspapermen that Her Majesty's Life Guard has retained the services of Colin Pendragon to bring a swift and just conclusion to the tragic murders of Captain and Mrs. Bellingham. And let them know that Mr. Pendragon will have an announcement to make at seventeen hundred hours this very Friday."

"This Friday, sir?"

"Yes, Corporal. *This* Friday."

And with that, the young man was gone, though I did notice he left the door ajar.

"I will solve this crime, Major Hampstead," Colin said with the simplicity of one discussing the weather. "I shall bring you the resolution Friday and we will see what gets delivered to the press."

"I admire a man of confidence," the major replied with a tense grin. "But listen very carefully, Mr. Pendragon, because if, at the end of your three days, you should find yourself stymied by this case, then I *alone* will decide what is told to those newsmen. You will say what I decide and you will walk away. Are we clear?"

Colin flashed an equally rigid smile. "You have been most clear, Major. And now I should indeed like an escort to the Bellingham flat so I may get started. Someone from Captain Bellingham's regiment would be my preference."

"Sergeant McReedy will take you. He reported to the captain." Major Hampstead's smile relaxed and I couldn't help but feel it was with the arrogance that comes when one perceives imminent success.

CHAPTER 2

—»‹•›«—

I joined Colin on the parade grounds as soon as I concluded the financial details of the condensed investigation he had bound us to. My negotiations with the major had gone well considering he was only hiring us for three days, the very thought of which set my stomach lurching. Nevertheless, he had meant what he'd said with regards to making sure Colin would be well compensated.

"Are we set then?" Colin asked as I joined him beside a young private with a mop of tight, curly brown hair hugging his head.

"We are in terms of money." A pained smile was all I could come up with.

"Have faith," Colin chided as he gestured to the young man beside him. "Private Newcombe here has been tasked to wait with us while Sergeant McReedy summons a carriage. A dreary task, I should think."

"I've done worse." The private flashed a mischievous grin. "And anyway, it's a terrible thing that happened to the captain and his wife. He was a good man. I'm glad they've brought you in to set it right."

"Well . . . yes . . . after a fashion." Colin tossed him a slight smile. "But let me ask you a question. Would you say your opinion of Captain Bellingham is the common sentiment within the regiment?"

"To be sure. He was a fair and decent man. I don't know anyone who didn't get along with him."

"You think the murders random then?"

Private Newcombe's face pursed slightly as he answered, "No, sir. You'll understand when you see the flat."

"Indeed? And did you know the captain's wife?"

"Gwen? I met her a few times. She was quite something to behold. There's just no reason for what happened. No reason at all."

"There is never reason enough for murder."

The sound of an approaching horse caught our attention and we all turned. "Here comes Sergeant McReedy," the private said. And sure enough we could make out his tall, slender frame atop a stallion, cutting a striking tableau against the steel-gray sky. Once again I had the needling feeling that a smile did not come easily to his face. He was cradling his metal helmet with its white plume in the crook of one arm, exposing close-cropped black hair, which he had shaved almost to his skull. The smudge of a mustache darkened his upper lip, adding a few years to what was otherwise a decidedly youthful face.

"Thank you, Private Newcombe." He spoke without inflection as he reached us. "There's a coach waiting in the side yard. If you will . . ." He didn't wait for a response, but immediately reined his horse around and moved off.

"He's as pleasant as he was at our flat," Colin muttered.

"He's taken the captain's death hard," Private Newcombe spoke up. "Served under him his whole career."

"Which, by the look of him, cannot be very long. And why is he so averse to my being brought in?"

Private Newcombe shrugged. "Who can figure those Scottish boys? They wear melancholy like an honor."

"Are you coming?!" Sergeant McReedy bellowed without glancing back.

"Twit . . . ," Colin muttered under his breath as we followed the sergeant around to the side of the building where a small coach was waiting. The two of us climbed inside and the driver set us lurching forward without a word.

"May I trouble you with a question, Sergeant?" Colin called to him as he paced beside us. The sergeant's answer came in the form of kicks to the sides of his mount as he surged ahead. "This little pisser is starting to peeve me," Colin grumbled as he pulled a crown out of his pocket and began rolling it between his fingers.

"Come now," I halfheartedly scolded. "You handled the major well enough; you can handle this one. What I don't understand is how the hell you came up with three bloody days for the resolution."

He shrugged. "I knew the major was in a hurry and it seemed a good number."

"Three?!"

"I didn't think he would go for thirty. Have you no faith in me?"

I scowled at him. "More than you deserve, I should say."

He nodded. "Well, yes, that's probably true."

"Do you really think you'll be able to solve this case that fast?"

He let out a chuckle as the coin continued its smooth rotation around his fingers. "It would seem that I must."

I shook my head but otherwise held my tongue. With nothing more than doubt and worry to contribute I knew it was best to keep silent. I turned my attentions to the window as we clattered around a steep bend in a neighborhood far removed from the palatial grounds of Buckingham. The buildings were brick and mortar and heavily stained by the ever-present soot. They were stacked so closely together that the concentrated scent of horse and human consequence made the air itself seem in need of a scrubbing. Street vendors hawked their wares— baskets of fruits and vegetables, a selection of freshly baked breads, white and yellow bricks of cheese, sprays of flowers— enticing the scurrying crowds with a warring cacophony of shouts, songs, and entreaties to gain their attention. It was a scene of bedlam that made me aware of just how far the late captain's Finchley Road flat was from Her Majesty's palace.

As our coach slowed, Colin flicked open his pocket and tossed the crown in with a flourish before glancing at me. "Do you think you might be able to coerce the sergeant into answering a few questions? You do have the better nature. I'm afraid I'm likely to just dislocate his jaw if he doesn't come around to cooperating."

"I'll try . . . ," I said, though I was not filled with conviction.

"Good enough, then. See if you can extricate anything at all from him." Colin gave me a smile as he climbed out.

I sucked in a deep breath and took my time alighting from the coach. A private with strawberry-blond hair held the door for me, offering a clipped smile as I stepped out. He was tall, with an aquiline profile, porcelain skin, and eyes the color of honey. I pegged him a novice and decided I just might learn something from him. "Did you work for Captain Bellingham, Private?"

"I did," he answered with tight formality.

"I'm going in," Colin called as he headed for the narrow three-story row house.

"Private O'Fallon!" Sergeant McReedy snapped at the boy-ish officer before me. "Stay with Mr. Pendragon."

"Yes, sir." He moved past me as he hurried to catch up with

Colin, stopping just long enough to mutter something to the two policemen posted at the stoop.

I watched Colin and Private O'Fallon disappear inside and knew it was time to try to engage Sergeant McReedy. Steeling myself, I went over to where he sat astride his horse and shouted up, "Might I have a quick word?!"

He glared down at me. "What?"

"I know the Guard would prefer to take care of this on its own—"

"That's right," he cut me off, making to swing his horse away.

"What I don't understand is why you seem so unwilling to be of *any* assistance."

He stopped, as I had hoped he would, and turned an icy frown on me. "The Queen's Life Guard does not need the two of you to help with its business." His eyes narrowed. "You do not belong here."

"So you're questioning Major Hampstead's decision?"

"I brought you here, didn't I?"

"And are you aware of Mr. Pendragon's reputation?" I pressed, trying to curb the edge of desperation snaking into my voice. "The papers have *never* reported a failure for him." I held the sergeant's gaze, his eyes so dark they looked like black pinpoints, and hoped I had struck my mark, but all he did was lean back on his horse and coax it away from me.

I was certain he was hiding something behind his umbrage. He had some knowledge of these murders and I determined I would keep an eye on him. I stared at his grim profile, but he took no further notice of me, so I cursed him under my breath before turning and pounding past the two policemen and into the flat. Neither of them paid me a whit of heed. They undoubtedly presumed I was welcome. They had no idea how utterly I had just been dismissed.

I let the door swing shut behind me and stood a moment in unexpected silence. I had assumed I would hear Colin or his parasitic private fussing about, but there was not a sound.

The drapes in the front room had been drawn against prying eyes, leaving the room dull and shadowed. I found it unsettling as I glanced about, and doubly so when I realized how immaculate the place was. In spite of the Bellinghams' having a young son, there was nary a toy or other plaything in sight, giving the room a distinctly unused feel.

Just beyond the front room was a small and equally pristine dining area. As I moved through I noticed four framed photographs atop an old wooden buffet. The first was a large portrait of a stoic but handsome couple on their wedding day, neither nerves nor excitement evident in the least. Two smaller photographs contained portraits of their son taken when he was no more than a toddler. He had curly hair and a chubby face, but even at this sprite age he appeared to be every bit the little man. The last photo showed the three of them together and I guessed it had been taken within the last year by the looks of young Albert.

I went through to a meticulously neat kitchen that was even more compact than the dining area, giving the sense that the flat was diminishing. What made it seem even more so was the staircase that rose along the wall to my right. Whoever had designed the flat, while skimping on space, had crafted it so that the smells of morning cooking would drift up to the bedrooms above, creating an irresistible enticement to get out of bed.

I grabbed the balustrade and made my way upstairs, girding myself for the remnants of the murders I knew I would find. As I reached the landing I found myself in the center of a small hallway that led off to three rooms, one of which had its door closed. Another staircase rose above me and I presumed it led to the attic. With any luck, I wouldn't have to go up there. Attics, with their dusty trunks and boxes full of fading lifetimes, have never appealed to me. It would be enough to stay down here.

The first room I approached had no door at all, and I remembered reading in the paper how the police had been forced to break the door to Albert's room down. When I reached the yawing doorway I spotted cracks in the molding and a ragged split where the latching mechanism should have been. The door itself, however, was nowhere to be seen.

I gazed into the small room and could tell at once that it belonged to a boy. There was a desk opposite that was cluttered with books, toy soldiers, and miniature dinosaurs. A nearby bookcase held a handful of little silver trophies and colorful ribbons proclaiming skills in calisthenics. Alongside were several softballs and a slightly worn leather glove. Only the bed revealed that something had gone terribly wrong, for it stood askew, most likely yanked from the wall in an effort to get at the little boy cowering beneath. No doubt some bobby had thought that the right idea, but I knew it would be a moment that would never again leave Albert's recall.

I had become so engaged with my thoughts that it took me a moment to realize that someone was trudging up the stairs. The rhythm of the tread assured me that whoever was coming was in no particular hurry, allowing me enough time to creep out of Albert's room and peer over the balustrade. I spotted an oval head with short, spiky black hair and saw that it capped a man of slight build in the uniform of Her Majesty's Life Guard.

"Hello," I called down.

A boyish face glanced up with all the guile of a pup. "Hello." He tossed me a smile. "Sergeant McReedy asked me to escort you through the flat." Or, more specifically, to keep an eye on me. I stuck out my hand and introduced myself.

"Corporal Hayward Blevins," he responded. "Captain Bellingham's aide-de-camp."

"I appreciate your willingness to show me around, Corporal," I said gamely. "I must confess to knowing little of what happened."

He nodded but held his silence, making me fear he was yet another guardsman loath to speak.

"The Bellinghams' bedroom is there," he announced after a moment, pointing toward a polished door some twenty feet away that I wasn't at all sure I had the temerity to go through.

"Is that where the captain and his wife were found?"

"Just Mrs. Bellingham. The captain was in the attic." My stomach curdled like milk. "You can go in," Corporal Blevins muttered, assuming, I suppose, that I had been waiting for him to tell me to do so.

"Yes," I heard myself reply with a noticeable lack of enthusiasm as I forced myself forward. I passed a compact bathroom with sparkling white tiles and porcelain fixtures, reminding me yet again of just how lovingly this flat had been maintained. Without particularly meaning to I stopped at the bedroom door and stared at the highly polished recessed panels with their circular grain visible within a warm sheen of oily wax. The meticulous attention of Mrs. Bellingham was everywhere.

Knowing Corporal Blevins must be wondering what I was doing, I finally reached out and twisted the cut-glass knob, pushing the door open with less determination than would ordinarily have been natural. As the room slowly revealed itself, a bed came into view, the covers appearing to be in a natural state of disarray until the far side was exposed. Here the blankets had been carelessly heaved asunder, no doubt by the coroner's extracting Gwendolyn Bellingham, leaving a large, rust-colored stain splashed across the pillow. It was obvious she had not been meant to survive.

A heavy *thud* on the staircase rattled me and sent me back out to the hallway, where I was surprised to find Sergeant McReedy bounding up. His face was grim and I wondered if

Major Hampstead had countermanded his orders of cooperation when I caught sight of a mane of white hair trailing in
McReedy's wake. Inspector Emmett Varcoe of Scotland Yard
bobbed into view hard on his heels.

"Where's Pendragon?" Sergeant McReedy's eyes shifted
from me to Private Blevins, who had snapped to attention.

"I haven't found him yet," I answered. "I suppose he is in
the attic."

"Right!" McReedy snapped, rounding the landing and continuing up.

Inspector Varcoe glared at me as he hurried past. "Don't you
touch *anything*, Pruitt," he seethed.

I held my tongue as I fell in line behind his accompanying
bobby as they ascended the narrow attic stairs. Corporal Blevins
did not follow but remained where he was and, I guessed, would
continue to do so until he received a command to do otherwise. I
glanced up and watched as Sergeant McReedy shoved his weight
against the attic door and barreled inside.

"The inspector demands a word," I heard him say as I
rushed up. Sergeant McReedy, Inspector Varcoe, and his dour
escort were standing in a broad semicircle around Colin and
Private O'Fallon. They looked like they were surrounding
their prey and I could see that Colin, the sergeant, and Varcoe
were indeed sizing one another up.

I took the opportunity to glance about and was amazed by
the number of boxes piled along the walls all the way to the exposed beams of the ceiling. Each was carefully marked: baby
clothes (boy), holiday ornaments, old clothes, linens, dishes,
winter things, and so many more that I could not begin to take
them all in. Half a dozen large trunks stood on my right with
several well-used travel cases. Yet even though this was a place
for storage, just as with the rest of the flat, it was immaculately
maintained. There was no film of dust across any surface or

aging grime marring the small, round window at the far end of the space. All of which conspired to make the scene at the center of the room that much more gruesome.

A straight-backed chair stood oddly canted, segregated from the neatly assembled artifacts nearby. Short coils of roughly hacked rope were haphazardly scattered about the chair's legs and there was a dark umber stain on the floor beneath it, demarcated in a great, violent spray. A large swath extended out behind the chair in what looked to be more than four feet in diameter. Even as I tried to process the sheer brutality, I noticed a horde of burnt matchsticks tossed about the base of the chair, caught in the viscous burgundy offal.

"*You*, sir . . . ," Inspector Varcoe bellowed at Colin, ". . . *are standing in the middle of a crime scene being investigated by Scotland Yard!*"

"I am here at the invitation of Her Majesty's Life Guard," he answered with remarkable restraint.

The inspector's normally translucent face purpled. "I don't give a piss, Pendragon. I haven't agreed to allow rabble off the street in here."

"Rabble, is it?" Colin exhaled blithely.

"*Officer!*" Varcoe barked as he wheeled on the young bobby he had brought with him. "Remove this interloper *at once.*"

"I don't think Major Hampstead will be pleased to hear you have thrown me off a case he has hired me to assist with."

"I don't give a bloody wank what he thinks." He turned and glared at his supplicant. "*Now, Officer!*"

"Just a moment, Inspector." Sergeant McReedy shifted his weight, allowing his tall, ramrod bearing to overtake everyone in the room by several inches. "*I* happen to care what Major Hampstead thinks. And if he wants Mr. Pendragon here, then I will ask you not to interfere unless I receive orders instructing otherwise."

Varcoe's face transcended to a black shade of plum as he whirled on the sergeant. "This is a Scotland Yard investigation, you little tosser! It falls under *my* jurisdiction."

"It is the murder of a guardsman and his wife," the sergeant brusquely corrected. "And Her Majesty views that as an attack on her own personage. So while Mr. Pendragon is in the employ of this regiment, you had best consider him a direct representative of our sovereign."

"You do *not* mean that."

"I do," Sergeant McReedy said simply. "He stays. You will not interfere with the Queen's business unless I receive orders from Major Hampstead. Make no mistake, Inspector, I can have you and your man forcibly removed."

Varcoe sucked in a long, reedy breath before abruptly spinning on his heels. "We shall see about that, Sergeant," he fumed, and then disappeared down the stairs, his uniformed escort fumbling behind in his wake.

Colin pursed his lips as he turned back to the single chair and its bloodied carnage. "It's not likely to take long for him to come back with the authority he'll need to permanently expel us, so I suggest we waste no time."

"This is the Queen's business," the sergeant repeated with the earnestness of one who has not yet fully realized the subtleties of Parliament.

"And so it is . . . ," Colin replied absently, kneeling behind the chair and poking at one of the frayed pieces of rope with the end of a small knife he'd pulled from his pocket. "But with Victoria at Sandringham, that lot of Yarders will have stomped this scene to uselessness before you can come up with a royal decree forbidding their intrusion. They *are* still the standard-bearers." He plucked one of the spent matches out of the coagulated smear with a pair of tweezers and carefully rotated it in front of his eyes. "Tell me, Sergeant, how were these matches used against Captain Bellingham?"

"He was burned with them."

Colin glanced up at the sergeant and flatly muttered, "Yes." He dropped the match into his handkerchief and plucked up another. "But *where* was he burned?"

Sergeant McReedy hesitated, and before he answered I knew what he was going to say. "His thighs and abdomen." He paused. "And his groin."

Colin ceased poking about long enough to look up. I could see a fire behind his eyes and suspected this information had not come entirely as a surprise to him. "Anywhere else . . . ?" His voice gave nothing away.

"You'll have to ask the coroner."

Colin stood up. "Of course. And might I trouble you to show me the bottom of your boot?"

"Pardon?"

"Your boot. May I see the bottom of your boot?"

"Are you inferring that I am a suspect?"

Colin flashed a tight grin. "I am not a man of inferences, Sergeant. You are *absolutely* a suspect, as is every person who came into contact with the Bellinghams within the last six months. Now may I see your boot?"

The sergeant scowled as he quickly raised a boot for Colin to inspect. "Satisfied?"

He nodded. "Indeed. I have only one last question."

"And what would that be?"

"Do you have any reason to believe that your captain might have been having an affair?"

"Really, Mr. Pendragon. Captain Bellingham was my superior officer. He was a good man, a fair man, and that's all I needed to know."

"It is a simple question, Sergeant."

"It's true," Private O'Fallon abruptly spoke up. "I knew him to visit a Lady Dahlia Stuart on several occasions. You should ask Corporal Blevins."

"That's enough, Private!" the sergeant snapped. "You will not tarnish our captain's memory with innuendo."

"Yes, sir."

"For what it's worth"—Colin moved out from behind the chair as he tucked the handkerchief with its bloodied matches into his coat pocket—"it is not my intention to denigrate anyone, only to solve these murders. The victims do not answer to me." He moved to the door and paused to study the carnage one last time before locking his eyes on me. In that instant I could see that he had already ferreted something out. There was something nestled in his gaze, if only no more than a hunch. "We are finished here," he said. "No need to see us out, Sergeant." He turned and headed down without another word.

"Thank you both," I said as I went after him, hopeful that he was right about the solution being there for the taking. I allowed a wave of optimism to lift my spirits, unaware that he had hatched a plan that would force me into a most dreadful place. And from there, it would only get worse.

CHAPTER 3

"I can tell you've already got some suspicion," I said the moment we climbed into the cab he'd hailed.

"I think you know me better than that," he answered vaguely, a glittering crown already spinning absently between his fingers.

"Meaning?"

"We're at the start of the case. Don't you think we would do ourselves a great disservice by jumping to conclusions just yet?"

"That may be," I cajoled. "But I can still tell you're considering something."

"I am considering the facts," he said with pointed finality. "So let us start with what we know. Someone arrives at the Bellingham flat late at night, late enough for Mrs. Bellingham to have already retired to bed, and yet he is granted access by the captain, as evidenced by the lack of a forced entry. That would suggest it was not only someone he knew, but knew well.

"Given that there seemed to be no sign that they dallied anywhere downstairs, I would say the captain took his visitor directly to the attic. Once there, the captain is overpowered and bound to the chair. After he is incapacitated, the perpetrator goes back downstairs and rigs young Albert's door to ensure he won't be able to open it, and then moves down the hall to the Bellinghams' bedroom, where he brazenly murders the captain's wife. She clearly had no idea what was about to happen, as she had not even gotten out of bed. Only then did the murderer go back upstairs to begin his ritualistic torture of the captain before finally, at some point, putting a bullet in his head."

"He was shot in the head . . . ?"

Colin glanced at me. "It's how he was killed. The matches . . . the burning . . . those are what the crime was about. If I can figure out their purpose, then I believe I shall know who did this."

"Why were you so intent on looking at Sergeant McReedy's boot?"

"There's a partial boot print in the blood beneath the chair. A swath that covers about three-quarters of the toe area. I wanted to see if the sergeant's boot was a match."

"And was it?!"

He nodded. "It is. But there's no telling how many guardsmen have been up there since the body was found." He resettled his gaze on the passing scenery, the coin continuing to flip smoothly between his fingers, and all I kept thinking about was how we had only three days left.

As our flat came into view I spotted a large forest-green carriage with four sidelights pulled by two roan stallions. There was a well-dressed driver perched on its top and the door had a regal-looking crest emblazoned upon it of wheat sheaves and arrow quivers. "Are we expecting someone?" I asked as Colin stuffed the crown back into his pocket.

"We are now," he said as he swung the door open and hopped out before the cab had come to a full stop.

I settled the fare quickly yet was not surprised to find that

Colin had already disappeared inside by the time I was done. With a heaved sigh, I pushed through the door, nearly barreling into Mrs. Behmoth.

"Always laggin' behind!" she groused as she stabbed her fists onto her hips. "You got a right lady up there wot needs yer 'elp on a case. She's breakin' me 'eart, so get up there with 'im and I'll fetch ya some tea."

"What case? We can't take a new case."

She narrowed her eyes as she stepped around me and stalked off to the kitchen, the swinging door her only response. I headed upstairs, knowing it would be difficult for Colin to refuse Mrs. Behmoth if she was demanding he help someone. In our nearly thirteen years together I couldn't remember her *ever* taking any sort of interest in a case. I only hoped Colin's better senses would overrule.

As I reached the landing I spied a heavyset older woman sitting on the settee across from Colin. She was outfitted in black crinoline, her wealth evident in both the volume of lace swirling about her neck and sleeves and the tiny offset hat with its black pearl lace veil that partially hid a soft, broad face. There were streaks of tears evident on the woman's face and her eyes were red rimmed, making our guest appear quite the sorrowful sight.

"Ah—" Colin jumped up as I moved around beside him. "Lady Nesbitt-Normand, may I present my partner, Ethan Pruitt. We are a package deal and you will find yourself ever the better for it."

The woman nodded and dabbed at her eyes with a handkerchief as Mrs. Behmoth came bustling back up with a tray of tea and biscuits. She shoved them at Colin before hurriedly turning back to our guest, asking after her as though we were not even there. Colin took no note of it as he fussed with the tea, dropping a lump of sugar and a healthy skosh of cream into our visitor's cup, which elicited the first sniffling words I heard her say: "May I have a bit more cream, please?"

"Of course." He started to add another dollop, but before he could right the little pitcher she leaned forward and seized the back of his hand, dumping in a good deal more. He gave an easy smile as he topped the cup with what tea he could fit before handing it to her. "There you are—"

Before she even properly grabbed the cup Mrs. Behmoth snatched up the plate of biscuits and held them out. "I make these meself."

"You're a godsend," our guest hiccupped as she patted the seat beside her. "Do sit by me. I find you such a comfort."

Mrs. Behmoth immediately slid in next to the woman and squeezed her arm. It was disconcerting, seeing our Mrs. Behmoth fuss over someone.

"I must apologize for my behavior," our guest continued in a cracked and wearied voice. "I have heard a great deal of you, Mr. Pendragon, though I never imagined that *I* would ever require your services." Her voice broke as she started to weep again. "Please forgive me—"

"You've nothing to apologize for," Colin soothed. "Take your time."

"It is the most awful thing," she went on after a moment, dragging the napkin across her eyes and leaving a gray streak of liner on one cheek. "It's the Lady Priscilla. . . ." She shook her head as she wilted against Mrs. Behmoth.

"That's awright, me dear."

Lady Nesbitt-Normand returned a feeble smile before finally managing to say, "She has been kidnapped. . . ."

"How awful." Colin leaned forward. "Is she your daughter?"

"Not as such—"

"Ah—" Colin nodded as his brow knit with a comprehension that escaped me. "Dreadful."

"She's only five and has *never* left the yard on her own before. Not ever. She's been taken. I just know someone has taken my little girl—"

"The yard . . . ?" I repeated foolishly, and even as I said it I realized what she was talking about.

"Of course," she sniffed, tossing an impatient glare at me. "She had gone out for her morning constitutional and disappeared. She is a prizewinning bitch, you know, though she's every bit a daughter to me."

"Of course she is." Colin gave a solemn nod.

"She's not just a two-time British champion; she is my pride and joy."

"Lady Priscilla . . . ," I repeated, glancing at Colin with disbelief and yet not at all surprised to see the frown blotting his face. He was forever on about our getting a dog ourselves, and perhaps I would consider it if I did not fear he would get along with it better than with anyone else.

"Lady Priscilla Elizabeth Windsor Hanover Nesbitt-Normand, to be precise." Lady Nesbitt-Normand beamed. "She is my *life*."

"Ain't ya just precious?!" Mrs. Behmoth cooed. " 'Ave another biscuit."

"You are a saint," our bereaved guest clucked as she reached out and swept up several more of the buttery treats.

"When was the last time you saw your Priscilla?" Colin asked.

"Early this morning."

"I must be honest. . . ." I cringed at what his honesty might entail. "It may be that your girl is only suffering a heat and has gone off to avail herself of the local houndage. You might wait a day and see if she doesn't come back all the better for it."

Lady Nesbitt-Normand recoiled. "She is a champion pug, Mr. Pendragon, not some street cur."

"No doubt. Nevertheless, our four-legged friends are not known for their selectivity." He stood up and moved to the fireplace, snatching up his little derringer.

"Do you mean to dismiss me, Mr. Pendragon?"

"You must understand . . . ," I cut in, worried that he might actually be considering taking the case, ". . . we've just this morning been requested to attend the Buckingham Life Guards on a matter that will preclude us from being able to do anything else for the next several days."

She popped up on the settee, her eyes bulging. "Are you referring to those awful Bellingham murders? That poor captain and his wife . . . ?" She shook her head. "Are you really to be on that case?"

"So it would seem." Colin's brow creased. "I can certainly understand your concern for your pup. I had a bulldog named Winston when I was a boy. . . ." His face lit up for a moment. "He was a scoundrel. Perhaps if you just wait a day—"

"No—" Lady Nesbitt-Normand nearly swooned. "I cannot, Mr. Pendragon. She is in peril and I can feel it in my bones." She stood up and barreled over to him. "Whatever Her Majesty's regiment is paying you, sir, I shall pay you four times as much."

"Really now . . . ," I started to protest.

She spun around and roared at me, *"Eight times!"*

"I shall do it for my regular fee." He said it so simply that I nearly didn't catch his words. "It will be my honor."

"But—" I started to say.

"I insist!" she blasted over me. "Eight times whatever the Life Guard is giving you. But you must come to my house at once."

"Of course." He set the reassembled derringer back onto the mantel. "And you are correct. In matters such as these time can make every difference—"

Lady Nesbitt-Normand swooned. "The very thought . . ." She gripped her chest as though attempting to calm her heart. "I shall go down and tell Fletcher we will be leaving at once." She started for the door but only got as far as the tea table. "Would you mind if I took a couple of these with me?" she asked Mrs. Behmoth as she stared at the remaining handful of biscuits.

"You must!" Mrs. Behmoth beamed as she wrapped them in a napkin and escorted her back to the landing. "I'm takin' this fine lady downstairs and givin' 'er the rest a the biscuits."

"You are too kind," our new client fawned as the two of them retreated.

"Those two don't need 'em anyway," I heard Mrs. Behmoth say as they disappeared from view.

"What are you thinking?" I turned on Colin the moment I heard the kitchen door swing shut. "We can't take that case. We've got these murders—"

He waved me off. "You don't know what it's like having a dog who's your best companion; trundling along beside you, adoring you, thrilled by even the faintest bit of attention. It's an indescribable gift and something you have to experience to understand."

"I have been around dogs," I protested.

"It's not the same. We can do this, Ethan. You're just going to have to trust me." He strode across the room and picked up his jacket. "Do you know if that bloke of yours . . . that Dennis Ruth . . . or Roth . . . or whatever the hell his name is, still runs the morgue?"

"Bloke of mine?!" I repeated with thick distaste. And only then did I notice the smile curling his lips.

"Is he still there?"

I frowned to be sure he knew I was not amused. "Denton Ross. Yes, he's still there. Where the hell else would someone like him go?"

"Excellent. This is just the sort of break we need if I'm to bring the Bellingham case to a successful resolution by Friday evening."

"And just what sort of break are you referring to?"

He gave me a smirk. "Why, you, my love. Given your history with the poor besotted troll, you shouldn't have any trouble getting me a copy of the autopsy report on Captain Bellingham." He chuckled, but I didn't respond in kind.

"Tell me you're not serious—"

"Well, he hates *me* and I should very much like to see that report."

"Oh, bloody hell," I exhaled. "And what about Mrs. Bellingham? Do you need to see her report as well?"

"No. I'm quite certain she's peripheral to the case. This is about Captain Bellingham." He reached into his pocket and pulled out the two spent matches from his handkerchief and studied them closely. "We must also find out about that woman Private O'Fallon mentioned. What was her name?"

"Lady Dahlia Stuart."

"Yes." He set the matches on the mantel and dropped to the floor, pacing out a dozen fast push-ups. "Everything is going to be much more difficult now that Varcoe knows we've been brought in. He's probably trying to convince some poxy magistrate to bar us from the crime scene this very minute. Even Major Hampstead could find himself castrated from the investigation once Varcoe gets finished. If that old sod were half as good at solving crimes as he is at mucking them up, we would be out of work."

"Fine," I muttered. "I'll go see Denton Ross."

"Good. You can go as soon as we've finished at Lady Nesmith-Norton's."

"Nesbitt-Normand."

"Right." He stalked to the window and stared down at the street. "And one of us is going to have to speak with young Albert Bellingham—" he tossed out as though a benign afterthought.

My heart sank. "Please don't ask me to do that."

He waved me off. "We needn't worry about that now. You

just get me that autopsy report and perhaps we won't have to bother the lad at all."

That was all I needed to hear. "I'll get it," I promised.

"Outstanding," he said as he bolted across the room and down the stairs without a backwards glance. There was no way I would fail at getting him that autopsy report. I would beg Denton Ross all afternoon if it meant I wouldn't have to speak with that boy. The thought of sitting across from him, hearing about what he saw and heard that night. The raw terror that would have gripped his throat, clawed at his insides, and set his heart pounding nearly out of his chest . . . It would bring up too many memories that I had worked too hard to keep safely packed away.

CHAPTER 4

"Please know that I realize ...," Lady Nesbitt-Normand hissed the moment she joined us in her massive library, "... that any of my staff is a potential suspect. I may treat them dearly and consider one or two almost like family, but I know better than to trust a single one." She looked at us as though we shared a clever secret. "You've a clean slate here, Mr. Pendragon. I'll not vouch for one of them." She stepped back and bellowed to a thin, elderly man who was hovering in the doorway, *"Hamilton!"* He snapped to attention. "Please have Mrs. Holloway assemble the staff in the main hall. I should like to introduce everyone to our guests."

"Right away, ma'am," he returned smartly as he took his leave.

"Hamilton has been with me since I was young. He's like a father to me," she said as she took a seat near one of the two roaring fireplaces in the room.

"He must be much older than he looks," Colin mumbled.

"What's that, Mr. Pendragon?"

He leaned forward and gave her a bright, dimpled smile. "I

certainly know how you feel, as our Mrs. Behmoth has been very much like a mother to me. The only one I've ever really known, actually."

"Such a dear woman. And quite the culinary artist. I'm afraid you are likely to find my chef quite unable to come up with anything as comforting as your woman's jam biscuits. She's a jewel, that one."

"That she is." Colin nodded, tossing me an amused glance.

I rolled my eyes as I looked about the library, finding its size and scope enough to elicit the envy of most scholars. The elderly houseman returned almost at once with a silver tea cart. Beyond the usual accoutrements, there were two Wedgwood serving dishes of three tiers each filled to overflowing with a display of petit fours in bright pastel coatings, little round chocolates rolled in cocoa the size of a thumbnail, warm mincemeat tartlets, tiny rectangular spice cakes no bigger than a finger and topped with a buttery frosting, lemon curd on golden pastry shells, shortbread cookies, and small ramekins of a warm apple mixture dusted with baked crumbles of brown sugar and butter. Next to these serving dishes sat a large silver bowl brimming with fresh strawberries and a small dish of clotted cream. It was the sort of abundance Mrs. Behmoth would be unable to provide with even a week's notice.

"It would seem . . . ," Colin drolled, ". . . that your *chef* manages well enough."

"I suppose . . . I suppose . . ." She waved him off glibly. "I must profess to a weakness for sweets, but oftentimes it is the simplest things that bring the most pleasure. Don't you think?"

I feared the answer he might give, so was relieved when a sudden rap on the door interrupted his necessity to do so. A soft, well-worn woman with graying hair wound into a tight bun peered in. "Everyone is ready, ma'am."

"Very well, Mrs. Holloway." The woman receded as Lady Nesbitt-Normand got to her feet. "I am most anxious for you to meet my staff, though I shall be positively adrift should any of them prove to be guilty of this horrid crime. They all love my little lady, but then she is irresistible." She shook her head wistfully. "Undoubtedly that's precisely why she's been spirited from her home. Come now. We must hurry, as her very person may be in danger even as we sit here prattling about."

"Of course," Colin tsked.

A minute later we were standing before a staff of better than forty in the oval two-story foyer that was greater than the size of our entire flat. "There are more people here than in one of Victoria's regiments," I would say to Colin later, and indeed there were.

Lady Nesbitt-Normand escorted us past the rigid formation of grim-faced workers, but it was Mrs. Holloway, shuffling along behind us, who stated the names and duties of each one. It gave me the distinct impression that our patron would have been incapable of that particular challenge. She did offer smiles and cluck over certain individuals but otherwise appeared to have little to say as we filed past her troops. The sole exception was a harsh, broad-faced woman named Elsa, who, we were informed by Lady Nesbitt-Normand herself, was Lady Priscilla's trainer. Elsa was compact and solid, with two muscular calves, like overfilled wineskins, poking out from the bottoms of her culottes.

She spoke in a thick German accent and bobbed her head stiffly. "You vill find our dear von, *ja?*"

"Of course they will," Her Ladyship scolded. "Elsa is the one who normally takes Lady Priscilla out for her morning constitutionals, but she was delayed this morning"—a withering look was lobbed at the trainer before Lady Nesbitt-Normand continued—"and I'm afraid our girl simply could not wait." She sighed. "I suppose it's my fault really. I shared some marmalade and a biscuit with her at bedtime last night and it unfortunately wreaked a bit of havoc on her system. I had to shoo her from my room well before dawn this morning. You can only imagine how *that's* left me feeling." Her voice caught as she spoke.

"You're being too hard on yourself," Colin soothed.

Lady Nesbitt-Normand looked about to succumb to a righteous spell as she brought a clenched fist to her mouth.

"Who was it that let her out this morning?" Colin asked.

"I did," Mrs. Holloway spoke up with the faithfulness of one who is long-suffering. "She was scratching at the door and yelping. I'm to blame. I should have gone out with her instead of fussing over the breakfast preparations. . . ."

"Was anyone outside when you opened the door for her? A deliveryman, perhaps? A groundskeeper?"

She shook her head. "There was no one. The morning deliveries were done and Mr. Simpson and his crew"—she nodded toward a short, squat, powerfully built man with a ruddy complexion—"they hadn't even gone out yet themselves. That's how I realized she was gone, when they *did* finally go out."

"How do you mean?"

"She doesn't care for Mr. Simpson. He sends her into fits of barking. As soon as she sees him she'll come running back inside to stand in the doorway and give him a good roust. So when he went out and she didn't come scurrying right back, I knew something was wrong."

"How long was she out before you realized something was amiss?"

Her eyes darted to Lady Nesbitt-Normand before she answered. "About ten or fifteen minutes."

Colin rubbed his chin. "How long was she normally out in the morning?"

"I'm not sure. Elsa would know that better than I."

"*Ja, ja,* dis ist *mein* fault."

"Now, now . . . ," Colin exhaled with singular patience. "No one is to blame. I am merely trying to establish the sequence of events."

"Let us adjourn back to the library," Lady Nesbitt-Normand interrupted. "I'm afraid my heart and feet are aching and I simply cannot stand here another moment."

"Of course." Colin stepped back and gazed down the assembled line of faces one more time. "I should like to continue speaking with Mrs. Holloway, Mr. Simpson, and Elsa. That will do for the time being."

"As you wish." She waved a hand at her staff, sending her upper arm into shivers of motion. "You heard what he said!" she bellowed. "The rest of you back to work." She turned a weary smile on us. "Come then, we mustn't let our refreshments get sour."

We followed her back to the library, the discomfort of her three selected staff members as evident as the reserve with which they so carefully held themselves. There was no wonder she held such affection for her little pup.

Mrs. Holloway set herself to pouring the tea as Lady Nesbitt-Normand slipped a tartlet into her mouth. "You were saying, Mr. Pendragon . . . ?"

"Yes." He flinched as crumbs flitted down her front. "Mr. Simpson . . ." He settled his eyes on the groundskeeper, who looked quite out of context in this part of the house. "Did you notice anything out of the ordinary when you went outside this morning? A gate unlatched? Fence boards pried aside? A bloodied patch of fur . . . ?" Our hostess gasped.

"No, sir. I didn't notice nuthin' 'til Mrs. Holloway came runnin' out."

"Were you aware that Lady Priscilla had been let outside?"

He shrugged uneasily. "I never paid 'er much mind since she didn't want nuthin' ta do wit' me." I saw him flick a surreptitious glance at his employer.

"Very well, Mr. Simpson." Colin stood up and paced over to the nearer fireplace as Lady Nesbitt-Normand devoured another mincemeat tartlet. "Let me not detain you any longer. If I could just have a moment with Elsa then . . ."

Mrs. Holloway and Mr. Simpson made a hasty retreat, but not before Mrs. Holloway refilled our cups.

Colin turned to Elsa as the other two took their leave. "You will permit me to ask if Lady Priscilla is in season?"

"I already answered that, Mr. Pendragon!" Lady Nesbitt-Normand sputtered through a hail of shortbread crumbs.

"You did," he acknowledged, "but I should prefer to have it confirmed from her trainer."

"*Nein,*" she answered with a note of disapproval.

"Are there other dogs in the neighborhood you allow her to run with?"

"Never."

"Anyone you meet while taking her for walks?"

"Absolutely not."

"Not once? Not ever?"

"She is a *champion,* Mr. Pendragon," Lady Nesbitt-Normand cut in. "She is not allowed to fraternize with street curs."

"Are there other show dogs in the neighborhood?"

"Not'ing close to de caliber of dis little lady. She ist a diamond among coal. Face of an angel *und* de heart to match."

"I have no doubt of that." He smiled as he turned back to our hostess. "Is she insured?"

"Most certainly. I am not a foolish woman, Mr. Pendragon. Lloyd's has a twenty-five-thousand-pound policy on her."

"That's an incredible sum for a dog," I blurted without thinking.

"She *is* a champion," Colin said before Her Ladyship could, digging a crown from his pocket and sending it winding casually through his fingers. "I'm sure you're quite proud. Are you the sole beneficiary?"

Lady Nesbitt-Normand scowled. "Of course I am."

"You must forgive the regrettable line of questioning, but I am simply trying to assemble the facts in order to ensure a quick and successful resolution."

"Yes, yes," she exhaled impatiently. "But how is any of this going to return my girl to me?" As though to punctuate her frustration she leaned forward and whisked up a handful of chocolates into her napkin. "I really wish you would go outside and *do* something. Make no mistake, Mr. Pendragon, I shall never forgive you if you fail."

Colin fumbled and dropped the crown he was spinning to the floor, his face withering. "I do not fail."

"Well then," she blustered, clearly surprised by such a pointed retort, "I'm certainly relieved to hear it. Now you will have to forgive me, as I must lie down. I am positively faint with worry." She slipped a chocolate into her mouth and I wondered if it was meant to give her sustenance to climb the stairs.

"You must allow me one request," Colin called after her. "If your Lady Priscilla *has* been kidnapped, then you will likely be approached with a ransom demand before the day is out. You mustn't respond to any such ultimatum until you have sent for me. It could mean the difference in your Lady Priscilla's life. I will have your word on that."

She sighed. "Yes, I suppose. But you had best be available then, Mr. Pendragon. I shall not have your absence be the cause of my never seeing her again."

"Blindly following a ransom demand is the surest way to have a thing like this end badly."

"*Oh!*" She went pale as she sagged against the doorjamb. "I cannot hear another word. My nerves are gone . . . just gone. . . ."

"If I may trouble you for one more thing, wholly unrelated . . ." Colin's tone eased as he knelt to pick up his dropped coin. "Are you familiar with a Lady Dahlia Stuart?"

Her brow furrowed as she shook her head. "I don't believe

so. I know a Stuart family, but there isn't a Dahlia among them. Two boys, William and Randall, both of them no-accounts, and three girls, Daphne, Mary, and Edith. I shouldn't think you would find any of the three of them interesting in the least. Is there anything else . . . ?" Colin nodded and she took her leave.

"You are finished vit me?" Elsa piped up.

"Not just yet." He flashed a quick grin. "Have there been any enquiries about Lady Priscilla lately, whether for purchase or breeding?"

"She ist a *champion*. Der are *always* people who vant her."

"Anyone who's been hanging around the area? Perhaps watching when you exercise her?"

"I don't know. I do not look around ven ve are together. She vould not tolerate such behavior."

Colin sighed. "And who are your main competitors?"

Elsa pulled herself up to her full height, her shoulders bulging like two monolithic slabs, her head held high and straight. "She ist a—"

"—champion," he cut her off. "I am abundantly aware of that, but if you do not give me the information I need, I won't be able to help."

Elsa heaved an exasperated sigh. "All pugs are mongrels compared vit her."

"I'm sure they are," he shot back, his patience thinning by the moment.

"You must understand." I stood up and placed myself between the two of them, staring at Elsa until she finally shifted her gaze to me. "We must investigate every possibility no matter how unlikely it may seem." I began to slowly sidle away from Colin, dragging her eyes with me. "Any information you give could be the key to getting Lady Priscilla back quickly and safely."

She faltered slightly, just as I had hoped she would, the solidity of her frame gradually deflating. "Of course. You are right." She tossed a hard glare back at Colin before looking back at me. "Der are three pugs who dream to be her. Von belongs to de Easterbrooke spinster: a slow, fat little beast called Buster Brown. De Rintons have a bitch named Bertha Omega, who is as mean und dowdy as your Qveen. *Und* Karl Steinmetz shows a young, schtupid pug named Cleavon. De Lady Priscilla has beat dem all."

"Are they all here in London?" Colin asked.

"Not Karl Steinmetz. He skulks about out in Stratford."

"Can you provide addresses for each of them?"

"Of course."

"One last question then. When you went outside after hearing your charge was missing, did you notice anything out of the ordinary?"

"No." She shook her head adamantly. "De gate vas closed *und* locked. Had it not been I vould have run out in search of her. Now, I vill get de addresses." She turned abruptly and stalked from the room.

"She seems to have pressed you into a mood," I cautioned.

"To hell with her." He waved me off. "I can maintain for the sake of that pup, because it's starting to sound like she truly has been stolen."

"Which *is* terrible," I started to say. "But do you really think now—"

His hand flew up to stop me. "You never had a dog. You cannot know how it feels," he said, settling a stern look on me. "Now isn't it time you got going?"

"Going where?"

"The morgue . . . ? You're going to get me a look at that captain's autopsy report. . . ."

I heaved an exasperated sigh. "Oh . . . that—"

His scowl eased. "You know I wouldn't ask if it weren't important."

"I know."

"Go on then. I'll tend to matters here."

I grimaced and left without a backwards glance, reminding myself that it was better to speak to the oafish Denton Ross, with his manner as coarse as the cobbled streets, than have to interview young Albert Bellingham. Even so, Denton had fouled my path when I was little more than fourteen, and I had never forgotten, nor forgiven.

CHAPTER 5

I sat on a hard bench in an unnaturally cold, utilitarian room with a knot in my stomach that threatened to throttle the whole of my sternum. Though electricity had been brought to this godforsaken place a year before, enabling the space to be kept ice-cold, it did nothing to stop the stench of death that still permeated everything here. I had been waiting almost half an hour to see Denton Ross, the city's primary purveyor of everything dead relating to *Homo sapiens*. This was his domain, his kingdom, and there was no one fighting him for the right of stewardship over this milieu. He had risen to the position of Chief Examiner based on the indisputable fact that few sought to build a career here. But for Denton Ross, the fit was as natural as tea and milk.

Six feet tall with the wide hips, distended belly, and sagging breasts of an elderly washerwoman, he shuffled along peering out at the world from behind long stringy hair that his clients took no notice of. His propensity toward excess, whether it be cheap wine or purchased companionship, was quietly tolerated, as it is understood that a decent society cannot exist without someone to perform his tasks. It enabled him to disregard how he was perceived.

To appreciate my distaste for Denton Ross you must look back twenty years to when I was in my early teens and he in his young thirties. I was on the brink of failing out of the Easling and Temple Senior Academy for spending more time trolling for opiates to still my troubled mind than concerning myself with the duties of higher learning. On the night I happened upon Master Ross I had suffered the entire day without benefit of a single handout. With the siren's song of opium demanding its due, I decided to go to a West End pub and try my hand at foraging through unsuspecting pockets. It was not a skill I had mastered, so I was forced to wait until the patrons became inebriated enough before attempting to relieve a few of whatever cash I could lay my fingers on.

I had spotted Denton earlier that night. I'd picked him out as looking soft and foolish and convinced myself that with enough ale he would surely prove an easy target. I kept my eye on him until deciding it was time to make my move. Sidling up in a crush of drunken revelers, I carefully slipped my fingers into the left front pocket of his pants, and almost at once he seized my wrist. Rather than yanking my hand out and hollering for help, however, he shoved it deeper inside, pressing it against the bare flesh of his aroused manhood.

"If you're going to play in there," he sneered in my ear, "you had best get to it."

I lurched back, struggling to pull my hand free, but Denton held me fast. The throng of laughing, screeching people smashed against us kept me rooted in place, and even if I'd had the temerity to cry out no one would have heard. He pivoted slightly, turning his body so my hand was wedged where he desired it most, and stared at me with a lopsided curl on his thick, rubbery lips. "You're a pretty one, you are"—he leered—"and don't you just have the softest hand."

I was panicked and struggling to twist away, but it only seemed to incite him further and not more than a minute later I felt a sticky wetness. "If it's money you're after," he burbled into my ear, "then I know how you can earn it." He released my wrist with a snicker and flung me backwards.

All I remember after that is shoving my way through the crowd, all the while holding my hand out as though it had erupted into flames. I threw myself out the back door and immediately heaved the contents of my belly into the alley. But what really caught the attention of the small mob of drunken people milling about was when I plunged my soiled hand into the puddle of horse piss. If I'd had a knife, I am certain I would have lopped my hand off.

The next time I saw him, more than a decade later, I was with Colin. One of our first cases together had precipitated a trip to the morgue and it came as quite a shock when it was *he* who came slithering out from the dissection room. He'd not said anything but had tossed a lecherous wink when Colin's back had been turned, and I knew that in spite of the passage of time he remembered me.

"Well, well . . . , " I heard his slippery voice anew. "Look who has come to visit a poor, old city worker."

I set my face and tried to keep my revulsion from showing. "Thank you for seeing me without notice."

He showed little interest as he flicked his eyes around the waiting room. "Where's your haughty little keeper? So like a laborer, that one."

"He's working another case."

"Good," he said as he headed back toward the inner rooms of his morgue. "And what brings you here?"

I followed him through a set of double doors and was struck anew by the freezing chill of the room. Bodies being kept for more than a few days were stored under gauzy covers atop cold metal tables. The floor raked toward a single drain in the center of the room, siphoning off water, chemicals, and effluvium that slowly leached from the bodies as they were being worked on. Most cadavers were kept no more than forty-eight hours, but there were some, and I knew Captain Bellingham's would be one such exception, that were held far longer.

Denton continued through the examination room to a small office at its far end. Without a door between the office and autopsy space, the tiny cubicle-like area was every bit as cold and dank as the main room and included the ever-present stench of formaldehyde and decay that clung to the walls with a pungency strong enough to sting the nostrils.

He flopped behind his well-used desk as I sat opposite in a sagging cane chair. The only other piece of furniture was a perilously drooping set of wooden filing cabinets inside of which was the file I had been sent to retrieve. "You were saying . . . ?" he muttered, though I had yet to say anything, as I was trying to draw a full breath without gagging.

I concentrated on a benign spot at the center of his forehead and noticed for the first time how haggard he looked in the buzzing electric light. Age had done nothing to improve him.

"I have come about Captain Trevor Bellingham and his wife, Gwendolyn," I started slowly. "Colin has been hired to solve their murders." He nodded but said nothing. "He would like to get a look at your autopsy report to see what conclusions you were able to draw." I hoped my feeble attempt at flattery might tickle his ego, but he only continued to stare at me, his eyes dark and unreadable. When I feared he was on the verge of refusing to engage with me whatsoever, I added, "Is his body still here?"

"Of course," he scoffed. He kept right on staring at me: measuring me, gauging me, thinking whatever thoughts a mind like his conceived at such a time as this, until I could stand it no more.

"Are you ill?" I blurted incongruously.

"Ill?"

"You don't look well and you have yet to respond to my request."

"Your request"—he leaned forward, a grim expression settling onto his face—"is not so easy. Inspector Varcoe sent a man around earlier today with explicit instructions *not* to share information with your Mr. Pendragon."

"Then you shall have done nothing wrong"—I tried to offer a smile but am certain it came off more a grimace—"as you will only be sharing with me."

"You?!" He chuckled as he leaned back and folded his arms behind his head, revealing great orange stains in his armpits. "You and your Pendragon are one and the same. I don't believe our good inspector meant for me to cooperate with you in lieu of your—"

"You'd be following the letter of his instructions," I cut him off, uninterested in whatever reference he was about to use. "He asked you not to cooperate with Colin and you won't be." I leveled my gaze on him and almost cringed as I heard myself utter, "This is between you and me."

A crooked smile snaked across his face. "And what's in it for me?"

"You would be helping solve this terrible crime," I answered.

"That's Varcoe's job and he's already *got* a copy of my report." He smiled gamely. "I'm afraid you have come all this way for nothing."

"It would mean a great deal to me if you could find some way to help me out. I don't want to compromise you with the inspector, but your help could make a great difference." I held his gaze with what sincerity I could muster and, to be fair, attempted to infuse it with the slightest hint of something more.

He eyed me for the longest time before abruptly pushing himself to his feet and sloughing over to his filing cabinet. "I keep it in here," he said with little inflection, yanking open the uppermost drawer and leaving it agape. "You can see it, but I *will not* hand it to you."

"Of course," I said quickly. "Would it be all right if I take a few notes?"

"You can copy the bloody thing verbatim for all I care, but if one of Varcoe's men comes by while you're pawing around in there, I will tell him you are doing so without my knowledge or consent."

"Of course."

"Of course," he mimicked snidely. "So agreeable, aren't you, when you think you're getting your way? But I think you know there is a price to pay for everything." He dug his hand into the cabinet's drawer and extracted a thick, scarred folder and then leaned over my shoulder, pressing himself against my side in a way that steeled my breath. "There it is," he clucked, tossing it onto his desk. "Do what you will while I prepare his body." He leaned farther, putting his lips close enough to my ear to assault me with his sour, oily breath. "You do mean to see the body, don't you?"

"Certainly," I fired back, but it was hardly the truth and I suspect he knew it. Still, it got him out of the room. I sucked in a breath and my nose curled against the foul smell of putrefaction cloying like overused perfume. Everything here, including Denton, was saturated with it.

I leaned forward and flipped open the Bellingham folder. I found myself staring at a grainy black-and-white photograph that showed Gwendolyn Bellingham lying on her left side facing away from the camera, her head held in place by her pillow. Behind her right ear was a single small entry wound from a gun that had clearly been fired at point-blank range. The front of her head, however, was burst like a melon; a hemorrhage of gray matter splattered across the whole of the bed in an uninterrupted pattern that assured me her husband had not been lying beside her at the moment of her death. The killing looked to have been committed quickly . . . thoughtlessly . . . and she had clearly been attacked with great stealth. She had most certainly never even realized that someone was coming up behind her. Her murder looked like a dutiful task completed with minimal fuss.

I paused a moment before pulling the second photograph out, the one of Captain Bellingham. His wrists and ankles were bound to the chair and he was slumped forward, his head having dropped far enough for his chin to be resting on his sternum. His nightshirt had been ripped wide from the neckline to the hem, its jagged edges visible despite much of it having been crudely shoved into the crux of the chair.

Small black dots were widely scattered across his abdomen, some of which oozed tiny black trails of blood, the result of the many spent matches tossed about the floor. The captain's knees were agape and I could see an even greater conflagration of the black marks across the insides of his thighs. Here the wounds appeared deeper than those on his torso, as there were innumerable streaks of coagulated blood crisscrossing his flesh. The number and severity grew exponentially as they got closer to his groin, which, I could now see, had been burned black.

I flipped the photograph over and stared at Denton's desktop for a moment as I struggled to settle my galloping heart. Only after I had managed to slow my breathing and convince my nerves to calm did I reach back out and nudge the photograph back over for one last look. It was important to do this, I told myself, as I was not likely to get a second chance.

Once again I was instantly assaulted by the brutalized sight of the captain's body. Even so, I forced myself to look closely at the wound on the near side of his head. Just like the one administered to his wife, this one had also been fired with the gun's barrel almost touching his skull, as the entry wound was as neat and pristine as what a surgeon might administer. And like his wife, the spectacle on the opposite side was one of utter wreckage. The delivery of such a definitive blow assured me that Trevor Bellingham had been alive when it was administered. He had suffered through the horrors of the burnings only to be murdered once the killer had extracted whatever he had been after. Perhaps Captain Bellingham had finally confessed for the solace of death, for while there was no mercy in his destiny, it had surely brought him peace.

I laid the photograph beside the other one, grateful to be done with them, and started flipping through the papers beneath. Perfunctory descriptions came first: height, weight, age, nationality, hair color, eye color, and so on, followed by the autopsy reports, the last one belonging to Captain Bellingham. With a hand less steady than I wished, I picked up a pencil from a jar on the desk and began scribbling some notes.

There were 371 match burns across the whole of his body. Of these, the greatest concentration were found along the insides of his thighs from his knees to his navel. His sex organs were charred and blistered, having been set afire. Deep lacerations and severe hemorrhaging encircled his wrists and ankles as a result of having been bound to the chair, with one area on the back of his right wrist cut so deeply that it revealed a spot of bone. The captain had endured immeasurable pain.

I let my eyes drift farther down the sheet, stopping when I found the description of the mortal wound to his head. It had been fired, just as I had figured, directly against his cheekbone. The bullet, a forty-four-millimeter arrow-shaped missile, had proceeded through his cranium on an upward trajectory, cleaving his cerebral cortex as it arced through his skull before exiting about an inch above his opposite ear, leaving an exit wound better than six inches in diameter.

"Your prince awaits . . . , " Denton Ross purred from out of nowhere, startling me enough that I dropped the sheaf of papers. He chuckled. "On edge, are we?"

"I'm fine!" I snapped too vigorously, and as though to prove my point I stuffed the papers back into the file and slapped it closed before pushing myself up onto legs that were, in truth, not quite ready to support me. "Let's go."

"You sure?"

"I've seen victims of violence before," I reminded us both.

"And so you have." He swept his arms wide like a carnival barker. "And this is one, I am sure, you will *never* forget."

I scowled at him as I started for the door. "It's remarkable, the pleasure you take from your work."

He chuckled again. "No one *ever* complains."

I pushed past him and back out to the frigid examination room. Little had changed save for the fact that there was now a draped body reclining atop the table at the room's center. It was a morbid sight, but then it always is, for there can be only one explanation for the cause of that shape beneath the cloth.

I tried to keep my breathing even as I felt my feet begin to drag. I desperately did not want to see Trevor Bellingham.

"Don't be shy," Denton clucked as he shoved his soft, pudgy hand into the small of my back, propelling me forward. But when we got within reach of the table he lurched past me and yanked the drape free, allowing the shattered, naked husk of Captain Bellingham to suffer one last humiliation.

Had I not gasped at the sight I would like to believe I would have turned on Denton Ross and pummeled him for his lack of propriety. But I did sink back, unable to say anything or even pull my eyes away from the travesty that lay before me.

Denton had split the body vertically at the center of the chest from the base of the neck to the midpoint of the groin so that Captain Bellingham's organs could be inspected. He had sewn the captain back together hastily, however, leaving him to look rather like a garment that has been buttoned incorrectly. Yet it was not this savage wound of enquiry nor its careless attempt at resuturing that was most horrifying, but rather the blight that covered the central section of this young man's body. He was spotted with an unfathomable amount of black dots and his sex was blistered beyond recognition.

"I apologize for the slipshod work," Denton muttered blithely, "but I really wasn't expecting gawkers." He snickered and I felt his breath strike the back of my neck.

I suppressed the urge to shiver and forced myself to concentrate on a spot at the far side of the table as I attempted to steady myself. I would not let this revolting man see me crumble. With a great deal of fortitude I made myself ask, "Are there any burn marks on his back?"

"*Oh!*" Again I was struck by the proximity of Denton's stale breath and sensed him leaning ever closer to me. "You *are* a randy one, aren't you?" he cooed. And then I felt one of his arms slither around my waist as he tugged me back against him.

Without a second thought, I reared back and shoved my right elbow deep into his sagging gut. He staggered backwards with a choked exhalation of wheezing breath before dropping to the floor.

"*You will never touch me again!*" I screeched as I stared down at his crimson face, watching him struggle to breathe. "And if you do, I shall split you open just as you've done to this poor man." He could only sputter and cough in reply. "And because you are such an offensive ruddy bastard," I railed on, "I am taking Captain Bellingham's autopsy report and if anyone asks any questions you will say it was *your* idea. *Do you understand?!*" There was more than a note of shrillness seeping into my voice and I knew I had best collect what I'd come for and get out.

I hurried to the tiny office and snatched up the captain's file, quickly tucking it beneath my arm. As I raced back through the examination room I saw Denton push himself up to his hands and knees, hacking so hard that I thought him on the verge of spitting blood. He deserved it, I told myself with a measure of pride. Yet that pride would prove to be very short-lived.

CHAPTER 6

By the time I got back home our flat was thick with the aroma of roasting lamb and potatoes. I was surprised to find myself tempted by food given what I had just seen, but my stomach was not to be deterred.

" 'Bout time," Mrs. Behmoth grunted from the kitchen doorway as I stepped inside. "Ya better be 'ungry. I been slavin' in 'ere 'alf the day."

I wanted to point out that was one of the reasons we paid her but decided to let it pass, as I was much more excited to show Colin what I'd accomplished. "Colin back?"

"Upstairs."

I hurried up to find him standing by the fireplace, his attention seemingly mesmerized by the flames even as his hands worked absently cleaning the barrel of a revolver he had taken apart and scattered across the nearest end table. "I have returned triumphant," I announced, presenting the file in the flat of my palms.

He glanced around, his eyes blank a moment, and then a broad, disbelieving grin spread across his face. "He *gave* it to you?!" He set the gun's barrel onto the mantel and rushed over to me, pulling me into a hug that threatened to choke the air from my body. "This is extraordinary! *You're* extraordinary!" He grabbed the file and immediately began thumbing through it as he headed back to the fireplace.

I watched him flip through the photographs without the slightest change of expression, continuously referring back to them as he read through Denton's report. Only after he had plunged into his chair, lips pursed and eyebrows tightly knit, did he finally look back at me. "Did you see the captain's remains?"

"I did." I told him everything I had seen, omitting only the last few moments of my time there. I saw no reason to rile him up when I had done a perfectly good job of defending my honor myself.

"Awful," he muttered when I'd finished. "Though it certainly offers insight into what likely happened that night."

"Does it?"

"Absolutely." He picked up the pieces of his gun and quickly began reassembling it. "When you went into their flat, what was the first thing you noticed?"

"How very clean and orderly it was."

"Precisely. It was faultless. Even with a young boy running about, it was pristine." He sighted down the gun's barrel before setting it between us. "And what does all that order imply?"

I gave a shrug. If there was something to be learned from the state of their flat it was lost on me.

"Whatever the killer was after was not *in* the flat," he supplied. "Nothing was disheveled. Which suggests one thing: The killer was after that most elusive of desires . . . information. Information that only Captain Bellingham could give. There can be no mistaking that fact."

"Which is why he was tortured . . . ?"

"And yet . . . what of it?" He glanced at me and I could almost see the cogs in his mind turning. "So specific. So . . . un-usual."

"An effective way to get a man to talk, I should think."

"Well . . ." He leapt up and stalked back to the fireplace. "I don't think that was the point." He snatched up the file and flipped through it again until he came to a specific page. "It says the captain endured three hundred and seventy-one match burns, and that his sex organs were nearly burned from his body. Do you really suppose he would suffer all of that and *then* choose to talk?"

"I could hardly think of a better time."

"I'm asking a serious question."

"I'm deadly serious—"

"You're being lazy." He scowled, folding his arms across his chest. "Apply yourself."

I let out a breath and tried to concentrate on what he had just gone over, but if he was expecting it to suddenly coalesce for me, he was woefully disappointed. "Why don't you just tell me what you think?!" I groused.

"What I think . . . , " he said, waving the file at me, ". . . is what I posited before. That Captain Bellingham invited the killer into the flat and took him up to the attic. Once there, the killer caught the captain unawares with a clip to the back of his head, knocking him unconscious long enough to bind him to that chair."

"A clip to the back of his head?" I repeated.

"Didn't you read the report?" He tossed the file at me. "I think you'll find it mentions a small hematoma less than two millimeters in diameter just below the left foramen magnum on the occipital bone." He pointed behind and below his left ear. "The cause was a blunt instrument, probably the butt of the very gun later used to kill him. Once he had the captain lashed to the chair the killer stole back downstairs, sealed little Albert in his room, and then murdered Mrs. Bellingham, dispatched without a second thought. And then, and only then, did he return to the attic to dispense his torment against the captain." He stroked his chin and dropped back into his chair. "But why . . ." He shook his head. "That's what I shall need to figure out."

"I thought you said he was after information?"

"If it was only information the killer was after, then why wouldn't he have used the captain's family as leverage against him?"

I shut my mouth and stared at him. That thought hadn't occurred to me.

"I'll tell you this . . . ," he went on. "The one person I should most like to speak with right now is the lady Private O'Fallon mentioned."

"Dahlia Stuart."

"Right."

"And do you have any idea how we might find her?"

He gazed into the fire a moment. "I suppose we could ask Private O'Fallon. He says he kept the captain's schedule. He should know where their visits took place."

"I hope so. But tell me." I finally settled into my chair. "How did you do at the Nesbitt-Normand estate? Did you find any traces of her pup?"

He shook his head as he seized his dumbbells near the bookcase by the door and began curling them to his shoulders. "I am afraid I found precious little. It's quite vexing and the more time that passes the greater the danger she's likely to be in. I cannot understand why no one has contacted Lady Nesbitt-Normand for a ransom yet."

"Then you're convinced she has been taken?"

"I am. I discovered two rib bones in the bushes by the side yard, and since Lady Nesbitt-Normand insists they never fed the pup pork, it would seem she has indeed been snatched."

"So where does that leave us?"

"With nothing but questions," he exhaled.

"I really wish you hadn't taken that case."

He frowned at me, the muscles of his arms flexing and relaxing in tandem with his movements. "You must stop saying that. You're supposed to be the one with the boundless compassion and yet you dismiss poor Priscilla as though she were a rodent. She is the woman's companion. A source of unconditional love in what must otherwise be a rather remote and dreary existence. Surely you can see that?"

"I suppose—"

"We should get our own dog . . . ," he muttered as he set the dumbbells back and crossed to the windows. "However, at the moment, it occurs to me that I have yet to ask exactly how you managed to get Captain Bellingham's file."

"The file . . . ?" The incongruity of his statement prickled the hairs on the back of my neck as I craned around to look at him.

"Yes. Your morbid Mr. Ross is downstairs with a couple of bobbies." He turned to me, letting the drapes fall back into place. "Is there anything you want to tell me before Mrs. Behmoth brings them up?"

"P-p-police . . . ?" I stammered. "He's brought police?!"

"Never mind." He waved me off as he hastily reassembled the file in its original order. "I've seen all I need." He tossed it on the table by the settee. "He can have it—"

A violent commotion burst up from downstairs, cutting Colin off. I hadn't even heard the door creak open before the thunder of multiple feet pounding up the stairs blunted all other sounds.

" 'Ere now!" I heard Mrs. Behmoth bellow with outrage. "Ain't ya lot got any bloody manners?!"

There was no reply as two navy-blue bobbies' domes bounced into view, followed closely by Inspector Varcoe, wearing his ever-present expression of profound distaste, with Denton Ross, red faced and breathless, bringing up the rear.

"*There!*" Denton howled as he gripped the handrail, pointing a fleshy finger in my direction. "*There's the scoundrel who assaulted me and stole my file!*"

Varcoe's gaze landed on me with a frown. "I thought you said it was Pendragon."

"Scoundrel?" Colin looked at me and I could tell he was restraining a laugh. "Did he just call you a scoundrel?"

"He's confused," I said smoothly. "I didn't steal his file. He loaned it to me. Isn't that right, Mr. Ross."

"There is *no* confusion!" he snapped back. "I was viciously attacked by this . . . this . . . "

"Careful now . . . , " Colin warned.

Denton reddened. "I was very nearly rendered unconscious for the sole purpose of stealing my file."

"Unconscious . . . ?" The inspector glared back at Denton. "By Pruitt?"

"Nearly . . ." His face flushed deeper as he repeated the word with less enthusiasm.

It took a moment before Varcoe realized he wasn't going to get the prey he'd been hoping for. So there was far less vitriol in his voice when he finally spun around and stared at me. "Well, Pruitt, what do you have to say for yourself?"

"Come now, Inspector—" Colin started to say.

"No one's talking to you, Pendragon!" he barked.

"Excuse me . . . , " Colin said, puffing out his broad, muscular chest like a rooster. "You cannot come in here spouting venom and expect that we are going to stand for it. Accusing Ethan of assault? That's mad and even you know it."

Varcoe's lips curled with displeasure. "Bugger the assault. I'm talking about a file that *I* ordered sealed, which is right now sitting on *your* damnable table!"

"He did assault me—" Denton Ross chirped from the doorway.

"Shut up!" Varcoe blasted without taking his eyes from Colin. "So how do you explain that, Pendragon?"

"Neither of us will explain anything with that formaldehyde-drenched pox standing in our flat."

"I don't have time for this, Pendragon."

"And neither do I!" he snapped back.

"*Inspector!*" Denton sputtered.

"Me lamb's ready fer servin'!" Mrs. Behmoth hollered from downstairs. "Ya best get that room cleared out. I ain't feedin' that lot a shites."

"Enough!" Varcoe bellowed. "We'll all take a ride to the magistrate's and let *him* sort this out. Grab that file!" he barked at one of his bobbies.

"You cannot be serious," Colin protested. "We haven't time for these games, Emmett."

"You will do as I say, Pendragon, or it will be my personal pleasure to have you *forcibly* removed!"

Colin gritted his teeth and looked about to throttle Varcoe as he fixed his gaze on me. "Let's make this fast!" he growled, storming across the room and yanking our coats from the hall tree.

"We'll see how full of spit everyone is when we get to the Yard," Varcoe crowed. Colin didn't say a word as he tossed my coat to me before bounding down the stairs.

"Wot's goin' on?" Mrs. Behmoth was standing in the entry with a ladle clutched in one hand and a wadded kitchen towel in the other. "Where do ya think yer off to with me supper ready?"

"We'll be right back," I mumbled, Colin having already stalked outside, his posture as rigid as I knew his mood must be.

"Ya can't leave now!"

I shook my head, avoiding her glare, as I closed the door and walked to the inspector's waiting carriage.

CHAPTER 7

—➤◆◄—

Colin and I were placed in a holding room for what felt like hours. The room was little more than a closet with a couple of chairs and a small table. More than an hour did creep by before Colin was finally allowed to send word to his father, and it took an additional three hours before Sir Atherton Rentcliff Pendragon, at long last, appeared at the door to our lockup, a great scowl on his broad, leathery face.

"What have you gotten yourself into this time, boy?"

"It's that bollocky bastard, Varcoe," Colin exploded, though I felt entirely culpable myself.

"Varcoe?" Sir Atherton yawned. "You mustn't pay him any heed." Though Sir Atherton is several inches shorter than Colin, he still retains an air of unquestionable authority due, in equal parts, to his years as Her Majesty's envoy to India and his wild mane of silvery hair.

"That man tries to thwart me at every turn!" Colin growled. *"And today of all days!"*

"Today? And why should today be different from any

other? Really now, boy, have I taught you nothing? You are such your mother's son."

"I'm afraid it's my fault," I confessed in the wake of Colin's glowering silence. "I've made a muck of things."

"Now, Ethan"—his father gripped my arm with a smile—"I find that hard to believe. And no harm's done anyway, as the magistrate's an old chum of mine. I'll cut this short and introduce the both of you to him. He could prove useful to you if this sort of thing happens again," he added with a wink.

Twenty minutes later we were standing outside Scotland Yard expressing our thanks to Sir Atherton. True to his word, he had not only gotten the case against us dismissed, but also his friend Magistrate Piper Cornwell had insisted we contact him should we ever have need of his services again. Considering Varcoe's propensity to impede us, that seemed more a matter of when than if.

Colin helped his father settle back into his carriage next to a lovely young woman. "My new secretary," he said by way of introduction before leaning forward and whispering, "Haven't the foggiest memory what her name is." He sat back with a cheery smile. "Do try to stay out of trouble, boy. And remember, you might try a little diplomacy now and then. It has certainly provided me a lifetime of work."

"I've seen you blast your share of men!" Colin groused.

"I said now and then." He flicked his eyes to me and gave a little shrug as he pounded on the roof of the carriage, sending it clattering off down the street.

As it disappeared around the corner, its wheels slipping easily into the well-worn divots in the cobbles, Colin turned to me. "What time is it?"

I fumbled for my timepiece. "Just past eight."

"Bloody hell! This whole day is nearly gone and we've learned almost nothing."

"I know. I'm sorry—"

"It isn't you," he said in a tone that didn't convince me. Heaving a frustrated sigh, he spun about and stalked off. I fell in step beside him and quietly waited to find out what was next. The fullness of night had settled in, a cool breeze drifting in on the shoulders of a massive cloud bank to one side of the sky.

"You have to find Lady Simpson," he said after several blocks, turning so suddenly that I nearly barreled into him.

"You mean Lady Stuart?"

"Yes. And anything you can about the men in Captain Bellingham's regiment. Where did they drink and whore? We have to learn something about them beyond their mutual respect and admiration for their sainted captain," he scoffed.

"All right." I nodded, though I had no idea how I would accomplish such a thing.

"It's imperative to find that lady."

"Yes, of course," I said.

"Very well," he answered brusquely, starting down the street again. "See if you can find her tonight," he tossed back over his shoulder.

"*Tonight?!*" I sputtered, certain this was my punishment for having lost us so much time. "How am I going to do that?"

"How indeed." He swung an arm out to hail a passing cab.

A two-seat hack pulled up and he climbed inside, taking up enough space to make it apparent I was on my own. "And where are you off to?" I called out.

"I've some poking around to do at Buckingham. Something is amiss beneath that bloody Guard's buttoned-up surface and I intend to get a notion of it. I need you to find that woman and anything you can about the off-hours of that lot." He thrust an open palm out at me.

"Right," I muttered halfheartedly as I handed over a fistful of sterling. "I'll see you later at the flat then."

"Best not!" he bellowed as the cab lurched forward. "Meet me at Shauney's at ten. Mrs. Behmoth will have thrown our supper to the alley cats by now."

"Fine," I called back, acutely aware that I had only two hours to accomplish the tasks he had set for me. As I gazed at the throngs of people scurrying about I decided I would concentrate on the guardsmen first, as that was an area I knew decidedly more about. Given the type of information I was after, there was only one place I could think to go. So I hailed a cab and asked to be taken deep into Whitechapel. To the place where I had once tried to annihilate myself.

CHAPTER 8

As we turned onto East Aldgate I noticed the driver's face sink into displeasure, so it came as no surprise when, less than a handful of minutes later, he abruptly pulled the coach up short at a corner some distance from where I wanted to go and announced that he would move no farther. I grumbled as I gave him nearly all the money I had left, shorting his tip for his cowardice, but in truth, I understood. These once familiar streets were troublesome and I knew that while the years had changed *me*, they had certainly not changed them.

I crossed the street at Shadwell on my way to Limehouse and was struck by how familiar everything looked. The same storefronts were sealed up by the same defaced wooden boards that lamented everything from taxes to graphic representations of the rumored relationship between Her Majesty and the late John Brown. It felt as though I had never left.

Every building was coated with a thick layer of soot, compliments of the chimneys clustered across their rooftops. The streets were no better, revealing what looked to be the same filth that had lain there when I had haunted these cobbled roads, which, were it not for the rain, would undoubtedly have been true.

As I picked my way along I couldn't help recollecting a time when my life, such as it was, felt simpler, if only because my sole desire had been to purge my head of the scourge that had driven my mother to murder. How I had feared the same fate.

There had been few friends back then, really nothing more than equally broken souls. We did the best we could to watch out for one another until someone overdosed, or got cut up, or simply disappeared. In the end, when I should have faded into the same anonymity as those around me, Colin had come from nowhere—a mere acquaintance on the occasions when I bothered to attend the Easling and Temple Senior Academy—and had quite literally changed everything.

I slowed and then stopped when I spied the rotted, brick-red door. It wasn't its condition that brought me to a halt—it looked just as it had the last time I'd been here—it was the circumstances under which I had last seen it. Addled and spent, tucked in Colin's intractable grip, I never thought I would ever come back. Yet here I was, facing the same door that had once compelled me so, beckoning me, urging me, promising the release that could only be found inside.

I glanced at the black sky and sucked in a deep lungful of pungent air, now tinged by the unmistakable scent of rain. As I reached for the broken doorknob I was suddenly overcome by the feeling that coming here was a mistake. Colin would be furious if he found out, and I was far from convinced that I was ready to confront these demons again. Yet I could see little choice. I had to do something and this was the only idea in my head. With grim determination, I pushed against the door and stepped inside.

It took my eyes a moment to adjust to the shadowed space beyond, but my nose was struck at once by the familiar, stale scent of decades of opium that permeated the walls more fully than the paint upon them. It caressed my brain just as it had once done, so I made myself move forward before it could force me to recoil back outside.

The place looked dingier than I remembered. It had never been a place one could describe as pleasing, but then no place built as a tenement would be. There had been tendrils of care about it at one time: fresh dabs of paint over the worst spots, a benign picture strategically placed atop the fist print of an unhappy customer, and inexpensive pillows in bright colors flung about to remind patrons that this was a place where exotic things happened. Now, however, any finery was gone, leaving the place looking indecently exposed. I could see a dusting of mildew on the barren walls and there were places where the paint had peeled off in great ragged chunks to reveal the uneven lath and plaster beneath.

As I stood viewing this once familiar room, I realized with a mixture of shame and relief that I had become quite coddled over the intervening years. Wasn't I the one forever grumbling about Mrs. Behmoth's behavior and the need for decorum? And yet I had once called this decaying den of debauchery home. I cursed my folly just as a gruff, scratchy voice called out from the darkness on the far side of the room: "Who is it? Who's there?!"

I recognized Maw Heikens's voice at once.

"It's Ethan, Maw," I called back even as my heart ratcheted up in my ears.

"Move into the light so's I can see ya," she said, her wariness evident.

I did as she asked, stepping into what little light filtered in from the streetlights outside. She hadn't lit any lamps, the price of oil no doubt being a concern. I knew gas wouldn't have been brought into the building. As I moved I caught a glimpse of her shadowy form hovering behind the oversized counter across from me.

"If yer who ya says ya is"—she did not move from the darkness as she spoke—"then what did I call ya when you was livin' 'ere?"

"Cuppy," I answered.

"Ah . . ." Her voice softened. "You was cute as a cupcake back then. Cute enough ta eat."

"And now?" I chuckled.

"Ach . . ." She waved me off, a bone-thin arm shooting out like a white blade from the blackness. "I'll bet yer just like the rest of 'em: growed up and worn down. Ya still with that peppery bloke?"

"Peppery?"

"Prancin' round like 'e ain't never stepped in 'orse shite. Ain't *nobody* never stepped in it, and that includes 'er almighty royal missus at the palace," she sniffed. "But 'e did get ya outta here, didn't 'e?"

"Yes." I couldn't help the smile that tugged at my lips. After all these years, she remembered. "We're still together."

"Course ya are. You was always soft. You wasn't ever gonna make it on yer own. That's why I let ya go off with 'im. 'E 'ad the cleanest boots I'd ever seen." She finally ambled out from behind the counter and I saw that she was stooped and pitched inelegantly forward, leaving her easily shy of five feet. Her body was as bony as the arm she'd swung in my direction, her skin mottled and opaque, looking like it was struggling to stretch over a conflagration of bluish veins. Her brown eyes were rheumy and watery, the left one clouded with the milky veil of a cataract. No wonder she had been leery of who I was.

"Siddown." She gestured toward the skeletal remains of a high-backed chair across from where she settled in. I thought for a moment that I remembered it, but the fabric had faded to something unrecognizable and I couldn't be sure.

"Where's everyone gone?" I asked without thinking.

She leaned back in the chair and looked as if she might be

swallowed by it. "Off ta better things," she said. "As I got old most a the girls wanted ta go off and do fer themselves. Ungrateful twats. And then one a them that stayed turned up with the pox. Went crazy before she died. Like a fool I let her stay ta the end. That ended me business right fast. All I got left now is me lack a teeth. Some gents like that, ya know," she chortled. "But I'll bet ya didn't come all this way ta listen to an ol' tart, did ya?"

"I'm sorry, Maw."

"I don't give a fig about you bein' sorry!" she snapped. "What good's that gonna do me? I own this place. Can't nobody throw me out 'less they pay me off and ain't nobody *that* stupid," she snorted. "So I just stay 'ere and take care a meself. Got a bit a money fetched up. Left ta me by that bloke used ta come by every Saturday, ya 'member?"

I nodded even though I had no recollection of any such man.

"Wouldn't 'is widow 'ave a bloody fit if she knew?!" she howled. "Get a nice check every month. Never fails. I was *that* good."

"You did fine by me."

She waved me off again. "You were a sorrowful little shite. I thought you was goin' daft. Just pitiful. All angles and limbs like one a them baby goats. Still, you did yer share round 'ere when you wasn't ripped outta yer damn 'ead, which was most a the time." She leaned forward and peered at me, studying my face as though trying to determine the person I had become. "Why you 'ere, Cuppy? I'll bet yer bloke wouldn't like knowin' you was 'ere."

"I'm sure you're right. . . ." I couldn't help smiling.

She chuckled and settled back in her chair. "Still soft."

I shook my head, but I knew she was right. I'd not even been able to properly obliterate myself all those years ago. "It's about a case Colin's working on," I pressed ahead. "A captain in the Life Guard and his family."

"You talkin' 'bout those Bellingham murders?"

I nodded. Of course she would know. There was little Maw didn't know. It's why I had come here in the first place. "I'm looking for any information you might have on the men of the regiment. . . ." I let my voice drift off so she could infer what I really wanted.

"Some a the boys come down this way from time ta time. Mostly to McPhee's on Haymarket. They don't come 'ere. Nothin' for 'em 'ere."

"I don't know McPhee's—"

"A right bastard wot overcharges for watered-down booze. But it's cheap. And he's got the young slags there. Mostly from them Slavic places. All exotic if ya don't look at 'em too close. Has a bit a gamblin' too, but no opium. You wouldn't like it." She laughed.

I ignored her barb. "The Guard's officers too?"

She shrugged her bony shoulders. "Not so much. A few a the sergeants, but no one higher up. They had some trouble a few months back . . . some sort a brawl . . . some a their brass had a rout with a bunch a Irish blokes. I don't think them big boys has been back since."

"What was it about?"

She shrugged again. "Prob'ly a piece a tail."

I suspected she was right, which gave me the idea to ask about my other quest of the night. "Have you ever heard of a woman named Dahlia Stuart? Lady Dahlia Stuart?"

She twisted her features in thought, her good eye losing its focus for a moment. "Dahlia Stuart . . . ? What the 'ell kinda name is Dahlia? She one a them American prigs?"

"She's titled. She can't be American."

"Ach . . ." She laughed. "Men get sloppy with the rules fer

the right bit a arse. You wanna find yer lady, then find the man wot give 'er that title: some fat little dowdy sod with more 'air in 'is ears than on 'is 'ead, I'd bet. I'll ask round, but I ain't 'eard of 'er and I've 'eard a everybody."

"True." I smiled.

"It'll give me somethin' ta do. Got no business anymore. Gave up the opium. Thank the good Lord I can still take the occasional slog a ale." She snickered.

I pulled out what little cash I was carrying and held it out to her. "Let me buy you some supper."

"Don't do me like that." She batted my hand away crossly, pushing herself back to her feet. "I been on me own since long before you was born. I don't need yer castoffs now."

"It's payment," I corrected. "For your time and effort."

"Bugger off." She turned and shuffled back behind the sagging counter. "I ain't takin' nothin' from you, Cuppy. Never 'ave and sure as 'ell ain't startin' now. You wanna give someone a bleedin' 'andout you go ta Saint Paul's. Those sots'll take anything."

"I'm only offering a meal. You fed me more times than I can count."

"Ya don't owe me nothin', ya little pisser. A couple cheap meals don't make up fer the things I did that was wrong back then. I wasn't no charity service. I was makin' plenty in them days." She glared at me, her good eye acutely focused as she seemed to size me up one last time. "Don't come back 'ere, Cuppy. I find anythin' on yer lady or them Guard blokes, I'll get ya a message." She turned and ambled through the doorway behind the counter.

"Thanks, Maw," I said to her disappearing back.

I stood there a minute feeling swallowed by a sense of melancholia, the cloying scent of opiate smoke and soured alcohol as ripe as the leavings in the streets. It seemed that stirring up old ghosts had done little for either of us.

I started back down the hallway with a heavy sigh and heard her call out, "Ya look good fer yerself, Cuppy!" I couldn't bring myself to look back. I knew coming here had been a mistake, but it would be another twenty-four hours before I realized how critical an error I had made.

CHAPTER 9

By the time I left Maw's building the cloud bank that had been assembling along the northern horizon had won its battle for the sky, leaving no stars visible. My mood was coinciding with the night. While I was pleased with the information I'd gotten about the regiment, I had no idea what to do about finding Lady Stuart. As I trudged back to Limehouse Street I swore I wouldn't be the reason Colin couldn't solve this case. No matter what, I was going to find the blasted woman somehow.

The wind caught my coat as I rounded the corner, slapping it against my thighs, but I gave it little thought as I concentrated on how Colin began every case he took, how he would start by assembling the facts, clinically and without prejudice. I tried to think of everything I knew about Lady Stuart. She had to be comely enough to attract a suitor such as Captain Bellingham, a young man of high regard with the promise of a long career in the Queen's service ahead of him. She was also likely either widowed or unsatisfactorily wed, given their affair and the apparent frequency with which they were able to carry it off. Last, she had to be a woman of questionable conscience to be involved in such an indiscretion with a married man. Which left me pondering whom I might be acquainted with who might know such a woman.

Few names came to mind. Abigail Roynton was one of them.

Mrs. Roynton was the well-connected neighbor of the Arnifour family and had been a valuable source of information in Colin's last case. If there was a highborn woman in this city, Abigail Roynton would almost certainly know something of her. So in spite of the fact that I had found Mrs. Roynton overbearing, unctuous, and wildly cloying where Colin was concerned, I could think of no other alternative as I crossed onto Shadwell Street, the demarcation between those who suffer in complete squalor and the merely downtrodden, and hailed a cab. The driver's dubious expression did not escape me as I instructed him to take me to the estates on the outskirts of the city's limits, so I made a show of jingling the coins in my pocket as I climbed into his carriage. Lucky for me that Maw had not accepted the last of my paltry funds.

Within thirty minutes we pulled up to the familiar iron gates outside the Roynton estate. I paid the driver and hopped out and was immediately struck by the overwhelming scent of rain. I looked up just as the sky shivered and rumbled with a staccato display of lightning, like a visual Morse code. Almost at once, the rain drew on me like a thief, tumbling from the willowy canopy of trees lining the long driveway. I raced the rest of the way up the drive but was well saturated by the time I reached the sanctuary of the porch. Stomping and sputtering, I reached out and banged the great looped knocker, conscious of the sight I would present to whoever answered.

"Yes?" Her houseman eyed me without expression.

I tried to coax a contrite smile as I gave my name and reminded him of my connection to Colin. As so often happens, his eyebrows rose at the mention of Colin's name, and he ushered me inside, bringing me to a library where a fire was thankfully ablaze. He offered me brandy, which I declined, but I did accept the chenille wrap he held out, grateful for its ability to blot my saturated clothing. I sidled up to the fire as soon as he left me alone, catching sight of the mantel clock. It was already nine: I had one hour left before I was to meet Colin at Shauney's.

As I warmed myself before the fire I tried vainly to keep from fretting about the time. Even so, I was grateful when a butler scuttled in with a tray of hot tea and a fresh blanket. He removed the wrap clinging to my shoulders, managing to avoid displaying an ounce of displeasure at its level of wetness, and replaced it so deftly that it was about me again before I realized the other was gone. He handed me a cup of tea before withdrawing with the stealth of a cat.

Within a few minutes I was able to shed the second wrap, and after the butler returned twice more to refill my tea and restoke the fire, and just before I was sure I was on the verge of apoplexy from waiting so long, the great wooden doors on the opposite side of the room swung wide to reveal the mistress herself. She was as striking as ever, her curly black hair piled up just so and wearing no more than a hint of makeup on her flawless skin. This was a woman who had clearly spent a lifetime protected from the harsh glare of the sun.

"Mr. Pruitt. What a pleasure," she cooed as she swept into the room. "I hope you've had a chance to dry off some?"

"I have, thank you. Your staff has taken care to see that I am both warm and dry."

"As they should." She gestured to a seat across from where she settled herself. "What brings you out on such a night as this? Might you be working on something for the enchanting Mr. Pendragon?"

No wonder he had liked her so much more than I. "Indeed," I answered rather coolly.

"And how is dear Colin? Pity he couldn't come himself."

I froze the smile on my face and forced myself not to launch my tea at her. "Yes . . . well . . . I'm afraid he has more important things to attend to tonight," I shot back cheekily.

She laughed. "I'm sure he does."

Her laughter made me feel foolish. "He wanted to come himself," I quickly backpedaled, "but he's quite involved in a new case, which is why I have had to impose upon you this evening. He's wondering if you might have knowledge of a titled woman he is most eager to find."

"How amusing!" Her eyes flashed with merriment. "Dear Colin sent you to ask me about another woman?"

I chuckled as though there was the slightest amusement to be found in her words before saying, "Her name is Lady Dahlia Stuart. Have you heard of her?"

"Let me think. . . ." She tilted her head and sighed. "Dahlia Stuart . . ." She turned and stared disinterestedly at the fire. "I do believe I have heard of a woman by that name," she conceded after what felt a protracted time. "Though I'm not at all sure about that title."

"It's what we have been told."

"No doubt." She gave a thin smile. "It may be what she calls herself, but then everyone knows how cheaply titles and a whiff of respectability can be had these days."

"Of course," I answered in a tone so dry it nearly caught in my throat. "Do you know her by some other designation?"

"I know her exactly as you refer to her, though I don't believe she has come by her title properly." She stared off vacantly. "I suppose she does have a vague sort of charm—"

I tried to keep the excitement from my voice as I continued to press her. "Would you happen to know where we might find her?"

"Lancaster Gate, I think. Not exactly the domain of those most noble, but I do believe you will find her slouching about there somewhere."

"Outstanding." And now an honest smile came easily. "I cannot thank you enough," I said as I set my teacup down and stood up. "Mr. Pendragon will be most grateful."

"Oh"—a Cheshire grin overtook her face—"I do hope so. Please give him my very best."

"Of course." I nodded as I headed for the door.

"Do let him know I'm here should he ever get lonely. . . ." She chuckled.

"Piss off," I hissed under my breath.

CHAPTER 10

━━━►✦◄━━━

Shauney's pub looks as likely a place for mice to seek solace as humans. Shauney himself is a rail-thin, black-haired Irish bloke from County Cork with skin the color of paste, enormous brown eyes, and a smattering of whisper-light freckles scattered across the bridge of his nose. He likes to brag that his modest upbringing taught him to thrive in squalid conditions, and so it is with his pub. Yet Shauney's generous demeanor encourages patrons to look past the stacks of empty bottles lining the walls, the spittoons full enough to reach the ankle of any unlucky sod who happens to plant a foot in one, and the utensils and glassware that have had little more than a passing acquaintance with soap and water. But it is the food that is the pub's greatest attribute. For despite Shauney's scrawniness, his wife, Kathleen, with her flyaway red hair and ginger-spotted complexion, is an extraordinary cook.

The moment I made my way inside, the scents of stewing cabbage and corned beef, lamb shanks simmering in a rich tomato sauce, and warm soda bread swamped my nose. There were five or six people deep at the L-shaped bar to my left, and the wooden booths flanking the wall to my right were equally overflowing. Even the tables running down the center were awash with happy, drunken people shrugging off the burdens of another day.

I looked about but did not spot Colin, which was hardly surprising given the crush of patrons. With a weary sigh, I began pressing myself between the clots of people, glancing from side to side as I struggled to find the top of Colin's dusty blond head. As I neared the back wall I finally heard my name above the din before spotting Colin beckoning me from the rearmost booth. He was wearing an odd, lopsided grin, and as I struggled to make my way over to him I glimpsed a bit of dark hair and the broad shoulder of someone sitting across from him. I changed my trajectory, barely avoiding one of the girls hauling two fistfuls of ale, before I was able to see, with great surprise, that it was the gruff Sergeant McReedy in Colin's company. He looked decidedly more amenable at the moment, and I could tell by the empty tankards on their table that they'd been drinking and, given the number, plenty.

"You remember Sergeant McReedy?" Colin popped out of the booth to let me slide in. "A credit to his regiment and a hell of a dipso."

"Ach . . ." He waved Colin off sloppily. "You flatter me." He slammed his pint onto the table and laughed so hard that a bit of ale dripped from his nose.

"We've been talking about the case," Colin said through a lethargic inebriation I spotted instantly as a fraud. "You've some catching up to do."

Sergeant McReedy snickered, turning in his seat to get the attention of a harried barmaid slamming ales onto a nearby table. "Let me get ya somethin'."

"Don't trouble yourself—" I started to say, but Colin's fist thumped my thigh and I knew he meant for me to join his mock revelry. "I'll get the young lady's attention myself. . . ." I gave a hearty chuckle as I beckoned for a server.

"That's better," Sergeant McReedy snorted. "I like someone who knows when ta give it up and join them that's gettin' blistered." He saluted his mug at me and tipped it back. A familiar barmaid weaved her way to us just as Sergeant McReedy flipped his empty glass upside down. The fifth one thusly arranged. "You got anythin' on that tray for me an' me friend?!"

She dropped two of the dark ales onto the table and held her hand out to Colin for payment. "You're really packin' 'em away tonight, Mr. P.," she said as she counted out change.

"Well . . ." He handed her a few extra pence with a pointed glare. "Nothing wrong with a bit of hops now and then." She took the pence with a noncommittal shrug and moved away.

"A touch a sass." Sergeant McReedy leered after her.

"A touch a sass," Colin echoed, hoisting his glass and toasting the sergeant, only to roll his eyes the moment the young man's head tilted back.

"Sass." I lifted my ale. I started to take a sip just as I caught Colin shifting his glass to his left hand and smoothly lowering it beneath the level of the tabletop. Before I could figure out what he was doing the glass reappeared, lower of volume, and gleefully banged onto the table as though he had just enjoyed a hearty pull. I leaned back and stole a glance beneath the table and spied a spittoon nestled between his feet.

"I'd like to propose another toast!" Colin reached over and grabbed my mug just as Sergeant McReedy slid his gaze back. Now aware of the game, I snatched up Colin's half-filled tankard and lifted it up and, with little more than a taste on my breath, appeared to be well on my way to getting bloody, buggery drunk. "To your Captain Bellingham," Colin said. "A kind and courageous man."

"A hell of a leader." The sergeant smacked his mug against ours.

"And to his wife," I felt compelled to add.

"Dreadful awful," Sergeant McReedy agreed before bottoming his glass and waving another barmaid over.

Colin waited until he'd been served again before speaking up. "The sergeant was just telling me he served under the captain for three years."

"That's right." He heaved a sigh and stared off. "You get to know a man in that time. He was solid. I never had any quarrel with him."

"Nor, it seems, did any of his men. But you mentioned his wife's brother. . . ."

"Ach . . ." He scowled and downed another slug of ale. "Thomas Mulrooney. A bastard sergeant in the Irish Guard. A real tosser." My ears perked at his mention of the Irish Guard, reminding me of what Maw had said about a brawl between them and the officers of the Life Guard a few months past. "Never had nothin' good ta say about the captain."

"Did they ever have an altercation?" I tried to ask blithely.

The sergeant's eyes flicked over to me with such intensity that I dropped my gaze and took a drink. "It's the Guard, not a schoolyard," he growled.

"Of course." Colin smiled. "And what about Major Hampstead? Did Captain Bellingham ever confide anything to you about the major? Something in passing perhaps?"

"The Guard doesn't natter like a bunch of old women," he scoffed, still holding himself tight. "If he had an issue with the major he wasn't talkin' to me about it."

"I just wondered if you heard any rumblings. Men have been known to complain from time to time, you know." He chuckled.

Sergeant McReedy stared off a moment and then drained his

glass. "I'm done," he said as he thumped his tankard onto the table and slid from the booth.

"One more?" Colin smiled.

The sergeant wouldn't meet his gaze as he shook his head and stalked off without another word, disappearing in the phalanx of people long before it would have been possible for him to reach the door.

"You certainly know how to empty a booth." Colin eyed me. "What was that about?"

"I heard there was some sort of brawl between some men in the Irish Guard and a few of the Life Guard officers a couple months back. Happened at a tavern on the east side named McPhee's. When he mentioned Mrs. Bellingham's brother being in the Irish Guard and not liking the captain"—I shrugged—"I thought there might be a connection."

Colin's brow creased. "Hard to believe there wouldn't be. And Lady Stuart . . . ?"

"Lancaster Gate."

He beamed. "What would I do without you?!" He reached under the table and squeezed my hand. "Let's go home. I've had quite enough of this place for one night. I'll get Mrs. Behmoth to scrounge something up for us and we shall share what information we've learned tonight, as I've not been entirely without success myself." He prodded me before I could press for a hint, and for the first time since he had accepted the case I allowed myself to consider that maybe, just maybe, he really would be able to solve these murders in the two and a half days we had left.

CHAPTER 11

In spite of her having been the family's scullery maid, it is true that Mrs. Behmoth served as the primary maternal influence for Colin after his mother's death when he was seven. She was not Sir Atherton's first choice for such a pivotal role in his young son's life, but after trying one nanny after another and seeing Colin pay them little heed, he'd finally had no choice but to resign himself to the attachment between Colin and Mrs. Behmoth. I am certain it was easier for Sir Atherton to simply give in. Some things have not changed.

To this day I do not profess to fully understand the bond between Colin and Mrs. Behmoth, and yet I would have bet that Colin could never have convinced her to sully her kitchen at this hour. And I would have lost that bet. Not only did she prepare sandwiches for us, but berries and clotted cream as well. Nevertheless, the moment our plates were empty we were summarily thrown from her kitchen with warnings not to return until beckoned for breakfast.

"Now tell me . . . ," Colin said with a yawn once we got up

to our bedroom, ". . . however did you manage to find the elusive Lady Stuart?"

"A most unlikely source," I answered as I slipped out of my clothes, carefully folding the clean things and placing them back in my armoire while my underthings got tossed into a straw basket Mrs. Behmoth had provided for that purpose. "You remember Abigail Roynton . . . ?"

"Ah." He smiled. "The lovely widow from the Arnifour case. An inspired thought on your part." He tugged his undershirt and breeches off, flinging them in the general vicinity of Mrs. Behmoth's basket. Before crawling into bed I ensured they completed their rightful journey. "Does she know the Stuart woman?"

"She said she's familiar with her and that she very much doubts the veracity of her title." I went on to share what little Mrs. Roynton had told me, adding in what I'd heard from Maw Heikens about the brawl between the guardsmen at McPhee's, though I was careful not to mention Maw herself. Luckily, he did not press me on where I had learned that specific bit of information.

"You have become quite the sleuth." He smiled as he reached out and pulled me to him. "One of these days you will be handling these cases without me."

"I very much doubt that." I chuckled as I rested my head on his chest. "And what did *you* learn this evening?"

"Nothing quite as useful as you," he muttered with a great yawn.

"I should like to decide for myself whose information is the more useful," I said, snickering, but he didn't answer and a moment later I felt his chest rising and falling in an easy rhythm and knew he had drifted to sleep. I was tempted to wake him, certain I would never be able to sleep without hearing what he had discovered, but before I could rally myself to do so found myself opening my eyes to morning light and staring at Colin's side of the bed, now vacant. Wednesday had arrived.

I peeked at our bedroom clock and found that it had progressed no further than six twenty-five. An unseemly time to start a day. I heaved a heavy sigh and I slid out of bed, recoiling irritably at the feel of the cold wood floor beneath my feet. Once cocooned in my robe and slippers, I headed for the study to see what he was up to. The smell of beans, sausage, eggs, and bread drifted up from below, which markedly improved my mood.

I found Colin already dressed and hovering by a voracious fire. There was a tray of tea and milk on the table, but his attentions were absorbed by the large hunting knife he was buffing to a meticulous sheen with a soft wad of cotton. "You're up early," I remarked with no more than a whisper of enthusiasm as I stumbled to my chair.

"I've a lot on my mind. Sorry if I woke you."

"You didn't." I seized his cup and took a greedy sip of the musky Earl Grey, grateful to feel it warming my insides as readily as the nearby fire worked on the rest of me.

"Mrs. Behmoth . . . ," he called downstairs, ". . . you'd best make that breakfast for two."

"Fine!" she bellowed back. "And if the mice in the walls want somethin' ta eat in another little while you be sure an' let me know that too. I'll just stay here cookin' breakfast all bloody day if it suits ya."

"Is there ever a time she isn't foul?!" I groused. "And just what is it you're off to so early?"

"The clock is ticking." He set the point of the knife blade down the mantel and spun it like a top, its freshly honed steel glinting like a jewel in the burgeoning sunlight streaming through the windows. "She's a beauty, isn't she?"

"She is almost certainly putting a hole in the mantel."

"Are you going to be disagreeable all day?"

I heaved another sigh as he headed for the staircase where Mrs. Behmoth could be heard pounding up. Cups, saucers, silverware, and china clanged precipitously until Colin managed to swoop down and seize the tray from her.

"Ya gotta put one a them damnwaiters in," she muttered, following along behind him.

"Dumbwaiters."

" 'Cause one a these days . . . ," she kept right on prattling, ". . . somebody's gonna fall down them stairs and I think we all know who *that's* gonna be."

He shook his head as he set the tray between us. "We'll look into it as soon as the week's over."

She glanced at me and said, "You look like somethin' a cat hacked up."

"Thank you!" I snarled.

"This looks delicious," Colin interrupted as he parceled out the food. "I'll bring the remnants down as soon as we've finished."

"I'll live fer the moment," she muttered as she headed back with her usual indelicacy.

"Do not say a word," he warned, handing me a plate. "There are far more important things to be discussed this morning than the state of her demeanor."

"What is the plan for today?" I conceded.

"First we're going to Major Hampstead's office. His cat-and-mouse games are irksome and it is time I extract some elemental details about Captain Bellingham from him or I shall demand to see the captain's personnel file. After that we will meet with Mrs. Bellingham's brother. We must determine whether there may be something amiss with him and his Irish Guard." He shoved his plate onto the mantel and took up polishing the hunting knife again. "Where did you say Lady Stuart lives?" he asked after a minute.

"Lancaster Gate."

"Excellent. Then we shall pay a visit to the captain's muse as soon as we have finished with his brother-in-law."

"Has anyone confirmed Captain Bellingham's affair with Lady Stuart?"

"Not precisely. All we have so far is Sergeant McReedy's assertion that Captain Bellingham had been seeing a good deal of Lady Stuart recently. He admitted that he'd not met her, nor did he know where she lived, but he did confess that the captain had spoken about her on several occasions recently."

"What had the captain said?"

He held up a hand imploring me to wait and let him tell the story his way. "Sergeant McReedy and Captain Bellingham went off to a pub recently, *not* a normal occurrence according to him, and after they tossed back a few ales the captain started asking the sergeant about his marriages."

"Marriages? That sour young man's been married more than once?"

"Twice. And twice divorced. The captain wanted to know why Sergeant McReedy's marriages had failed."

"Why would he want to know that?"

"The sergeant didn't know. And while he says he didn't probe for information in return, he told me the captain volunteered that his wife had been distracted lately. *Ill-tempered and dismissive* were the words he said the captain used."

"And what does that mean?"

Colin shrugged. "Hard to say. But he said Captain Bellingham credited his dear friend, Lady Stuart, with being the sole person helping him keep his wits."

"His dear friend? Is that how he referred to her?"

"So the sergeant tells it."

"It all sounds very odd to me. Women can be wives, acquaintances, fiancées, lovers, and the occasional dalliance, but dear friends?! What kind of thing is that to say?"

"I've been wondering myself. But I should think we will find some of these answers when we visit the enigmatic lady herself."

"Shouldn't we *start* our day with a visit to Lady Stuart then? Doesn't it sound like she would be the person best able to comment on the state of Captain Bellingham's life?"

"Perhaps. But I doubt she would be willing to offer much usable commentary if we show up at *this* hour of the morning." He chuckled. I glanced over at the mantel clock: quarter past seven. He had a point. "And then we simply *must* turn our attentions to Lady Nesbitt-Normand's lost pup. I quite fear for her safety with every hour that goes by. If I didn't have this damnable deadline . . ." He let his voice drift off as he snatched a coin from his pocket and began spinning it through his fingers.

I didn't have the heart to remind him that the deadline had been self-imposed. "And what about the men in Captain Bellingham's unit?" I asked instead.

He sighed. "We must interview them. With only fifty-seven hours to go we are not only at the start of this case, but very much in its middle. We must raise the stakes by noon. Now get yourself dressed, and while you're doing that see if you can remember how Private Newley referred to Mrs. Bellingham yesterday."

"Newley?"

"Yes, yes. The eager young lad who waited with us in Buckingham's forecourt while Sergeant McReedy fetched a carriage."

"*Newcombe*," I corrected. "His name is Private Newcombe." I recalled the slender young man with the tight, curly brown hair. He, of everyone we had met, had been the most pleasant. "I certainly don't remember him referring to her in any particular way—"

"Well then," he challenged as he shooed me off to the bedroom. "Let us see if you notice today."

CHAPTER 12

By the time we got outside the day revealed itself to be bright and warm. Anything feels possible when the sun is out, which contributed to a renewed sense of optimism for me. Yet, as we pulled up to Buckingham's massive gates for the second day in a row, I stared up at the crystalline sky and could not help but remember that this was another day Captain Bellingham and his wife would never see. The sun's generosity would have no impact on them.

This time we were ushered in with little scrutiny and escorted back to Major Hampstead's office. As before, the major's youthful attaché, Corporal Bramwood, expressed great enthusiasm at having Colin pay another visit. The corporal was clearly more keen about Colin's involvement in the case than his superior officer was. It left me suspicious of the major, and as we took the seats offered by his corporal I knew Colin felt the same way.

Corporal Bramwood fussed over tea and a tray of scones before informing us that the major would join us shortly. He stepped back to the door with a smile for Colin and said, "Let me know if you need anything," hanging on Colin's gaze as though he were Sarah Bernhardt herself.

"You have been most solicitous," Colin answered, his eyes sparkling with mischief. "I cannot imagine another thing you could do."

I wanted desperately to roll my eyes but managed to restrain myself. The corporal nodded and pulled the door shut. I glanced over at Colin and found a wide, sloppy grin covering his face. "He seems to be quite the fan of yours. It's a wonder your reputation has gotten down to his generation."

Colin's smile curdled. "Oh, thank you ever so—"

Before I could taunt him further the door burst open and Major Hampstead stepped in, resplendent in his full red and white dress uniform with his great white plumed helmet seated atop his head. "Sorry to have kept you waiting," he said, pulling the helmet off and setting it on the corner of his desk. "I always inspect the troops first thing." He unbuttoned his tunic and heaved a sigh as his soft middle sprang free, settling behind his desk and suddenly looking much more the middle-aged man he was than the military officer who had just entered. "Do you have news for me?" he asked, and I would have sworn I heard a note of trepidation in his voice.

"Not just yet." Colin offered a thin smile.

The major returned what I thought was meant to be a look of disappointment but was undercut by the contented way in which he suddenly leaned forward and slathered strawberry jam onto a scone. "It does seem a fat lot to accomplish in three days, Mr. Pendragon. I don't envy you. I don't envy you at all."

"I shouldn't worry for me, Major."

"Of course not," he muttered as he devoured the scone.

"But as we are conscious of time, I would ask you for some assistance."

"Anything at all."

"I should like a letter of introduction compelling each member of your regiment to cooperate fully with my investigation, no matter the time of day or their present duties."

"Ah." He seemed to consider it a moment. "You're lucky the Queen's at Balmoral or I would never be able to agree to such a thing. But as it is"—he waved a hand dismissively, crumbs raining down from his lips—"I shall have Corporal Bramwood prepare something for you. What else?"

"I need for you to arrange a time for Mr. Pruitt to meet with Captain Bellingham's lad, Albert. It shouldn't take long and they can do it right here, but I should feel ever better to cover all ground. Perhaps this afternoon . . . ?" His voice trailed off as my heart ratcheted up. I had been hoping Colin might have given up that notion, but it was clear he meant to make me do this.

"Of course." The major waved a hand again. What did he know of my discomfort or that boy's horror? "Will that be it then?"

"No. There is one other thing. I would very much like to see Captain Bellingham's record of service."

The major paused in the midst of a bite from a second scone and stared at Colin. "You mean his personnel record?"

"I do."

Major Hampstead took his time dabbing thoughtfully at his mouth before answering. "I'm afraid that would be out of the question, Mr. Pendragon. A man's file is never privy to the civilian population. It is simply not done. I trust you understand."

"Not seeing that file could impede my investigation."

"That *would* be a pity," he sniffed, his voice dense with mock concern.

"I'm glad you understand. . . ."

The major affected a look of consideration as he downed the rest of the second scone and followed it with a sip of tea. "I'll tell you what. . . ." He stood up and headed for the door. "I shall personally check Captain Bellingham's record to see if there is anything that might prove of value to you. If there is"—he gave a wink as though sharing an intimate secret—"then I will get you a gander at that specific bit. If there is not"—he spread his arms wide at the sheer simplicity of it all—"then no harm will have been done."

"But you won't know what to look for," Colin answered flatly. "I hardly know myself."

He laughed. "Then I can certainly do no worse than to search for something you yourself are uncertain of." He yanked the door wide and bellowed to Corporal Bramwood, "I need you to put a letter together!" as he passed into the anteroom, effectively ending the matter.

Within ten minutes Corporal Bramwood had provided the promised letter and escorted us to a small conference room in which Major Hampstead agreed we could interrogate whomever we wished. To my amazement Colin selected Sergeant McReedy first, stating that he hoped to find him more willing with a clear head, though that seemed less likely to me.

"What do you make of Major Hampstead?" I asked once Colin and I were left alone. "Do you believe that twaddle about civilian access to personnel records?"

"I suspect it's true, though conveniently so," he answered as he blithely rolled a crown through his fingers. "It seems to me he's hiding something."

"And what do you suppose that could be?"

"Something to do with the Guard's reputation, I would guess. Just imagine if the captain and his wife were killed by a member of the Guard itself . . . or perhaps a cadre of them? Now *that* would be something he would be anxious to keep from the press."

I wrinkled my nose. "A conspiracy?"

"Be careful of dismissing what we have yet to prove false."

"But really, murderous vigilantes in the Guard? Do you really think such a thing could be credible?"

"Anything is credible."

"You suspect no one yet?"

He scowled. "I suspect everyone. Haven't you been paying attention?"

I was on the verge of an exceedingly arch reply when Sergeant McReedy burst into the room with an expression of unmistakable gall. He stood at attention, his powerful chest straining against his red tunic as he held his plumed helmet in the crook of one arm. His eyes were riveted on nothing, staring vacantly behind our heads, and his lips were pinched so tightly that they appeared to be receding from his face.

"Sit down, Sergeant." Colin gave a quick smile as he slid the crown back into his pocket. "There's certainly no need for formalities."

"I would rather stand," he shot back.

"Is there something preventing you from joining us or have you decided our company is only acceptable after dark?"

"I have already said everything I have to say. If you persist in singling me out then you will have succeeded in nothing more than earning me the distrust of my men. I cannot do my job under such conditions." He held his gaze rigidly forward as Colin stood up and moved around behind him.

"Really now, Sergeant—"

"I wouldn't expect you to understand," he hissed with quiet force.

"Very well. Then I shall need to see every man who was serving directly under Captain Bellingham at the time of his death. How many would that be?"

"About a dozen. But there were over four hundred under his command."

"I'll start with the dozen." He circled back by me. "Did you count yourself in that number?"

"Am I a suspect?"

"Everyone is a suspect."

"Is that why you plied me with ale? To see what stories I might let slip?"

"Is that what I did?"

"I'm not daft, Mr. Pendragon."

"I never thought you were. Just tell me one thing. Why is everyone in the Guard so unwilling to see me solve these murders?"

"Because we take care of our own. We don't need *you* to settle our business."

Colin leaned across the table, his voice low and hard. "The slaughter of a captain and his wife in their own home while their young son cowers nearby is hardly taking care of your own. And I find your sudden change of attitude most disturbing, Sergeant McReedy. So you will bring me those dozen men in quick succession or you can tell your major I will be going to the press to divulge how the Queen's Guard refuses to cooperate in the resolution of these murders. Do not trifle with me."

Sergeant McReedy sucked a breath in through gritted teeth before turning and stalking out.

"Why is he being such an ass when he was so accommodating last evening?" I asked.

"Either your reference about a brawl between the captain and his Irish Guard brother-in-law has permanently set him off or the disingenuous Major Hampstead has rolled out a fresh edict this morning. I wouldn't be the least surprised if he has instructed his men to cooperate only so far as they must in order to keep us mollified."

"That would be a travesty."

Captain Bellingham's aide-de-camp, Corporal Blevins, abruptly rapped on the doorjamb. He had shown me around the Bellingham flat the day before until Inspector Varcoe's ar-

rival had put us all off. But before the skinny black-haired corporal could join us, Major Hampstead appeared behind him in
the doorway and quickly shooed the young man out, pulling
the door closed behind him.

"I have just been told the most disturbing thing, Mr. Pendragon," the major said in a tone that sounded very much like
scolding. "I thought we agreed your investigation was to be conducted with the utmost discretion. That no statements would be
released until Friday evening with my express input."

"Unless I solve it before then," Colin corrected.

"Solve it?" His eyes narrowed. "Are you telling me you
think you have solved these murders in a single day?"

"Had I solved them"—Colin folded his arms behind his
head—"would I be on the verge of torturing that young corporal with questions?"

"Of course." I could feel the major's demeanor ease. "We
also agreed you would report any findings to me before you
engaged the press, did we not?"

"Yes, Major."

"Very well then." He smiled. "As I said yesterday, my desire
is solely to protect the reputation and honor of both Her
Majesty and the Guard."

"Noble." Colin's smile was rigid and forced. "May I get on
with my investigation now?"

"Of course." The major turned and yanked the door wide,
but before he stepped out he paused and with his back still toward us said, "I will have Corporal Bramwood set up Friday's
conference." He glanced back at Colin. "I look forward to having this behind us."

"Yes . . . ," Colin said to the major's disappearing back, "you
smarmy ass."

"Now, now . . . ," I cautioned, "don't let him get to you."

He glared at me foully and called out, "We are ready, Corporal Blevins!"

"Yes, sir." The thin young man entered the room but remained hovering by the door.

"It seems your major believes the Guard's business should be kept out of the papers even at the cost of a truthful resolution." Colin waved him to a seat.

"Thank you, sir. The Guard will find the truth. We take care of our own. It is the honor of being in Her Majesty's service."

"Do you believe the perpetrator is a member of the Guard?"

He blanched. "No, sir."

"As the captain's aide, is there anyone who gives you pause?"

"No one, sir."

Colin stood up and moved toward the young man, taking a circuitous, sauntering tack. "How long did you report to him?"

"Five months, sir."

"Ample time for a bright young corporal to see and hear things. Whom was he having problems with?"

"No one, sir."

"Who complained to you about him?"

"No one, sir."

"Whom was he angry with . . . ? Whom had he recently disciplined . . . ? Whose character was he worried about . . . ?"

"No one, sir. There was no one. No one at all."

Colin stopped behind Corporal Blevins and leaned in close, lowering his voice to a near whisper. "What about his wife's brother, Corporal?"

He sat motionless, not even drawing a breath as he answered, "I don't know him, sir."

Colin remained as he was a minute, looming over the young man's shoulder, before abruptly pulling away. "Thank you," he said warmly.

Corporal Blevins nodded as he jumped up and hurried from the room.

In quick succession we met a Second Lieutenant Dwight

THE BELLINGHAM BLOODBATH / 99

Hanover followed by two more second lieutenants, three lieutenants, two sergeants, another corporal, and two lance corpo-
rals. The verdict of the men was unanimous: Captain Bellingham
had been a first-rate leader who inspired his troops, treated his
men fairly, provided clear direction, and never asked anything he
himself was not prepared to do. He seemed a man without ene-
mies or conflict, other than the fact that someone had murdered
him in the most brutal way.

"Are they all lying?" I couldn't hide my frustration after the
last man said his final memorializing words and took his leave.

"They can't be. They had no idea whom we would want to
speak with until we got here." He dropped to the ground and
hastily knocked out a dozen push-ups before springing back to
his feet. "I'd say most of these men believe exactly what they're
telling us: that Captain Bellingham truly was a man of virtue
and substance. But I suspect we are being led astray in what
they are *not* telling us." He turned and strode to the door with
fresh purpose. "*Sergeant McReedy!*" he hollered down the hall.
"I should like to speak to Privates O'Fallon and Newcombe,
and to Corporal Bramwood, in that order, please." He turned
back to me. "Did you bring Lady Stuart's address?"

I pointed to my temple.

"Fine. And I have requested a meeting with Mrs. Bellingham's brother, Thomas Mulrooney, as soon as we leave here.
We are to meet him at the Parliament building where he's stationed." I nodded.

"Sir?" Private O'Fallon presented himself at the door, his
expression as contrarian as ever.

"Private . . ." Colin went over to the young man and pumped
his hand with considerable vigor as he ushered him in. "Thank
you for taking the time to speak with us."

"I wasn't aware I had a choice."

"You don't." He waved him to a chair. "But your willingness to cooperate will be looked upon most favorably."

"By whom?" Private O'Fallon stared at him blankly.

"By me." He flashed a smile that was, as usual, not returned. "Now tell us about your duties for Captain Bellingham."

The private ran a hand through his pale red hair as though the question somehow hurt his head. "I tended to his personal matters," he said after a moment. "I handled his correspondence, scheduled his meetings, and made sure messages were delivered in a timely manner."

"I see." Colin leaned back and stroked his chin. "Is that how you became aware of his association with Lady Stuart?"

Private O'Fallon's milk-white complexion exposed his immediate discomfort. "I was wrong to speak of that. I don't know anything and should have held my tongue."

"Are you having second thoughts, Private? Or is someone having them for you?"

He scowled but said nothing. We sat like that, silent and distrustful, for what felt an interminable amount of time. Colin did not lift his gaze from Private O'Fallon and I understood that he meant to wait the young man out. For his part, the private remained stiff, his eyes affixed to the tabletop.

I wondered how long we could retain this unnatural peace before the slowly creeping time became too much for Colin to ignore. I glanced over at him and found him looking decidedly content and knew I could stand it no more. "I hate to be the voice of dissension . . . ," I spoke into the silence, ". . . but you gave us Lady Stuart's name yesterday and confided that there had been some sort of connection between her and the captain."

The young man looked vexed as he turned to me, his eyes filled with a mixture of surprise and admonishment. "I know," he muttered, "but ours is a brotherhood that protects its own."

"So I have heard ad nauseam," Colin said as he shifted in his chair. "May I remind you that your Major Hampstead hired me to solve this case. He invited me into the sanctity of your brotherhood, unbidden, to do that which I am renowned for doing. Your unwillingness to help would appear to be counter to your senior officer's wishes. Is that what you would have me believe?"

"Not at all!" he snapped. "I'll answer your questions, but you will find that I wasn't privy to much."

"You may have been privy to more than you know. But what interests me right now, Private, is what you know of Lady Stuart."

"All I can tell you . . . all I know . . . is that Captain Bellingham went to visit her from time to time over the course of several months."

"How many months?"

"Five . . . maybe six."

"And how often?"

"Weekly. Sometimes less, never more."

"Did you accompany him?"

He scowled, his face flushing pink. "What are you suggesting?"

Colin offered an eager smile. "I meant only to enquire if you ever rode out to her home with him? Perhaps to wait with his horse while he went inside?"

"Never," he said. "Captain Bellingham was a private man."

"And yet you knew of his visits to this woman."

"I kept his schedule. It was my duty to know where he was."

"Did you record his appointments with this woman in some sort of ledger?"

Private O'Fallon heaved a labored breath before admitting, "It was my job."

"Didn't it strike you as odd that a woman you believed Captain Bellingham to be somehow involved with was noted on his weekly calendar?"

"It wasn't my business to consider such things."

"Come now, are you telling me you subverted your sense of propriety?"

He shifted his eyes back to the tabletop.

"And the lady lives on Surrey Ridge?"

"If you say so."

"You're lying to me, Private," Colin replied quietly.

"I have told no lies," he tossed back.

"And what of the captain's brother-in-law, Sergeant Mulrooney? Do you know him?"

"I met him a time or two."

"I've heard he and Captain Bellingham were at odds."

"Sergeant Mulrooney is a hotheaded mick. Nobody likes him."

"And what was it between him and the captain?"

The private's gaze hardened. "I'm sure I don't know."

"And do you know anything about a brawl between several members of the Irish Guard and a few of your Life Guard officers? Happened at a tavern. . . ."

"McPhee's," I supplied.

"No."

Colin exhaled. "Very well. I believe we have finished for the moment."

The private threw Colin a cold look as he quickly made his way out.

Private Newcombe came in right behind him, a lopsided grin upon his face, his uniform slightly disheveled in an apparent attempt to achieve some greater level of comfort. "You wanted to see me . . . ?"

"Yes. . . ." Colin motioned the young man to the same chair Private O'Fallon had so readily vacated. "I should like to ask you a few questions. I trust you'll be willing to cooperate . . . ?"

Private Newcombe beamed. "I'll cooperate all day if it'll keep me off those blasted parade grounds." He plopped his mighty plumed helmet onto the table and rubbed a hand through his short, wiry brown hair.

"We'll see what we can do." Colin smiled. "How long did you work for Captain Bellingham?"

"I've only been with the Guard for eighteen months, but I unofficially reported to Captain Bellingham for the last six."

"Unofficially? How so?"

"I fill in for Gavin—Private O'Fallon. I help him out. I also assist Corporal Bramwood when he needs help with the major."

"A man of many talents."

"Not really." He laughed rakishly. "My pop was a captain in the Guard. Served until his death six months ago. See any connection there?" He leaned way back in his chair. "Major Hampstead and my pop started in the service together 'bout a hundred years ago. When my pop got himself killed the major reassigned me to Captain Bellingham and himself. I know what you're thinking"—he snickered—"that the major was looking out for me, but I think it was more outta guilt."

"Guilt?"

"Oh yeah. Major Hampstead and my pop were drinking buddies. They went to the taverns three or four times a week and never failed to get bloody buggery drunk every time. Thank god my mum didn't live to see what a ruddy wanker my pop turned out to be." He shook his head. "One night the two of them got into a brawl with some Irish blokes and somebody pulls a knife and guts my pop. The major walks away without a scratch and my pop dies in hospital a week later. And just like that"—he snapped his fingers with a twinkle in his eyes—"I've got a cushy job reporting to him and Captain Bellingham."

"What tavern was it?"

"McPhee's. Down in the East End."

Colin flicked his gaze to me. "Was there anyone else with your father and the major that night?"

"Captain Bellingham was there and one of my pop's men, Captain Morgesster."

"Was it unusual for your father and the major to be joined by others?"

He shrugged. "Nah."

"And who was the other captain?"

"Edmund Morgesster. A fat old sot. Always piss faced."

"I see. And did you know Captain Bellingham before you reported to him?"

"I knew who he was."

"Had you met?"

Private Newcombe frowned. "I knew him 'cause a my pop, but I didn't have anything to do with them."

"Am I detecting a touch of animosity, Private?"

His scowl deepened. "Think what you want. I had nothin' to do with any a them until I got the job helpin' Captain Bellingham and the major."

"A job you like?"

"It's easy. That's all I'm sayin'. I had nothin' to do with any a them otherwise."

"So you keep saying. . . ."

Private Newcombe slowly rocked his chair forward again. "Why are you gettin' all slick and oily all the sudden?"

"Am I?" Colin stood up and moved behind me, surreptitiously reaching down and touching the middle of my back with a single finger. "I have a theory," he said. "Would you care to hear it?"

He continued to frown. "I suppose."

Colin stepped away, his finger sliding off my back as delicately as it had alighted there. "The Bellinghams' son . . . , " he said in a faraway voice that sounded better suited to a stage drama. "What is his name . . . ?" And I suddenly understood the poke to my back.

"Albert," Private Newcombe answered.

"Yes, of course, Albert. And his wife . . ." Colin let his voice trail off again.

"Gwen," the private quickly filled in.

"Yes." He turned to the young man and eyed him closely. "I

wonder how it is that you speak of your captain's wife with such familiarity? You did the same thing yesterday. *Gwen,* you said. Not *Mrs. Bellingham,* not *Gwendolyn,* but *Gwen.* Rather like an old school chum."

He didn't answer for a moment and I could see something clouding his eyes. "She said I could," he said offhandedly.

"Did she?"

"This is bollocks!" He slammed a hand on the table and jumped from his seat with such fervor that he sent it tumbling backwards to crack against the floor in a climax to his statement. "I am guilty of nothing."

"And I don't believe I have accused you of anything, Private—" Colin spoke slowly.

"I'm finished here!" Private Newcombe barked, reaching out and snatching up his great plumed helmet. "I'll not sit here and be laid into with a bunch of bloody nonsense." He turned on his heels and stormed out the door.

"Well," Colin said as the young man's footfalls receded down the hallway, "if he wasn't having an affair with Mrs. Bellingham then he certainly wanted to."

"Do you suppose?"

"It hadn't occurred to me until he became so sticky, but we may have slipped onto something quite unexpected."

Corporal Bramwood came up short at the doorway. "Did you wish to see me?" he asked tentatively.

"Please." Colin gestured him in. "I've only a couple of questions for you and you can be on your way."

"Very well." Even the young man's smile seemed uneasy.

"Sitting just outside the major's door as you do, I should think you hear a great many things."

His eyes flicked from Colin to me. "I hear some."

"Well, I shouldn't want you to divulge any state secrets." Colin grinned coyly. "But I do wonder if you have heard anything about an incident at a tavern named McPhee's? Your Major

Hampstead was apparently involved and Private Newcombe's father was mortally wounded. What was his name?"

The corporal looked down at his hands before answering. "Wilford. Wilford Newcombe. I heard about it, but I wasn't there."

"A terrible thing."

"Yes, sir. It certainly was."

"What was the outcome of it?"

"The Irish lot were discharged without honors."

"I see." Colin scratched his chin and slowly sauntered back over to me and sat down again. "Must've been hard on Private Newcombe. . . ."

"I suppose, sir."

"What do you make of him? Is he a good help to you?"

"He's fine, sir."

"Was he especially close to the Bellinghams?"

The young man shifted uncomfortably but kept his eyes down. "I guess he thought he was."

"How so?"

He shrugged. "Acting like he was the captain's confidant. It used to bother me."

"No doubt." Colin smiled conspiratorially, though he wasn't fooling me. "He seems the type of chap who doesn't know the boundaries—"

The corporal's eyes flipped up. "That's what I thought too, sir. Thinks he's better than the rest of us."

"Especially concerning Mrs. Bellingham. . . ."

Corporal Bramwood shifted again. "I wouldn't know about that."

"But you heard things. . . ."

He shrugged once more and let his gaze drop, and though I could tell he wasn't going to say anything else, I knew he had said more than enough already.

CHAPTER 13

We got from Buckingham to Parliament in less than ten minutes and signed in with a captain of the Irish Guard, a portly older man named Brady. He was indeed expecting us and took us immediately to the basement of the building, where rows of discrete little offices lined either side of a vast hallway. He brought us to a small cubby with a single desk and two chairs and beckoned us to settle in. "I've been informed ya only need ta see Sergeant Mulrooney, is that right?"

"It is," Colin answered. "We won't take but a few minutes of his time."

"Well, see to it. They ain't payin' us ta be idle."

"Of course." Colin smiled as he settled into one of the chairs. "But might I trouble you with one quick question before you go?"

Captain Brady gave a quick exhalation. "I s'pose."

"Are you familiar with a tavern fight that took place some months back with some men from the Life Guard that cost a captain his life?"

The man's face puckered. "You talkin' about McPhee's . . . ?"

Colin maintained a look of naïveté. "Yes, I do believe that was the name of the place."

"Wot of it?"

"Can you tell me anything about it? How it started, perhaps?"

The captain thrust his hands on his ample hips. "Is that why ya come here? Ta ask about that rot? Well, I'll tell ya somethin'. I lost three good men 'cause a that bloody row. The lot a them booted outta my regiment. And you know what I say . . . ?" He leaned forward, coming precariously close to Colin's face. "My men were all noncoms while that lot a Life Guarders were almost all officers. Now who do ya think shoulda been held responsible fer a thing like that? I'll tell ya what I think." He forged on without waiting for a reply. "Them that earned the titles, that's who." He glared at Colin a moment before straightening up and turning to the door. "I'll send Mulrooney down. Just see ya don't waste his time." And with that, he was gone.

"I've never seen anyone so passionately not answer my question," Colin said with a scowl.

"I guess it's to be expected. Still, you were the epitome of decorum while he ranted. I'm proud of you."

"I'd be prouder if I had ceased his rant with my boot," he grumbled.

"Come now," I reminded. "You'll get more aid with berries than brambles." He flicked his eyes to me and I could see he was in no mood for my grandmother's chestnuts.

Not more than a minute later Thomas Mulrooney joined us, a grimace already set upon his face. I could see he was a young man, not yet over the quarter-century mark, with a broad, otherwise handsome face, a solid frame, and close-cropped deep brown hair. His visage was so sour that at first I thought perhaps he had stumbled on his way into the room before I realized that the sourness was, in fact, meant for us. Whatever he contrived might be our motivation to speak with him, it was clear it made him unhappy.

"Sergeant Mulrooney . . . ," Colin began, waving toward the chair he had just vacated.

"What's this about?!" the sergeant snapped back, standing firm just inside the doorway. "I don't appreciate being summoned when I'm in the middle of my shift."

Colin's eyebrows inched up. "We have come about your sister," he said flatly.

"Gwendolyn?" He shook his head but held Colin's gaze. "Gwendolyn is dead. Will that be all?"

"Have I done something to offend you, Sergeant?" Colin pressed with remarkable restraint.

"Offend me?" he scoffed.

"I have been hired by Her Majesty's Life Guard to ensure that justice is brought to bear in the murders of your sister and brother-in-law, and yet—"

"Justice?!" he sneered. "And what would those British bastards know about justice? They're tossers, they are, every one of them."

"Nevertheless," Colin started again, "they *have* hired me to—"

"Be their lapdog!" the sergeant snarled. "That bunch of degenerate trolls doesn't want justice. They're too busy hiding behind their skirts. I wouldn't piss on them to save their lives."

"And your sister . . . ?"

The question seemed to catch him, just as I knew Colin had intended it to, causing him to draw a labored breath before he answered. "My sister made her own choices and look where it got her. She was stubborn and foolish. At least her boy will have a chance at a new life now. I'm taking him back to County Cork to be raised by my mum."

"Do you know how your sister died, Sergeant?"

The young man's face went very still. "She was shot, Mr. Pendragon, facing the wrong way. Just like she lived her life."

"An interesting detail for you to have, given that the press has yet to be informed of that fact."

For an instant the sergeant looked taken aback before quickly recovering. "I'm done here, Mr. Pendragon. Will that be all?"

"I have heard you had some issue with Captain Bellingham—"

"Trevor was a liar and a fraud. Anyone could see that. Anyone with half a mind."

"But your sister—"

"There was no reasoning with my sister," he shot back. "Gwendolyn made her choice and it cost her her life."

"What if I told you your sister was having an affair with one of the guardsmen?"

"I only hope she was," he sneered.

Colin stared at him a moment before dismissing him with the wave of a hand. "That will be all." Sergeant Mulrooney didn't need to be told twice, as he quickly disappeared from the room without a further word. "What in the hell was *that* all about?!" Colin groused as he sat back down.

"It seems we have finally found someone who did not admire the sainted Captain Bellingham."

"But why such vitriol?" He swept a crown out of his pocket and began worrying it between the fingers of his right hand. "It's almost noon and I'm more confounded by this case than I was this morning."

"Confounded? The man practically handed you an entreaty for murder. It's obvious he hated his brother-in-law and had little kindness for his sister. And what do you make of that bit about how he knew she'd been shot from behind? It would all seem to suggest—"

He caught the rapidly flipping coin and stared at me. "Do you really think it will be so easy, Ethan? That he will just deliver himself into our hands?"

"Why couldn't it be that simple?"

He continued to stare at me as though my brains had abruptly liquefied. "Have you never worked a case with me before?"

"Sometimes a thing can be just what it seems," I said rather more defensively than I had intended.

"Are you trying to help solve this case or just look for the easiest possible solution?"

"I mean to be helpful."

"Well, you're not."

I knew he was under enormous pressure, but such was the state of my ego that I could not stop myself from blurting out, "Then perhaps you would prefer if I left you on your own until Friday."

"Perhaps that *would* be best," he sallied right back as he got up and headed out the door.

CHAPTER 14

Minutes later we were back on the street hailing a cab with nary another word between us. I sucked in a lungful of fresh air and decided to abide by my hasty offer in spite of my almost immediate regret at having done so. "I'll stay at the Devonshire," I announced determinedly as we headed off following the imprecise directions I had gotten from Abigail Roynton.

"What's that . . . ?" he muttered, the same silver crown once again rotating effortlessly between his fingers, making it obvious he was paying me little mind.

"Until Friday. I'll stay at the Devonshire. It'll give you time to yourself." I spoke breezily, with assurance, as though I really thought the idea a good one.

"Fine," he muttered distractedly.

It wasn't the response I'd been seeking, so I decided to let it drop in hopes that I might get a reprieve if I let the whole thing be for a while.

As we continued north to Lancaster Gate, I started to wonder precisely how we were going to find which home belonged to Lady Stuart. It seemed we would either need to beg assistance from the local postman or, worse, be forced to pound on random doors until we found our quarry. We had certainly done such things before, though the latter was one of my least favorite tasks.

Colin had shifted to the far side of the seat and I heard yet another sigh escape his lips as he stared out at the passing scenery, the crown weaving smoothly between his fingers as though propelled by its own force. It appeared he really *did* need to be left to his own musings, so I diverted myself by watching the tightly packed flats of Piccadilly gradually give way to the gently rolling expanse of emerald fields that abutted the gracious homes lining Green Park. As we turned onto Lancaster Gate the lush properties began to abbreviate as the homes drew closer again in a deferential nod to discretion.

Our cab slowed and the driver dragged his cap from his head, scratching his fingers on his shaggy pate. "This 'ere's the street ya asked for," he said. "You know which 'ouse yer after? I'll take ya up if ya point it out."

"This will be fine," Colin answered, slipping the crown into his pocket as he climbed out and began eyeing the houses lining the short street.

I paid the man his fare and sent him on his way before joining Colin, who looked to be focusing his attentions on several houses kitty-corner from where we stood. "Should we start knocking on doors?" I asked with what enthusiasm I could muster.

"There'll be no need," he said at once. "I'd say the lady's house is right over there." He pointed toward a cottage-like home with a densely thatched roof partially covered by ivy. It was slightly smaller than the rest of the homes on the block but meticulous in its upkeep.

"And why do you think that?"

He cocked an eyebrow as he turned to me, a rogue's smile curling his lips. "I don't think it, I know it. Do you see the chimney?"

"Of course." It was thick with the spade-shaped ivy but still revealed whimsical swirls of oat-colored plaster as it rose up beyond the height of the home's rooftop.

"And do you see the wrought iron fastened near its top?"

I hadn't, but now that he pointed it out I spotted the slender bit of black metal in the shape of a half circle protruding from beneath a spray of ivy. "It looks like a backwards *C*."

"Upon closer inspection I believe you will find that it's the bottom half of the letter *S*. Apropos for a woman named Stuart, wouldn't you say?"

We crossed the street until I could indeed see the entirety of the letter *S* peeking from beneath the greenery. "Interesting," I allowed. "But perhaps the Smythes live here, or the Sandersons, or the Westcott-Simpsons."

"Who?!"

"It doesn't matter. You get the point. You cannot tell me you're certain based on a single letter hanging on the chimney."

"Ever the doubter." He chuckled. "Look at the flowers running along the pathway to the door."

"Miniature roses, aren't they?"

"They do look something like a rose, but they aren't. They're dahlias. They come from the mountains of Central America and Colombia. You don't often see them in our dreary city. Rather expensive to import. For someone to have this variety and quantity I should say the owner of this home is most fond of this particular bloom. Most fitting for a woman named Dahlia, wouldn't you say?"

I grinned. "Now that *is* convincing."

"Exactly." His eyes sparkled. "Shall we?"

He pounded on the door, and given the diminutive size of the house, it took only a moment before an elderly gentleman in an elegant tuxedo answered. "May I help you?" he enquired in less than impeccable English.

I was surprised to find a houseman of his caliber in a home as unimposing as this. Even though the woman who lived here was titled, I had not thought she would engage more than a house-keeper and cook, like our Mrs. Behmoth, as she was clearly trying to live within some particular means.

"Good afternoon. I'm Colin Pendragon and this is Ethan Pruitt."

"Yes, sir. I am aware of who you are."

"Ah." Colin's face revealed a hint of satisfaction. "Very well. Then I would be most obliged if Lady Stuart could spare us a few minutes of her time."

"Is Madam expecting you?"

"She is not. But I can assure you it is a matter of the utmost urgency, hence our unannounced arrival."

The old man pursed his lips. "While it is human nature to believe one's business always urgent," he stated simply, "I am afraid Her Ladyship will not consent to meet with anyone un-less they have an appointment. It is the only way to maintain order in her days."

"I see. . . ." Colin flicked his gaze to me a moment. "The lady is so in demand then?" He kept his tone light, but his in-ference was evident.

"She is," the man stated innocently, either missing Colin's intent or choosing to ignore it.

"I wonder if I couldn't impose upon you to ask Her Lady-ship if she might make an exception to her otherwise sensible rule. If you could inform her that I am here on an official mat-ter, a matter of great delicacy that reaches all the way to Her Majesty's household, I would be most grateful. And while I ap-preciate your homespun platitudes, I assure you I am not over-stating my urgency."

The man didn't move for a moment and I worried that Colin

had pushed too far, so it was a relief when he finally said, "I must ask you to wait here—" And with that, he shoved the door closed and reseated its bolt.

"If that old hump doesn't nip right back," Colin immediately hissed, "I'm going to set fire to the roof and smoke them out." But nothing of the sort was necessary, as almost immediately the door was again unbolted and pulled open and the two of us were ushered inside.

We entered a small white hallway adorned with wainscoting that stretched halfway up the walls. A rough-hewn beamed ceiling crisscrossed above our heads, very much in keeping with the cottage motif evident from the outside. We were shown to a sitting room not more than a dozen paces down the hall that also served as a library, much like our own front room, though Lady Stuart's was appreciably larger. Bookshelves lined the side walls and a large plaster and brick fireplace stood at the center of the wall across from the doorway. The fireplace was framed by a row of arched windows with filmy white drapes pulled across them. There was a high-backed sofa in the center of the room covered in a whimsical fabric of leaves and thatch that had four wing-backed chairs flanking it, two on either side.

"If you wouldn't mind waiting here," the houseman said, "Her Ladyship will be with you shortly."

"Of course." Colin bothered with only the briefest smile.

The man nodded and disappeared the way we had come.

"Don't you find this a peculiar home for a woman of nobility?" I asked quietly as I wandered over to look at the photographs on the mantel.

"I do," Colin muttered as he perused the nearest wall of bookshelves, quickly fingering the bindings without pulling any of them free. "I would say the lovely widow Roynton was right: Our good lady was neither born nor raised of money, but came to it sometime later in her life. Likely either a good marriage or an adept con."

I swung around to look at him, wondering if he was teasing, but he remained focused on the books, pursing his lips and nodding his head from time to time. "A con?!" I hissed.

"Anything is possible."

I decided not to risk any further questions, so turned back to study the framed photographs. One was a head shot of a beautiful dark-haired woman with black eyes and satin skin who looked to have a touch of something exotic in her ancestry. The next was of the same woman standing before a creek in a wood next to an elderly man. The woman appeared to be some years younger in this photo and the man looked like her grandfather, so similar were their features. They shared the same oval face and striking cheekbones underscored by a solid, square jaw, but while the elderly man, with his shaggy white hair and ragged, untrimmed beard, wore the garb of a Gypsy, the young woman did not. They did, however, both wear brilliant smiles, which spoke to the certainty that they were *not* British.

The last picture was of Her Majesty in an appropriately dour and sanctimonious mood. With her gray hair tugged tightly beneath her tiny crown and her thin lips and heavy jowls as rigid as granite, she was clearly demonstrating for the whole of the empire what became her people most.

"I trust I have not kept you waiting too long?"

I turned and found myself staring at the same beautiful face I had just been looking at in two of the photographs, although she was older now. I guessed her to be about the same age as I, though I was finding it difficult to be certain given her pristine complexion and the mane of rich black hair pinned up above her shoulders. Her bearing was graceful and assured, an obvious display of breeding, and she moved with the delicacy of a woman trained in dance.

"Absolutely not," Colin enthused, a great smile breaking across his face that assured me that he too had been caught by his first impression of her. "We are grateful you have agreed to meet with us at all."

Her smile came easily. "How could anyone refuse you, Mr. Pendragon? You've quite the reputation. And I understand you have come on a matter of some urgency?"

"Quite so."

"Please." She gestured to the chairs by the fireplace as she settled on the sofa. "May I offer you tea?"

"You mustn't go to any trouble. We are merely seeking information regarding a man I am told you were familiar with—" But before Colin could finish his thought she lifted a hand to stop him as she reached out and picked up a tiny bell from the table in front of her.

"You must indulge me," she said as she flicked her wrist, setting off a sweet tone. "If we're going to have the discussion I believe you are here to have, I simply must have some tea."

"Madam . . . ?" Her elderly houseman stepped through the archway.

"Fetch us some tea and shortbread, Evers. And don't be stingy."

"Yes, madam." He nodded, disappearing as quietly as he had come.

"I must profess a bit of curiosity . . . ," Colin said the moment he was gone, ". . . as to just what you think we are here to discuss given that I have yet to pose so much as a single question?"

"Oh, come now, Mr. Pendragon." Her eyes sparkled with amusement. "You're being coy. You have already confessed your intention to seek information regarding a man I was familiar with. Past tense. Unless I am mistaken I would presume that man to be the late Captain Trevor Bellingham. No doubt it wasn't a secret among his men that he came to see me from time to time—"

"You are most astute, Lady Stuart."

"And I shall hear no more until our tea has been served," she said.

Evers returned almost at once with an elegant tea set atop a tray that also held a plate of shortbread and a small crystal decanter half-filled with an amber liquid. He placed it on the table nearest Lady Stuart and poured our tea, raising the little decanter to his mistress and staring solely at her.

"A spot of brandy?" she offered, but we both demurred. "Quaint." She gestured to Evers, who poured a dollop in her cup before preparing the conventional version for Colin and me. "I have a hunch today is a day when I shall enjoy the warm embrace of a touch of brandy."

"Be assured I am not here to cause you distress," Colin said. "Yet I am certain you understand the need to learn all we can about the Bellinghams in order to guarantee these murders are quickly solved."

"Of course." She sipped at her tea before settling her gaze on Colin. "I suspect you wish to know the nature of my relationship with Captain Bellingham."

"I do," he said gently, "as well as anything else about him you might care to confide. And I hope you will permit me to ask a few questions along the way."

"You are like velvet, Mr. Pendragon." She grinned over the lip of her cup. "Soft, silken, and seductive."

"You flatter me."

"I think not." She chuckled as she set her cup down. "Let us not forget that velvet is also coarse and rough on its opposing side, without which its more sanguine face would never hold together. Something of a conundrum, wouldn't you say?"

His smile held firm, but I could see the enjoyment in his eyes slowly waning. "I suppose it is something of a conundrum at that," he allowed.

Lady Stuart released a deep, sonorous laugh. "Forgive me for teasing you so. And you such a good sport."

Colin's pallor slowly deepened as he waved her off with the nonchalance of a man trying to prove he is at ease being the brunt of mockery. It was all I could do to keep from laughing alongside her.

"My apologies." She nodded with a delicate smirk as she reached for her tea again. "How I wish we could avoid the topic at hand, but I know we cannot." She cast her gaze at the ceiling a moment before settling her eyes back on Colin and speaking in a clear, if halting, voice. "It is fair to say that I do not relish talking about Trevor. I find it almost intolerable to speak about what happened to him and poor Gwendolyn. I have known him for ten years, Mr. Pendragon. He was a corporal when I first met him. He and Gwen had only just married."

"You were close with Mrs. Bellingham?"

She sighed. "I was. And I was also godmother to little Albert. That poor child." She glanced away again, clearly trying to cling to her composure. "I was newly widowed when Trevor and I met. Not at all in mind of a romance despite what you may have heard. Trevor and I were more like brother and sister."

Colin flashed the thinnest of smiles before asking, "Exactly how did you meet?"

"At a hunt." The recollection seemed to lighten her mood. "My husband had been friends with the Duke of Brynhaven. After my husband's death I was occasionally invited up to his estate for the running of the hounds. While it's not actually to my taste, I used to go because I knew it was better than sitting about feeling sorry for myself.

"As you are likely aware, the Duke is a member of Parliament and a former colonel in Her Majesty's service. He is also not the slightest bit averse to availing himself of free labor from the military whenever he sees fit. Trevor was one of several men he had arranged to work at his estate that weekend. His job was to attend the foxes. He was to keep the poor creatures well until they were released to be hunted. Such a gallant pastime," she murmured.

She fussed with more tea for all of us before continuing, her manner once again relaxing as she continued to recount the story. "I was wandering the grounds behind the stables in a wretched mood while the men prepared their mounts. For no particular reason I had headed into the woods just beyond where the hunt was to take place when I came upon Trevor hidden in a thatch of weeds and brambles cradling this poor terrified fox in the crook of an arm." She laughed outright. "He had doused it quite thoroughly in the Duke's cologne and was wrapping it in thin strips of cloth from one of the Duke's old shirts. I knew at once what he was up to and absolutely adored him for it.

"As you can imagine, I gave him quite a start, but once I assured him of my like sympathies we combined our efforts. He ripped a large chunk of cloth from the bedding in the fox's cage and handed it to me. I hurried off with this rupture of material dangling from my hand, marking the terrain as I rushed in a diagonal arc away from that section of the woods.

"When I started hearing the baying of hounds, I altered my course and went as deep into the forest as I could, hoping our ridiculous charade might actually work." She shook her head as a playful smile curved her mouth. "I was surrounded by barking, snarling, befuddled hounds within minutes, sniffing about trying to figure where they had gone wrong. The men were no better." She released another low, throaty chuckle. "It was the beginning of a friendship I knew would last a lifetime." Her smile faded. "I just never imagined . . ." She did not finish the thought.

"And what of Mrs. Bellingham?"

Lady Stuart glanced back at Colin, the expression on her face unreadable. "Gwendolyn and I met shortly thereafter, but it was Trevor who was so very patient and understanding of my new widowhood."

"Consoling, was he?"

She laughed and shook her head. "Such subtlety, Mr. Pendragon. I can only imagine the sort you must deal with, with whom such tactics work." She took another sip of tea before looking back at him with the same grace and confidence that seemed to infuse everything she did. "Trevor gave me invaluable guidance with respect to my business affairs and wouldn't allow me to give him so much as a farthing for his efforts. Had he not stepped in as he did I am sure I would not now be living as well as I do. That's our shared history, Mr. Pendragon. We communicated without artifice and cared for one another with the purity of family."

"I understand," he said, and unlike me, I knew he would. "Did he ever confide any fear for his safety or that of his wife?"

"Never. And there was little we did not discuss."

"Did he mention any business dealings he was concerned about? Someone new to the regiment he was having an issue with? Any recent disagreements weighing on his mind?"

"Nothing at all. And I assure you, Mr. Pendragon, nothing would please me more than to be able to tell you of such a thing."

Colin nodded grimly as he stood up and set his teacup on the tray. "Will you permit me one last question?"

"Of course."

"How did you learn of the murders?"

"Like every other disaffected member of this city, Mr. Pendragon: on the front page of the *Times*."

CHAPTER 15

The early afternoon was proving to be cool and there was a midnight-blue bank of clouds creeping across the horizon that once again carried the portent of rain. With this threat hanging over us, Colin methodically turned his attentions back to the disappearance of the furry Lady Priscilla. As we hiked past a yawning gate and up to the large Stanford and Hildegard Rinton estate, I was struck by the excess of lacey moldings dripping like frosting from its woodwork, making the house appear to be almost edible. It was painted a startling shade of yellow with the trim piped on in variations of cream, tan, and burnt umber. An oversized front porch bound by an explosion of latticework ran the length of the house and wrapped partway down the far side.

Not only did the Rintons live here but also one Bertha Omega, a reportedly dowdy cur who had spent nearly all of her showing years in Lady Priscilla's formidable shadow. At least according to Elsa. We spotted dubious traces of the perpetual also-ran courtesy of uprooted flowers on either side of the porch steps and small yellow circles of poisoned grass that defaced the otherwise velvety green lawn.

"It would seem this bitch has picked up a host of unseemly behaviors," Colin noted as we climbed the porch steps.

"I should say." I chuckled. "We had best mind our ankles."

Colin pulled the bell next to the door and immediately set off a barrage of yapping that was as dogged as a murderous scream. "Incessant barking," he tsked. "Hardly the sign of a champion."

A woman's voice could be heard scolding the dog to no avail and a moment later there came a high-pitched yelp that was followed by utter silence. It took another minute before the door finally swung open to reveal a tall, slender man with a rapidly receding hairline, a great, curved nose, and a chin that seemed to be hiding somewhere within the confines of his neck. "Yes?" he asked in a twitchy voice as he planted his frame, such as it was, in the center of the doorway.

"I'm Colin Pendragon and this is my associate, Ethan Pruitt." Colin flashed his stellar smile, but the man's gaze remained vacant. "I have been retained by Lady Nesbitt-Normand to investigate the disappearance of her pup, Lady Priscilla. Might I have a word with either Stanford or Hildegard Rinton?"

The man began to blink furiously as though fearing a poke in the eye before stammering, "Are H-H-Hildegard and I suspects?"

Colin shot out his hand. "Mr. Rinton, I take it?"

"Who is it, Stanford?" a sturdy female voice belted out from somewhere nearby. "Whom are you talking to?"

The man flinched, his knuckles white where he gripped the doorjamb, as he turned and called back into the belly of the house, "It's Colin Pendragon and some other chap. They want to speak with us about Lady Priscilla."

"Well, for pity's sake let them in. Our little girl's about to jump out of her skin with curiosity."

He stepped back to allow us to pass, retaining an unflappable stoicism as he did so. The moment the door clicked shut there came a sudden, frantic scratching on the floor that picked up intensity as it drew nearer, culminating in a pudgy tan and black pug torpedoing into the foyer from a side corridor as though having been shot from a cannon. The dog stopped no more than three feet away before wholly rebuking us with a fresh barrage of barking.

"Bertha Omega, you stop that this instant!" A short, plump woman of slightly more than middle years lumbered into the room at what must have counted for full speed. "We do *not* bark at guests."

"She's fine," Colin said as he knelt down and held out a hand.

But the lady of the household was not to be deterred, as she came up behind the pup and swatted her rear with a mighty flail of meaty palm, causing the poor thing to spin almost completely around before abruptly squatting and relieving herself on the foyer rug. *"Stanford!"* she wailed. "Just look what you've made her do. Really . . . I should think you would have more sense when you answer the door. Now get that cleaned up." She fixed her gaze on us with evident annoyance. "Stanford has never understood our little girl in the least." She snatched up the dog and nuzzled her face in its belly while making a host of sloppy sounds, all of which only seemed to further agitate the pup. "Please come in and sit down," she said at length as she led us to a large front room that appeared to encompass nearly half of the downstairs area. "We are positively *destroyed* about Lady Priscilla's disappearance."

"As is Lady Nesbitt-Normand." Colin flashed a tight smile. "We certainly appreciate your willingness to see us."

"But of course," our hostess enthused as she dropped into an overstuffed chair by the fireplace. "An attack against any pug is like an attack against every one of us. Isn't that right?" she cooed to her pup.

"You did show against Lady Priscilla, didn't you?" Colin asked with seeming nonchalance as we sat down across from her.

"Well, of course we did," she clucked. "She beat us two years running. I must admit *I* find her the barest hint of high-strung, but she does have the most perfect stature when they can get her to stand still. And her face!" She nearly purred. "Such symmetry if you look at her from *just* the right angle." She leaned forward and set her wriggling pug on the floor by her feet. "Please don't mind my little one. She gets so excited when company comes. She only wants to sniff your shoes. She means no disrespect."

Colin leaned over to scratch the dog's head, but she would have none of that, leaping back each time he reached out and letting loose a growl of warning. Only after he sat fully back did the pug dare to reel forward again, taking full inventory of not only his shoes but the cuffs of his pants as well. Once the dog had satisfied herself with her inspection of Colin, she turned and came over to me, but I was apparently much less intoxicating, as I was quickly dispatched after a cursory examination so the wearying Bertha Omega could return to Colin.

"Oh, look," the proud Hildegard Rinton said with amusement. "She likes you, Mr. Pendragon."

This time he managed to coax the dog over and it fell prey to his ministrations almost at once. "She really is quite the love bug." He chuckled as he scratched behind the pug's ears.

"I am so pleased that you can tell, Mr. Pendragon." She beamed.

We all watched transfixed as the pup licked and nestled against Colin for a minute, before quite suddenly, without any warning whatsoever, lurching toward me and sinking her teeth into my nearest boot. Without even thinking I shot my leg out and sent the unfortunate pug in a brief airborne arc that landed little Bertha Omega in a belly skid by the fireplace. Hildegard Rinton screamed as the pug stood up, shook herself off, and started yowling with renewed vigor, all of which brought Stanford Rinton racing into the room with a look somewhere between fear and mortification.

"Ethan—" Colin cringed as he bolted up. "I'm terribly sorry, Mrs. Rinton. I do believe we have overstayed our welcome. You've been most gracious."

Mrs. Rinton looked apoplectic as she heaved herself to her feet and hurried over to her pup. "My baby . . . My little darling . . . ," she fretted as she snatched the dog up into her arms. "Is my poor little girl okay?" She glanced over the scruff of her squirming dog. "Well, show them out, Stanford."

"I am so sorry," I said, but no one seemed to hear me as Stanford Rinton rushed us back outside. I kept quiet as we fled down the driveway and managed to hold my tongue until we were climbing into a cab Colin had waved down. "I feel awful," I muttered.

"You would have thought she was an Irish wolfhound the way you reacted."

"I know—"

"Never mind. There was nothing to be learned there other than the fact that Stanford Rinton would likely do just about anything to keep that wife of his at bay."

"So you think he could be responsible for the theft of Lady Priscilla on his wife's orders?"

"I wouldn't find that difficult to believe, but it's all just idle conjecture. It would be unwise to discount anything at this point." He pulled out his pocket watch and glanced at it. "Next is the home of one Buster Brown. What's the name of the spinster who owns him?"

"Edwina Easterbrooke."

"Yes. And then we must pay a visit to Lady Nesbitt-Normand to see if she has had word from anyone seeking payment for the safe return of her little lady." He turned and set his gaze out the window, idly fiddling with his watch fob as he stared out at the rows of passing townhomes abutting Regent's Park.

"And I really should get a room at the Devonshire before the whole of the afternoon gets by."

"What?" He glanced at me for an instant, but his eyes quickly shifted back outside as his thoughts failed to engage with my inanity. "Whatever you think is best," he mumbled.

I let out a muffled sigh and cursed myself as we rattled up to a large four-story town house not far from our own flat. I paid the driver and then joined Colin as he stared up at the towering redbrick building with its tiny rectangle of perfectly manicured green grass out front. Red geraniums bordered the stamp-sized porch and window boxes overflowed with the same scarlet flowers. The boxes and casements were painted a snowy white, but unlike the Rintons' home this one displayed no signs of a malcontent pup on either the gardens or lawn.

Colin rapped on the door and we waited several minutes before a rotund man with a flush face and pink jowls hauled it open. "Yes?" he said in a labored voice that made me fear he had been on the top floor when we'd knocked.

Colin made the introductions, informing him that we were there on an urgent matter, and I noted the look in the man's eyes as he registered Colin's name. I supposed he suspected why we had come just as the Rintons had. "I'm afraid I must ask you to wait a moment while I ascertain if Madam is available," he said officiously, in spite of whatever he may have been thinking.

"Of course." Colin smiled easily. "Ascertain away."

The man closed the door and Colin and I were left to our disparate musings for several minutes. It was enough time for Colin to check his watch—twice. I was afraid he might be on the verge of barreling in uninvited when the door finally swung open again.

"Your patience is appreciated," the houseman announced as he did his best to move aside and allow us entry. "I am afraid the volume of stairs are getting the best of me as the years press on."

"Be wary of laying too much blame on your age," Colin offered carelessly as he crossed the threshold.

I tried not to blanch as I added, "We certainly appreciate your mistress granting us a bit of her time."

He nodded perfunctorily, thankfully too professional to remark on Colin's insinuation. He led us up a single flight to a large open space that stretched the entire length and width of the flat. There were several seating areas spread across the floor, making it look more like the great room in a hotel than a living space for a home. A large carved fireplace of white marble stood at the far end of the room, a tumbling pattern of ivy accentuated in bold relief across its face. We were shown to chairs in front of it as the corpulent man went huffing back downstairs to fetch some tea.

We sat in silence until I began to hear a strange, methodical clicking coming from overhead. It sounded like an overzealous clock, but when I caught the delicate tread of a woman I realized what it was. I turned away from the blazing fireplace warding off the chill in this great space and found Colin already on his feet looking at the staircase behind us. I stood up just as an unusually tall, rail-thin woman with a harsh, angular face made her way down the steps in the wake of an obese pug.

"Mr. Pendragon . . . Mr. Pruitt . . . ," she said, her voice as thin and frail as her frame, yet quite incongruous with her towering height.

"Miss Easterbrooke." Colin returned a generous smile as he glanced up at her before bending and scratching the ears of the dog, who had dropped at her feet in a flurry of labored panting. "And you, little man, must be Buster Brown."

"You have heard of him?!" Her face lit up as she perched on the edge of a chair across from us. "He was a champion once, when he was younger, and has caught the eye of many a judge through the years." She too leaned over and scratched between the pug's ears with a hand that dwarfed his pudgy head. "He can be quite the charmer."

I stared at the dog as he hoisted himself back on his derrière, which was twice the width of his head, and struggled to give him the benefit of the doubt.

"I can see that he's certainly able to charm his way into table scraps." Colin grinned.

"Oh!" Miss Easterbrooke offered a polite twitter that came out oddly harsh. "I'm afraid that's my fault. I cannot bear to see anyone go hungry."

"An admirable quality," he mused, though it was clear she did not feel the same about herself.

"Thank you, Alvin." She turned to her houseman as he set out a tray of tea. "I think I will do the honors myself today. That will be all." He withdrew far more silently than someone of his bulk should have been able to. Miss Easterbrooke leaned forward and rearranged the cups and saucers on the tray to suit some inner demon before looking over at us and asking, "Tea?" We both agreed and watched as she started mixing the tea, milk, and sugar with the focused precision of a chemist. She topped off the process by placing each cup on its matching saucer and twisting it just so to ensure the handle faced us properly, and only then did she hand them across to us. For herself she poured a mere half cup, adding nothing more than a light squeeze of lemon. "You will tell me if it doesn't suit you," she said.

"It is perfection." Colin smiled.

She reached for a small plate of gingersnaps and shortbread fanned out like a deck of cards and delicately segregated the two sweets with a small knife before holding them out. "Biscuit?"

"Very kind. . . ." Colin nodded, sweeping up one of each and willfully causing opposing crumbs to drop as he did. Miss Easterbrooke's brow furrowed the slightest hint, but she said nothing. When she turned the plate in my direction I shook my head with a smile, unwilling to get involved with the whole sordid mess.

"Are you certain?" she prodded, and I'm sure I detected a note of distress in her voice. When I declined yet again, she set the plate on the floor and the heretofore knackered Buster Brown leapt up and bolted forward, sucking down the remaining half-dozen biscuits with evident passion. "That's my boy." She chuckled. "I simply cannot refuse him anything." She stuck her fingers out and the dog greedily lapped at the salts on her skin.

"He seems to have a sweet nature to go along with his sweet tooth."

"Indeed he does. . . ." She giggled, picking up a napkin and carefully wiping her fingers one after the other. "He was a Dorchester County champion at three. After that . . . ," she sighed, ". . . he started putting on a bit of weight. I do think the judges insist the dogs be too thin these days." She continued to wipe her fingers with the napkin, folding it in half each time she used it. "And then Lady Priscilla started to be shown. Buster Brown simply didn't have a chance after she came along."

"Which is precisely why we are here."

"I presumed. I heard about her disappearance. Dreadful, simply dreadful. Who would *do* such a thing?"

"That's what we're going to find out. Have you known anyone to make threats against Lady Nesbitt-Normand or her pup?"

"Absolutely not. Lady Nesbitt-Normand is a lovely woman and a formidable challenger."

"Still . . . ," Colin prodded, "I know things can happen in the passion of competition."

"You don't understand the show circuit, Mr. Pendragon. We are quite like a family really, with our four-legged dears as much our children as if we had borne them ourselves." She leaned forward and wedged the tiny square that was left of her napkin under the teapot, compelling it to stay in the minute shape she had forced it into.

"Understandable. And what is your Buster doing in his retirement?"

"Well"—she hesitated—"I should very much like to breed him . . ." As though to approve her intention to roll her Buster Brown out to pasture, the pug suddenly began digging at the carpet in what I felt sure was a desperate attempt to free any crumbs he had not already inhaled from the plate. "Now you stop that," she scolded, reaching out and shaking a finger in the dog's face. "You know better than that." He stared at her a moment, apparently deciding she meant no ill will, and immediately resumed his frantic digging. *"Alvin!"* his mistress hollered, rising from her chair as though it had suddenly become quite hot. *"Come and get Buster."*

She shooed Buster with her arms, herding the pug toward the stairs even as the poor pup cast mournful glances backwards. By the time she managed to coerce him across the room, her houseman, Alvin, bobbed into view, moving with a rapidity that seemed to suggest he had been fearing just such a summons.

"Take him upstairs," Miss Easterbrooke commanded. "Put him to bed."

"Yes, ma'am." He stooped and swept up the dog. The pup craned its head around to keep us, or the room, in view for as long as he could, which lasted only a moment before he finally disappeared aloft. Miss Easterbrooke came gliding back to us.

"I am so sorry." She settled on the edge of the same chair again, her face now quite flush.

"You've nothing to apologize for and I shall only trouble you to answer one more question."

"You mustn't rush off. More tea?"

"No, thank you. I'm just wondering if you have made any plans yet to start the breeding process?"

"Oh!" She stiffened, flicking her eyes between Colin and me. "Such a topic for mixed company." Her face pursed uncomfortably as she looked down at her hands. "Not yet, Mr. Pendragon. It's just so hard to find a good bitch."

"I'm sure it is." He stood up and slid his teacup onto the tray. "We have taken up more than enough of your time, Miss Easterbrooke. You have been most kind and I only hope you will allow us a further visitation should it prove necessary."

"But of course." She smiled, casually pushing Colin's cup into a more symmetrical placement. "We are at your service." She took my cup and settled it with equal care before standing up and brushing at her dress, ridding herself of crumbs that only she could see. "None of us will rest until Lady Priscilla is home again. I won't even allow Buster to go outside by himself anymore and you can just imagine how he hates that."

"I really don't think you or your little charge has anything to worry about," Colin soothed. "I'm quite certain that Lady Priscilla's theft was very specific."

"Oh dear. . . ." She hugged her bony arms around her thin frame as though they could actually be of use in protecting her. "Somehow that makes it even worse."

We were outside hailing a cab within minutes, my mood plunging at our lack of progress, when Colin abruptly seized my elbow and said, "That was outstanding."

"What was outstanding?"

He ushered me into the coach and called out our home address. "We have solved the case," he announced with a hearty grin, his dimples alight.

"What?!"

"Edwina Easterbrooke and her corpulent henchman are holding Lady Priscilla prisoner in that flat," he announced with great self-assurance.

"You cannot possibly know that."

"I absolutely do."

"Then why didn't you say something?"

"Because now we have to prove it."

CHAPTER 16

I was sitting on a too-hard chair back at Buckingham Palace in a small room in which the only sound I could hear was the drumming of my heartbeat in my ears. Major Hampstead had gotten word to us the moment we returned home that I could come and speak with young Albert Bellingham. The very idea had immediately sunk my mood, and it had only spiraled from there as I'd been forced to gird myself and head back. I had thought of entreating Colin for a reprieve this once; after all, hadn't I gotten that blasted autopsy report for him? And on the heels of that very thought I had realized this was my chance to redeem myself. We would not end up in prison when this conversation was done, though I wondered if that mightn't be preferable to the mental state I was quickly descending into.

Footsteps echoed from the hallway and a moment later a little boy with curly white-blond hair, brilliant brown eyes, and a wide, open face entered with a tall, lanky woman at his side. She wore the white uniform of a nurse and a sour expression that alerted me to the fact that she hated what this lad was about to be subjected to. I couldn't have agreed with her more.

The woman did not introduce herself, nor did I care, but after settling the boy in she pointedly let me know she would be back in fifteen minutes—fifteen minutes exactly—and that would be all the time I would be allotted. I nodded, dispensing with the sham of a smile, and she left, her shoes clicking reproachfully as she disappeared back down the hallway.

Albert looked drawn and tired, and I knew he wasn't sleeping well. I could see it in his eyes. I could remember those first nights myself.

"I'm sorry for what you've been through," I mumbled so disconcertingly that it even startled me. The boy just stared back. I could hardly blame him. "My name"—I took a deep breath—"is Ethan Pruitt. I have been asked to help make sure that whoever hurt your mum and dad gets captured. I know that's what you want, isn't it?" If I could have bit the words back, I would have. They were inane and stupid, and I wasn't at all surprised when the boy kept silent.

"I need to ask you about the night your parents died, Albert, because you might know something that could help—" And once again I blanched at my own words as I realized they were the same ones that had been used on me so many years before. I was repeating them as if they had been said to me yesterday, still so fresh even after twenty-seven years. Every bit as much as the sound of someone calling me. A woman. My mother.

"*Ethan!*" she was hollering, her voice high-pitched to the point of shrillness. "*Ethan!*" she bellowed again, and this time I could hear the note of desperation.

"Leave him be," a man's voice soothed. My father's voice.

"I want him," she answered harshly, her tone distorted by the talons of her hysteria. "We should be together. We *need* to be together."

I was aware that I was trembling, my whole body quaking as though trying to rid itself of a fever, but I wasn't sick, I was scared. No, I was terrified.

"Come back in here," my father was urging, his tone as soft and calm as a breeze, but even I could hear the worry coloring his words. "Bring the baby and come back. We'll be fine. Just the three of us."

Oh god. Oh no.

My throat clenched and I couldn't draw a breath. I wanted to scream and tell my father not to go in there with her, not to take the baby, that poor innocent baby, so beautiful and pure, but no sound would escape my mouth. Nothing at all. I longed to move, to run, to flail about, to do anything to make some noise and stop what I *knew* was about to happen, but my legs and arms were as seized as my throat and I could not will them to cooperate. It felt like I had been drugged or cast into a mire from which there was no hope of escape.

And then I heard the door shut. It wasn't a slam, it wasn't done with anger, but there was a definitiveness about it that I would always remember. It was only a sound—*click!*—but it was crisp and tidy and signaled the end of everything.

I tasted the tears before I realized I was crying. My nose was running, slick and viscous, and I cursed myself for cowering there, unable to move, unable to yell, unable to do anything but leak snot and salt water. My shaking had become so severe that at some point I wrapped my arms around myself as if I might be about to fly apart. Selfish to the end. And still I did not move, *could* not move. The silence in the flat was deafening. Taunting me. Extending itself languorously because it knew that *I* knew what was about to happen. Even so, I could not unravel myself from my hiding place.

Pop!

My body jerked and in that same instant my bladder released.

Pop!

I flinched as though I had been hit, my back arching up and hitting something, something hard and unforgiving. Wood. My eyes focused and I remembered I was under my bed. I had crushed myself into the farthest corner and could not move because I had wedged myself between the walls on two sides and the bottom of the frame just above.

Pop!

And suddenly my feet heaved against the corner where the walls met and I was able to propel myself forward, bursting out into the moonlight streaming through the sole window in my room. But still my limbs would not cooperate, my knees and arms scrabbling about, struggling for purchase on the shiny wood floor. My face was streaked with wetness and I was soiled. And there was something else. A heavy smell: dark, burnt, metallic. Gunpowder. And just like that my voice roared back and I screamed. From the depths of my soul I hollered so hard and so long that I feared I would never stop. . . .

I stared across at Albert a moment, unaware of whether I had said or done anything. His face remained impassive however, leaving me grateful that my terrors had not escaped my lips. As I drew in a long breath I understood that I could do this. I *would* do this. So by the time the woman came back to fetch him, we had finished our conversation and I prayed he might sleep better this night.

CHAPTER 17

By the time I returned home, Colin's mood had dipped. I could tell his initial enthusiasm was tempered by the enormity of the task at hand around both the Bellingham murders and the Nesbitt-Normand case. What made it worse was that I had nothing to offer him from young Albert Bellingham. The boy had heard the two gunshots, those innocuous *pops* he would never forget, and the occasional muffled cry of his father overhead, another sound that would haunt him until his own death, but had seen no one and heard no other voices.

"Have you given any more thought to Sergeant Mulrooney?" I prodded Colin, concerned about the poor lad being under his uncle's vitriolic stewardship if even for a few weeks. And if the sergeant proved to be involved in the murders . . . I could not help the glare I leveled on Colin.

"In what way?" he responded with a clipped abruptness, clearly driven by unsettling thoughts of his own.

"He has to be considered," I said.

"He *is* being considered. They are *all* being considered. What *are* you prattling on about?"

I didn't take his bait, deciding it was indeed best for me to leave him to his brooding for the next couple of days. Without a further word, I went straight to our bedroom to collect a few things for my stay at the Devonshire Hotel.

"What the bleedin' 'ell are you doin'?" Mrs. Behmoth startled me as I stuffed my writing into a valise before even bothering to consider clothing.

"I'm leaving Colin alone for a bit. This Bellingham case is crushing and I'm afraid I have been more distraction than aid."

"That's daft. 'E ain't no good without you underfoot."

"Oh, come now." I scowled as I stuffed a few things into a sack, certain she was having a laugh at my expense. "You shouldn't let him hear you say that."

"I'll tell 'im meself!" she snapped as she turned and left.

I should have told her to leave him be, but she was gone before I thought of it and, truthfully, there was still a part of me that hoped he might come back and insist I stop my foolishness. Heaving a sigh of annoyance, I finished pulling things from the armoire and set my sights on the top of the commode.

"You're bein' a ruddy arse!" I heard Mrs. Behmoth growl from the other room.

"If you *please*," Colin shot back.

A moment later I felt him lurking in the doorway even before I looked up to find him standing there. "You don't have to do this . . . , " he said, but there was little conviction in his tone.

"I'll be two minutes down the street and shall do any bidding you need." I gave him an earnest smile. "I just need the rest of my things from the loo." I moved past him, confident that I was indeed doing the right thing, and quickly grabbed my few toiletries, taking care not to disturb any of Colin's face creams or hair oils. I looked at the little shelf and felt the void of my presence for the first time as I stared at my empty side.

"You needn't take everything . . . ," he piped up from behind me.

"*Objets de beauté.*" I smirked.

He gave a small smile as he stepped in and shut the door. "I'm sorry. I know I've become intolerable about this Bellingham case—"

"You haven't." I took his hand. "There's enormous pressure on you and I do *not* wish to contribute to it any more than I already have by landing us in prison and kicking the Rintons' dog. . . ." I sighed heavily as he snickered and slid his arms around my waist.

"I wouldn't have you any other way," he said, his hands beginning to drift.

"What are you doing? Where's Mrs. Behmoth?"

He looked at me, his eyes sweeping my face with amusement. "Downstairs, I suppose. Why? Did you want her to join us?"

I laughed as his powerful arms squeezed me as though trying to fuse the two of us together. And in that moment nothing else mattered, not the cases, not my blunders, not even the incessant sweeping of the clock's hands; there was only the two of us, fitting with ease and surety.

Such pinnacles are as ethereal as the beating of a hummingbird's wings, however, for in what seemed the span of a breath I was down on the street, my bags in tow, waiting for Colin to hail a cab. He had decided to come with me to the Devonshire before we went our separate ways, me to see Lady Nesbitt-Normand while he headed back to Buckingham.

"To the Devonshire," he called up to the driver as we settled in for the short ride. "Are you sure about this place? I don't remember it being very enchanting."

I laughed. "I shall be perfectly fine. Heaven knows I've stayed in worse places in my life."

"Hmmmm . . . ," was all he said, and I knew he didn't like the reference to my years in the East End.

In less time than it took me to consider my task ahead at the Nesbitt-Normand estate, our coach was swinging around in front of the Devonshire. As I stared up at the dilapidated structure I realized that my recollection of it had been far too forgiving. A flat-fronted brick building without benefit of any ornamentation, its austerity was surpassed only by its overall dereliction. The paint around the windows was cracked and peeling, and the front door was in such sorrowful shape that the interior could be spied through the splits between its lashed boards. Even the sign no longer correctly reflected its name, revealing a bizarrely truncated version that read: *De on ire Hote,* with nothing but sun-bleached stains where the missing letters had been.

" 'Ere ya be," the driver called as he brought us to a stop. "Not one a yer finer places."

"We really don't require any commentary," I shot back as Colin began hoisting my few pieces of luggage down. I paid the man and went into the lobby with Colin on my heels and found that it consisted of little more than a narrow pass-through with the front desk tucked in beneath a staircase. A series of oddly lopsided wood cubbies were trussed up along the wall behind the counter and there was a smattering of wallpaper hanging in irregular patches displaying a repetitious pattern of roses that had faded to the color of ancient parchment. Worst of all, however, was the cloying aroma of mildew that assaulted the nose.

"This will not do," Colin said the moment he stepped inside.

"Nonsense." I waved him off, determined to prove my mettle as I moved to the counter and slapped at the misshapen bell rotting there. "I wasn't raised among the nobles in India. I didn't have an elephant for a plaything—"

"She was *not* my plaything."

"I'm staying," I decreed with finality, completely aware that my stubbornness was accomplishing little more than earning me a night in the sort of place I thought I had left far behind.

He shook his head as he yanked out his watch and scowled at it. *"Bollocks!"* He stabbed an arm out and assaulted the raggedy bell with a great deal more determination than I had, adding to its overall disgrace.

A heavyset woman in an ill-fitting robe came through a door on our left and plodded back behind the counter. She moved with the determination of someone to whom motivation is as foreign as zeal. Gray circles enveloped her eyes and her skin matched the color of the wallpaper remnants. She had a poorly rolled, unlit cigarette hanging from a corner of her flaming red lips and an explosion of black hair piled high upon her head that was barely being contained by a pitted dinner fork. As she squeezed behind the counter I felt her eyes rake across us as though gauging our worth. "One room er two?"

"One," I said.

She stared at me a moment with an expression I could not place. "How many hours?"

"Two *nights*," I corrected.

"Two of ya cost extra."

"It'll just be me," I said, sliding the posted fee across the counter.

Her eyebrows knit as she shot a withering glance at Colin. "Suit yerself, but remember, two of ya cost extra."

"We shall remember it like the gospels themselves," Colin enunciated pointedly.

The woman scrutinized the money I had given her carefully before stuffing it down the front of her robe. She snatched a key from beneath the counter and shoved it back at me. "Ya turn yer key in before ya go out or it'll cost ya extra. And if ya want someone ta clean yer room or change the bed—"

"It'll cost bloody extra!" Colin snapped. "Thank heaven the bugs and mold are free."

The woman sucked in a tight breath before slamming a fist down on the key just as I was about to pick it up. "That kinda attitude will get yer arse thrown out."

"He's not staying anyway," I grumbled back as I reached for

the key again, stopping just short of her fleshy mitt, until she finally, grudgingly, lifted it and took a step back. "Thank you," I said with what charm I could muster, grabbing my valise and leaving the bag for Colin. "Which way?"

"Upstairs." She gestured with her chin before tossing a smirk at us. "Top floor."

"Fine," I said quickly, heading for the stairs before Colin could add anything else.

We made our way up the five flights without talking. At first it was a choice, but eventually it became a necessity as the climb took its toll on our lungs, although it was certainly truer of me than Colin. By the time we reached the uppermost landing we were both out of breath and I could tell he was even further out of sorts.

"She put you up here on purpose," he seethed.

"Perhaps there'll be fewer bugs on the top floor," I muttered, getting the lock to release by giving the door a boot.

I tossed the valise onto the lumpy bed shoved against the wall before walking over and yanking the threadbare curtains wide. Sunlight filled the room, and for a moment I wasn't at all sure that was a good thing. A single chair leaned against the far wall, looking to be in a losing battle with gravity. There was a cracked washbasin streaked with the calcified remains of yellowed minerals pitched awkwardly next to it. The room held no other furniture, which, given what was there, seemed like a wise choice. "Sparse," I said.

"If you—"

"I'll be fine," I waved him off haughtily, turning back to the window to let in a bit of fresh air. To my utter consternation, however, it held fast. I checked for a lock or dowel rod before trying again, but still it defied me. "Would you please open this blasted thing?!"

"Of course." He stalked forward, grabbed the bottom of the window, and threw his considerable strength into it, but it still would not give so much as a millimeter. *"Dammit to rotting hell!"* he shouted. He tossed his coat and vest onto the drooping bed and rolled up his sleeves. With his face set in a scowl of heroic indignation, he turned back to the window and seized the small wooden handle, struggling against the frame to the point that I could see the muscles of his arms straining against his upturned sleeves even as his face surged to a cautionary shade of crimson. And then, all at once, the window gave with a shuddering *screeeeeeeeeeeeeech*, ratcheting up so abruptly that it shattered the instant it slammed against its upper casement. *"There!"* he roared as tinkling shards of glass rained down onto the floor. "That should give you a nice breeze."

"And *that* ... ," I muttered, "... is going to cost extra."

CHAPTER 18

Colin had given me the most specific of instructions before sending me back to the Nesbitt-Normand estate. While he hadn't bothered to explain *why* I was doing what he'd decreed, I knew it had to be critical, as he had been keenly disappointed not to be coming himself. Lady Nesbitt-Normand also freely displayed her disappointment when I showed up alone. Only a hastily jotted note from Colin that I'd insisted he write had cheered her spirit and ensured he was still fully engaged. Too engaged, in my opinion, given the relentless ticking of the clock on the Bellingham case.

I shifted my feet and allowed an inaudible sigh to escape as I watched Lady Nesbitt-Normand dab at her eyes. "I was hoping . . . ," she uttered between sniffles, ". . . that you were coming to deliver good news."

"Nothing would have pleased me more, but it is encouraging to hear that no extortion demands have been made. Whoever has done this thing seems not to have done it out of greed, so you should find some comfort there."

"But why would someone take her if not for money?"

"Almost certainly to breed her," I said, offering what I knew Colin had come to suspect.

"Well"—Lady Nesbitt-Normand dabbed at her eyes again—"I do suppose there can be some solace in that. But I shan't be happy again until she is returned to me."

"I don't know how you could feel any other way," I said with a smile I hoped she would discern as empathy. For despite what Colin insisted, I couldn't help feeling her the slightest bit overwrought.

"I hope he won't be unduly detained at Buckingham," she muttered. "Did I mention that Victoria met Lady Priscilla once? She was quite fond of her."

"I'm sure she was. I look forward to the pleasure myself."

"Are you certain what Mr. Pendragon wrote is true?" she asked, her eyes boring into me.

"Absolutely," I soothed, though I felt a knot grip my stomach as I reiterated, "Your little one will be curled up in your lap before day's end tomorrow."

"But what of today?" she sniffled, her round cheeks making short work of her already-slivered eyes.

"Today is about trapping the thieves. That is why I've come to collect a personal effect of Lady Priscilla's. It will ensure we bring this case to a swift and joyful conclusion."

"Are you certain?"

This time my smile was genuine. "Without question. Mr. Pendragon does not tolerate failure."

"He may not tolerate it, but it *is* a fact of life," she said, tossing me a pointed look. "I shall live for tomorrow then." She pushed herself off the settee and nodded for me to follow as she trod back to the foyer. "*Elsa!*" she bellowed as she headed to a small side chair near the front door. "*Elsa, where are you?*" She lowered herself onto the seat, virtually concealing it beneath her.

A long minute tiptoed past before Lady Nesbitt-Normand seized a bell from the side table and rang it with the fortitude of a well-schooled night crier. It seemed impossible that a response could be so prolonged in a household as filled with staff as hers, yet there we waited. I was beginning to fear that everyone had fled the estate when Mrs. Holloway came scampering in.

"Where *is* everybody?!" Lady Nesbitt-Normand blasted.

"Sorry, mum. Is it Elsa you want?"

"Well, I'm not calling her name looking for you!"

"Of course, mum." Mrs. Holloway nodded without the glimmer of a reaction before scurrying away again. Elsa came barreling in almost at once, an appropriately mortified expression pasted on her face.

"Didn't you hear me calling?" Lady Nesbitt-Normand shoved herself to her feet, scowling ferociously.

"I vas in de yard. You vill forgiff me, madam."

"I cannot imagine why you were out there given that Lady Priscilla's missing!" she snapped, causing the woman to cringe slightly. "Mr. Pendragon needs to borrow something of my little dear's. Go and fetch her pink blanket from my bed. She loves that more than almost anything."

"Right away, madam." Elsa nodded curtly and headed for the stairs, bounding up two at a time.

"Honestly"—Lady Nesbitt-Normand glanced at me as she sat back down—"I don't know what has gotten into this staff. Not one of them seems to appreciate my suffering." With a great sigh, she sagged against the wall as though it were the only thing keeping her from sliding to the floor. "I hope none of them ever has to go through what I've had to endure these past twenty-four hours."

"I'm sure they mean well," I answered offhandedly.

Elsa returned at once with a small pink blanket folded under her arm. "Here you go," she said, thrusting it at me.

The unmistakably oily scent of dog struck my nose as I took it from her. "This is ideal. Mr. Pendragon will be very pleased."

"Then tell him to be done with it already," Lady Nesbitt-Normand sniped. "I cannot stand much more of this."

"I give you my word." I nodded.

"You must relax, madam," Elsa cooed. "I vill show our guest out."

Lady Nesbitt-Normand responded with a dismissive flick of the hand as she heaved herself up and headed back to the parlor.

"You are getting close?" Elsa asked as soon as we were outside.

"I believe we are. Mr. Pendragon is quite certain he is on the verge of solving this case."

She shot her arms out and seized my shoulders in a powerful grip, her eyes on fire. "Do not play vit me. Dis dog ist *mein* life. Who does he suspect?"

Even though I eclipsed Elsa by more than a handful of inches, her shoulders were considerably broader and her extended arms greater than the circumference of one of my thighs. Clutching me in her steely grip, she had my attention as surely as if she were dangling me upside down by my ankles. "I am not playing with you," I blustered. "But Mr. Pendragon has not confided in me," I lied. She studied me closely and I knew she was trying to discern the level of my honesty, but it was hardly a fair contest, as she had no way of knowing that I had learned to be quite convincing years ago. Maw had seen to that.

"So be it," Elsa warily conceded before suddenly leaning forward close enough for her breath to rake my face. "But if you learn something, you vill tell me," she demanded. There was a tight smile on her face but no warmth in her eyes. "I *vill* have my revenge."

I gave her a stilted nod but did not exhale until she finally released me from the vise of her grip.

CHAPTER 19

As I headed back to our flat to deliver Lady Priscilla's keepsake, the sun slid into a steely black layer of clouds, hastening the end of the day and further stirring my dread around the intrepid passage of time. I wrapped myself deeper into my cloak as the smell of rain, fresh and slightly metallic, hung in the air.

I bounded up the steps to our flat and let myself in. Immediately the scent of roasting chicken mixed with the pungent aroma of garlic struck me and I had to stop by the kitchen to shake off the low-slung moodiness of the late afternoon sky. Mrs. Behmoth was washing and chopping crowns of broccoli and feeding them into a boiling pot. She glanced at me with a curious expression as I rid myself of my cloak. "It smells like heaven," I said.

She grunted. "You'll find it less like 'eaven upstairs."

"Why?"

She nodded toward the ceiling. " 'E's in a right foul mood. 'Ad a visitor. Put 'im all outta sorts."

"Who?"

She tossed me a look of annoyance. "Some young bloke. Stop pesterin' me like a bleedin' owl and go ask 'im."

"Of course—" I hurried back out with Lady Priscilla's little blanket tucked under an arm, hoping I would be able to put him right when he saw what I had achieved. I wondered which of the young guardsmen had stopped by and what he had said to have so sullied Colin's mood.

When I reached the landing upstairs I found Colin standing by the fireplace curling two heavily laden dumbbells over his head. His mood was palpably sour and, as he allowed the dumbbells to slam to the floor, I knew he meant to be both imposing and confrontational. It brought me to a halt as I caught the animosity firing behind his eyes. Somehow, someway, it seemed *I* was responsible for his mood.

"What's happened?"

"We've had a visitor." He spoke slowly, sourly, as though the words were bitter on his tongue. "An urchin from Whitechapel."

"Whitechapel?"

"*Whitechapel!*" He punched the word, freezing my gut as I instantly realized what this was about. "And who do you suppose was sending us a message from Whitechapel?"

I knew who it was. I had been careless to think I wouldn't hear from her again. "Maw Heikens." I tried to say it with nonchalance even as it threatened to stick in my throat.

"*Dammit!*" He pounded his fist on the mantel. "Why in the *hell* would you go back to see that drug-addled dreadful old slag? It's an insult. It flies in the face of everything we have built together."

My pulse thundered and my heart felt like it had leapt into my throat. "I went to try and get information about the Life Guard like you asked. *She's* the one who told me about the brawl they had with the Irish Guard at McPhee's," I stabbed back defensively. "She knows that world down there. She always has. And given the shortage of time I thought she could be of help."

"She's a lecherous pariah who would sell her own child for a farthing."

I shook my head. "She did me a service at the most miserable time in my life."

"She used you and everyone else she came into contact with. You're a fool if you can't see that."

"Well, we weren't all born to the Queen's colors, you know."

"Neither do we all choose to drown our fears in opiates and pandering."

"That's not fair," I shot back.

But without another word, he turned his back to me.

I opened my mouth to say something, to defend myself, but to my utter dismay I knew he was right and so I was left to stand there mutely. It took a moment before the stink of the little cloth tucked under my arm began to strike me. Unable to think of anything better to do, I tossed it onto the settee and said, "There's Lady Priscilla's blanket."

And then I left.

CHAPTER 20

The clouds let loose their fury by the time I got within a block of the Devonshire Hotel. It seemed as incapable of containing its rage as everyone else this evening, sending a great crack of thunder shivering across the city just before unleashing a mighty torrent. Had I been in a better frame of mind I would have dashed the rest of the way, but I did not so much as quicken my pace, so that by the time I reached the Devonshire I was as saturated as if I had taken a bath in my clothes.

I trudged through the dismal lobby and the same woman, still clad in the checkered robe she had been wearing that morning, tossed me a disapproving look as she slid the key across the counter. Her withering gaze made me feel accused of some wrongdoing and I half-expected her to tell me it would cost extra if I didn't stop dripping on her sorrowful floors.

The oversized key fit the lock loosely, which only made matters worse as the lock itself partially rotated within its circular cutout. I was on the verge of kicking it in with the full extent of my pent-up anger when the bolt suddenly slid back and the door swung wide. The room stared back at me with the same disinterest I was feeling, requiring all my determination to step inside and boot the door closed.

Home. *Temporary* home: Though considering the way I had left things with Colin, it suddenly didn't feel all that temporary.

It took a moment for my eyes to adjust and, in the interim, I could feel cold air rushing in through the window Colin had shattered. Determined to find some way to keep the storm from raging inside my room, I tugged the sheer drapes closed only to be slapped by them as they immediately whipped back at me. I slid on the damp floor, nearly tumbling down, but the sound of glass crunching beneath my shoes was enough to convince my brain to seize control and hold myself upright. I was already wet to the skin; I hardly relished adding a web of cuts.

I glanced around to find something to staunch the flow of weather into the tiny space, but nothing caught my eye. There was nothing to *catch* my eye. Only the pitiful chair, tilting precipitously to one side, and the matronly-looking bed, all plump and sagging, looked back at me. With little else coming to mind, I wedged the chair beneath the gaping window, effectively pinning the sheer drapes against the void. It would have to do. Perhaps tomorrow I would mention it to the woman beneath the stairs. Then again, perhaps not.

I herded the bits of scattered glass into a small pile and scooted them beneath the chair with a sigh and then collected my small bag and trudged down the hall to the communal bath, grateful to find it vacant. I twisted the gas sconces and latched the door before casting my gaze about the utilitarian space. With great relief, I found a rag and small bottle of bleach hidden behind one of the tub's claw feet, so was able to set to cleaning the tub until beads of perspiration leached onto my forehead, all the while thinking how proud Mrs. Behmoth would be of me. The task wore me out, which was exactly what I had hoped for.

While hot water cascaded into the now pristine tub I peeled

off my wet things, leaving them in an unaccustomed pile on the floor. The steam and heat of the water felt soothing as I eased myself in, urging my mind and heart to release the crux of their concerns, but they were not so willing. Thoughts of Colin continued to swamp my mind: his disapproval . . . his anger. After all these years I could still be stung by the errors of my youth, all I had done and feared. Could I not finally forgive myself, if not also the illness that had been my mother's?

A sudden rattling at the door brought me upright, sloshing water onto the dingy floor. " 'Ow bloody long ya gonna be?!" a husky female voice called out.

"A while!" I snapped back.

"Well, some a us got business to attend to and I ain't walkin' down a bloody flight a stairs ta do it, so you'd best get yer arse outta there before I get back."

"Piss off," I mumbled.

"I'm pretendin' I didn't 'ear that."

"I said piss off!" I hollered, but got no further response.

Quite done with myself, I yanked the plug and climbed out, watching the water gurgle down the drain as I wrapped myself in my robe and gathered my pile of wet things. It occurred to me that the woman might be waiting to pummel me for my surliness and determined she would get a face full of sodden garments if she tried, but there was no one there.

The rain was still pounding determinedly when I got back to the room and the frail drapes were so thoroughly drenched that they now stuck to the wall without any help from the chair. I threw my wet clothes onto the floor at the end of the bed and tried to convince myself it would be good to settle in for what I knew would be a long night.

I pulled back the thin bedcovers, tossing my robe over top, and slid onto the mattress only to find it even lumpier than it looked. Even so, I pressed my eyes shut and pretended I was going to sleep while my restless mind continued to impose visions of Colin, Lady Nesbitt-Normand, and, most of all, the Bellinghams. With little more than forty hours to go, I feared the possibility that we might never find the truth of what had happened. It was unthinkable.

I rolled into a tight ball to shield myself against the damp chill of the storm as my thoughts stole back to the sight of Colin's back and the unkindness of his last words. I had no idea what the morning would bring, whether he would seek me out or if I would wait all day in this godforsaken room for some word that might never come. We had never traversed such territory before.

At some point I drifted off. I know it because somewhere well within the belly of the storm, in between the deepest hours of night but long before the first hint of dawn, I was awakened by a clap of thunder that imploded upon my wearied mind as having been particularly close. The incessant pounding of the rain had yet to renounce its vigil, leaving me with little to do but roll over and try to find some position on the mattress that would do the least amount of damage to my spine. Another immediate drumming, louder and even closer, seized me fully out of my dopey cocoon and bolted me upright in fear that I might actually be struck. I rubbed my eyes with the heels of my hands, attempting to clear my addled brain, when another crash rocketed me to my feet, leaving me naked and shivering at the side of the bed.

It wasn't thunder; someone was at my door.

I stumbled to it just as another pounding cracked through the storm's tirade, and, without even thinking, yanked it open. At first my eyes refused to adjust to the diffuse gaslight flickering in the hall, but as my brain caught up to the signals being relayed through my retinas I found myself staring at Colin. His hair was matted flat and there was water dribbling down the sides of his face. It took a moment before I registered the expression on his face and the dark, sunken look in his eyes.

"I can't sleep," he mumbled.

I stared at him a moment before saying, "Oh," my voice cracking as a fresh wave of exhaustion swept over me.

He kept staring at me, his gaze unwavering, and when nothing else would come to my mind I finally stepped back and gestured him in. He shuffled inside without another word and I closed and bolted the door behind him, all the while trying to think what I should say. I sucked in a deep breath and turned around, set on lighting a few candles, only to find that he had already peeled off his saturated clothing and was climbing into the bed. My brain heaved with relief as I stumbled back and climbed in beside him.

I resumed my former position, curling into a tight ball, but before I could properly settle in he moved against me, gently tucking himself within my arms. He pressed himself so completely that I was certain a wisp of wind could not come between us. I held him, the cool dampness of his skin warming at once, as he reached out and clasped my nearest hand, pressing it to his chest.

The next thing I knew I felt his lips on mine and as I smiled and opened my eyes I was stunned to find the sun streaming in and him standing beside the bed fully dressed. He straightened up while fumbling with the buttons on his vest, the poor thing as wrinkled as a centenarian, while I tried to coax myself to wakefulness. The rest of his clothes had fared little better, leaving him looking ready for a day in pursuit of charity.

"Rise and shine," he said cheerily, his face lighting up with his dimpled smile. He stepped over to the glassless window and whisked the sheers aside, allowing an effervescent swath of warm sunshine to stream unimpeded into the room. "There's much to be done today."

"Maybe so," I said, kicking the covers free and stretching lazily. "But you certainly can't do it looking like that."

"No?" He swept his jacket off the floor and shrugged into it. "Something amiss?"

"Unless dishevelment became the fashion overnight."

"You were wearing much less than dishevelment when you opened that door last night. What a sight." He chuckled as he tugged at his clothes as though that might encourage them to lie flat. "Now get up and get yourself dressed before you're the cause of further delay this morning."

I laughed as I sat up. "You really aren't going out like that, are you?"

"Only as far as our flat," he said, bullying his feet into his shoes without even looking down. "Can you be out front in ten minutes?"

"I can."

"Then I shall get us a cab."

Sunshine made the Devonshire appear almost agreeable, or perhaps it was my mood. The room seemed almost vaguely charming in its stark simplicity, with the well-worn bed more a comfortable old friend than the hazard to the spine I had first pegged it to be. Even the gaping window commanded a compelling view of the hopscotch of rooftops with their chimneys and pipes.

The fresh morning was so relieving that I didn't even mind the brief wait for the bathroom. Even so, within ten minutes, my spirits soaring, I was bounding down the stairs to join Colin.

"Well . . . well . . ." The accusing words erupted out of the dark space beneath the stairs so unexpectedly that it caused me to miss the final step and lurch jarringly onto the ground floor. "Look 'oo's up," the voice sneered.

"Morning." I offered a quick smile as I glimpsed the haggard face of the black-haired woman still wrapped in the same robe she apparently spent her life in. While everything else about the day looked brighter, nothing of her had altered a whit, including the fork still holding her mop of hair aloft.

" 'Oo do ya think yer foolin'?" She stood with her arms folded across her chest, the sly smile on her face revealing more gaps than teeth.

"Pardon?" I started to say before realizing that she had likely discovered the shattered window the day before. "Oh. You mean the window."

She slammed a hand onto the dust-laden counter and snarled at me, "I'm talkin' 'bout 'im that spent the night in yer room! I told ya a thousand bloody times that two a ya cost extra and I don't give a bloody shite if he *was* only there part a the night. 'E's extra and ya gotta pay." Her eyes narrowed. "And what about the winda?"

I pulled out some coins, trying to ignore her withering glare. "Of course."

"Damn right." She snatched some of it before seizing my wrist. "What about the ruddy winda?"

"It was stuck," I said. "When I tried to open it the glass broke."

She puckered her face. "It was rainin' last night. What the 'ell were ya openin' the bleedin' winda for?"

"The room stank," I grumbled.

She was clearly unimpressed. "That'll cost ya," she sneered, snatching a few more coins before releasing my wrist. "And if 'e comes back tonight, you'll be payin' fer 'im again. I ain't runnin' no buggered charity 'ouse."

"A charitable organization would never stand for these conditions." I scowled.

By the time I stepped outside and breathed the clean air, now washed free of its customary soot, smoke, and animal detritus, I felt rejuvenated again. Even the grimy buildings looked almost renewed.

We got back to our flat in minutes and I remained with the driver while Colin ran up and changed. He was gone an astoundingly brief time yet looked ever so much more dapper by the time he returned.

"Let's be quick," he called to the driver as he climbed aboard. "There is money to be earned if you proceed with all due haste."

"Bribing drivers, are you?" I laughed.

"Without question. We've a full day ahead and I don't relish continually searching for transportation, so I have offered the fellow a bonus if he provides his services solely to us today."

"A bonus . . . how extravagant."

"It will be wisely spent. Especially given the neighborhood I've coaxed him to start in."

I looked at Colin curiously. "What neighborhood?"

He picked up a small leather satchel that he'd brought from our flat and opened it so I could peek inside. Nestled within lay the little pink blanket belonging to the missing Lady Priscilla. "This will be our second stop." He grinned mischievously. "It will provide the proof we need to bring the little pup home to her mother. But our first stop"—he flipped the satchel closed and looked at me—"shall be Limehouse Street."

"Limehouse?!"

"I may have been a mite hasty about your visiting that Heikens shrew. She sent that urchin to let us know she had learned something about Lady Stuart." He shrugged with uncustomary remorse. "If she really has come up with information on her then I'm a fool not to hear her out." He turned his gaze to the passing scenery, placing a protective hand over mine.

"I should have just told you I had gone there—"

"No . . ." He removed his hand and dug a crown from his pocket, flipping it easily through his fingers, a contented smile settling on his face. "You probably did the right thing. If she hadn't sent that boy . . ." He shook his head with a smirk on his lips. "But I'll tell you what. Later on we're getting your things from that infernal hotel. You'll not spend another minute there. That was a terrible idea."

I laughed, happy to comply and wholeheartedly in agreement. If he needed time to himself in the future, I would just keep my mouth shut. And so it was that we didn't speak again until the cab pulled alongside the alley behind Limehouse.

"Wait here," Colin ordered the driver as we climbed from the cab.

"You'll pay me somethin' before I let ya outta me sight."

"We'll give you half," I spoke up, slipping some cash into his upturned hand. "You'll get the other half when we return."

"If we're not back within the hour, notify Scotland Yard!" Colin called out as he headed down the alley.

"Yer holdin' half me fee. I'll come get ya meself."

"Reassuring," Colin muttered, following me through the unmarked door that had once led to Maw's teeming establishment. Other than the toxic smells of liquor and opium clinging to the structure, it pained me how little it resembled its former life. "I haven't been back here since the night I dragged you out," Colin muttered as I led him down the narrow hallway to the main room.

"I barely knew you back then. I had no reason to trust you."

"You knew who I was. I'd seen you plenty of times at Easling and Temple."

"Plenty of times?!" I laughed. "I didn't attend classes enough for that to be true."

His nose curled as the lingering scents assaulted us. "My getting you out of this place is the best thing that ever happened to you."

"It is. But the same can be said for you too," I needled before turning and calling out, *"Hello!"*

"Cuppy . . . ?" Maw's raspy voice drifted right back and I realized she was sitting among the shadows behind the counter.

"Yes, it's me."

She stood up and came ambling out, and I heard Colin suck in a hard breath as she made her way around the counter. Her obvious frailty had the effect on him I knew it would. This was no longer a daunting woman, though I had never thought her to be so. While she had not been one to be trifled with, neither had I ever seen her be cruel.

She moved to within a few feet of me before casting her good eye over at Colin. "Brought '*im*, didja? Knew 'e'd wanna see what was left a me."

To my relief, Colin kept quiet.

"How are you, Maw?"

She waved me off. "Same as I look." She gestured us over to the set of well-worn chairs and slowly lowered herself into one of them. "Ain't this somethin'?" She snickered. "The three of us sittin' 'ere jest like ol' times." She looked at me with a smile that seemed almost wistful. "Two days in a row, Cuppy . . ." She let her voice trail off, leaving me to wonder whether she thought it a good thing or bad.

"You sent for us?" Colin spoke up, an edge in his tone.

"Always 'bout the business, ain't ya?" Maw shot him a glance, her good eye raking him carefully. "I 'ope 'e's been good to ya, Cuppy. 'E never was one fer words."

"Yes, Maw."

"Don't!" he snapped.

She clucked and shook her head. "Still full a 'isself, I see."

"This was a mistake." He stood up, his body tense, and threw an agitated glance at me. "We're done here."

Maw shrugged and leaned back in her chair with a chuckle. "Jest like ol' times," she said again.

"Sit down, Colin. We haven't heard what we came here for."

"She's just fiddling with us. We've already found Lady Stuart anyway."

"Found 'er, didja?" Maw chuckled again as though she was the only one who understood the joke. "That ain't nothin'. It's knowin' 'er that counts. Didja get ta know 'er? Didja get the truth?"

"And what do you know about truth?" he shot back.

Maw went still a moment before turning to him and speaking in a low, even tone. "I never lied ta nobody. Weren't my fault everybody was so eager ta lie to themselves. All I ever did was help people believe they was seein' what they wanted ta see: the prettiest girls . . . the 'andsomest boys . . . the finest opium . . . the smoothest scotch. If that's the way a customer saw it, well then, that's the way I saw it too. So where's the 'arm in that?"

"You degraded people. You made them addicts." His gaze slid over to me and I could see his outrage lurking there.

"I didn't drag nobody 'ere. All I did was offer services. Weren't none a me business why anybody did what they did." She studied him a moment. "I didn't try ta stop ya when ya took Cuppy outta 'ere. And I coulda." A smile broke across her face. "So don't act like me judge and jury. Tell me, ya like them that judges you and Cuppy?"

"That's different."

"It's always different. Was different to those that came 'ere too. But 'ere you are tellin' me what I did was wrong and what you do is fine, yet there's those that hate us both jest the same. That don't make ya think . . . ?"

"*Please* . . . ," I interrupted. "We came to hear about Lady Stuart."

Maw waved a bony hand and sucked in a wheezing breath. "There ain't no damn Lady Stuart," she announced with a great deal of self-satisfaction. For a moment I thought Colin would surely leap up and strangle her, but he contained himself, remaining as rigid as a molded soldier. "Name's made up. Did she tell ya that when ya met 'er?" Maw grinned wickedly. "Did yer right proper lady tell ya she's jest a ruddy Gypsy? That 'er real name is Magdala Genovesse?" She clucked happily. "She married some ol' sot for 'is money and that shite title. Didn't get much a the former from what I 'ear, but did end up with a place off Lancaster Gate with 'er father actin' the 'ouseman. Calls 'im Evers. Maybe that's 'is name." She shrugged. " 'Ell if I know."

"Are you sure?" Colin frowned.

"Ya really askin' me that . . . ?"

I couldn't help chuckling as Colin went on. "Why the ruse then? What's she hiding?"

"She's tellin' fortunes to them society ladies fer money. The *real* ladies. 'Ear she makes a tidy sum at it too. Seems some a them ladies won't do nothin' 'til they check with your precious lady. Only way she can be doin' that is ta make 'em think she's one a them."

"Of course," he said, absently running his fingers through his hair. "Is it only the ladies? Does she tell fortunes for the men as well?"

Maw laughed. "Ain't ya learned nothin', boy? Money don't give a shite what's between the legs. Ya do what ya gotta do fer whoever's willin' ta pay. True a you, true a me, true a Magdala Genovesse no matter what the 'ell she calls 'erself."

"Has she been linked to anyone?" he pressed. "Have you heard anything about someone she might have been carrying on with?"

Maw dismissed him with a wet explosion of her lips. "What woman ain't been linked with a 'undred different men? Don't mean nothin'."

"Humor me."

She leveled her sharp brown eye on him, the slightest curl

tugging at the edges of her lips. "I been humorin' you since the day ya first walked in 'ere 'bout a thousand years ago."

"Maw . . ." I leaned forward, placing myself between her and Colin. "Was there any particular man you've heard mentioned?"

Her watery eyes flicked back to me and her smile widened. "Always the one in the middle, ain't ya?"

"Maw—"

"She ain't with no one!" she groused. "I'm tellin' ya she ain't got no need fer a man. She's makin' all the money she wants and got 'erself all set up nice and proper. Not everyone needs a man, ya know." Her words came out harsh and disapproving, and I knew what she was inferring. She had always set a powerful example of strength. Even now—half-blind, stooped, and looking as frail as a baby bird—she still managed to learn anything she wanted to know. And I was certain the information had cost her nothing. She never owed anyone.

"I also 'eard that Bellingham woman 'ad 'erself a tosser of a brother in the Irish Guard name of Mulrooney. 'Ad no use fer 'is brother-in-law."

"We've met him," I said, shooting a pointed glance at Colin. "I didn't think much of him, either."

"Ya 'member I told you 'bout that brawl at McPhee's? I 'eard 'er brother 'ad everythin' ta do with it. A bunch a officers from the Life Guard and those Irish cads. 'Eard the officers took the worst a it."

Colin stood up for the second time, only now he did so slowly and without anger. "Thank you for your help. You must allow us to pay you for your time." He looked grave and sallow, but Maw only laughed.

"I don't want yer money." She kept right on chuckling as she looked up at him. "But there is somethin' you can do fer me."

A second passed before Colin said, "And what would that be?"

166 / Gregory Harris

"Ya be good ta Cuppy. Don't let 'im end up alone. If yer lives change, if ya fall away from each other, don't let this 'appen to 'im, 'cause 'e ain't got the stomach fer it."

Colin's face went slack as he stared at her, but I couldn't tell what he was thinking. "I'm going back to the cab," he announced disconcertingly. And before I could say anything he left the room, and a moment later I heard the alley door creak open and closed.

" 'E's a good man," Maw said. "A bit 'arsh about 'is edges, but that keeps 'im interestin'." She tottered unsteadily back to her feet. "Now get outta 'ere. 'Elp 'im solve 'is case. And don't come back 'ere. I ain't tellin' ya again."

I smiled at her as I stood up, wanting to reach out and hug her, but she moved away before I could do any such thing and did not stop until the worn counter was between us. That's when it struck me that in all the years I had lived under her roof, when she had given me a place to sleep, and made sure I had what I needed to survive, and put me to work, and given me a sense of my own value, even when she had hollered at me to hurry up or pay more attention, that in all those years I had not once, not ever, hugged her.

"Go on." Her voice, edgy and determined, shook me from my thoughts. "Get out."

"Right," I muttered.

"That's right!" she snapped.

I knew she had done us a great service just as I knew I would never get the chance to properly thank her. She would have none of it. That was her way. That had always been her way.

CHAPTER 21

Our next destination had also been prearranged, as the cab began moving the moment I climbed aboard. While Colin's distraction was evident as he stared absently out the window, I couldn't resist asking, "Are you okay?"

"Of course," he answered.

"Then are we on our way to see Lady Stuart . . . ? Or whoever she is?"

"Shortly. But first we must pay a visit to that Captain Morgan-something. The other officer involved in the McPhee's brawl."

"You mean Edmund Morgesster."

"Right." He nodded. "I find it curious that two of the Life Guard officers from that night are dead and the third, this Morgesster, has been put out to pasture. That leaves only the tight-lipped Major Hampstead apparently unscathed. I've also got to find out what that Irish bloke, Mulrooney, had to do with it all. Interesting how his name keeps coming up."

"Haven't I been saying from the start that he seems too venomous to not be involved?" I reminded.

"Yes . . ." He slid a wry glance to me. "You have."

I tried not to look too pleased with myself as our cab came to a stop in front of a soot-blackened building with a yellowed sign above its door that read: *Regiment Arms Retirement Hotel*. "This is it," he said as he hopped out.

There was no issue with the driver waiting for us this time, as the neighborhood had improved significantly. Nevertheless, I doled out another half portion of our fare before following Colin into a foyer that was as immaculate in its upkeep as it was stark in its décor. White walls displayed nothing but a single cross of two modest sticks lashed together by thin strips of reeds and a plainly framed portrait of our Queen in her standard mourning regalia. Wooden chairs adorned with flattened cushions were arranged about the space in small pods, many of which were already cradling lonely-looking elderly gentlemen. Some of the men were reading while others seemed content to stare into space with a pipe or cigar clenched between their teeth. A few were huddled in tight groups around a card game or chess set, but none was so enamored of his activity that he didn't pause to gawk as we entered.

A long counter stretched across the back of the room, behind which a middle-aged man worked stuffing mail into myriad little slots. Colin strode purposefully through the smattering of aged faces watching him with rapt attention, going right up to the counter and leaning across it to tap the attendant and announce our names. The man turned to consider us, a dearth of interest in his eyes, as Colin announced that we had an appointment with Captain Morgesster.

"He's on the sunporch," the man answered in a flinty tone. "Round back." He gestured with his chin in the opposite direction from which we had come. "You can go on through"—he glared at us—"but don't get him riled up. He's too difficult to calm down again."

"You make him sound like a miscreant hound." Colin smirked

tightly, making no promises as we headed out to the glassed-in portico.

The room extended from the back of the building into the center of a small, meticulously tended rose garden, giving the feeling that one was actually sitting in among their splendid brilliance. Several gentlemen in various states of slumber were seated about the atrium and yet Colin walked directly up to a heavyset man with a shiny red face and hairless pate. He looked like any of the other men here, some rounder, some leaner, some with white wisps of hair on their heads, but when Colin introduced us and the man bothered to look up I saw he had indeed selected the right one. I hadn't realized the significance of his ruddy pallor or the spiderweb of blood vessels burst across the swollen tip of his nose. Private Newcombe had described him as a *sot* and the evidence of it was most clearly there on his face.

Colin dragged two wicker chairs over and we seated ourselves, cozying up to the doughy-faced former captain who did not appear to have the slightest curiosity as to why we were there. He continued to stare out the windows at the trim yard and I wondered if he was studying the roses or just not looking at us.

"I appreciate your meeting with us," Colin said.

The man harrumphed.

"No doubt you are wondering why we've come." There was no response. "We would very much like to ask about the night your friend, Wilford Newcombe, was attacked."

"Attacked and *killed*," he grunted. "Died a few days after it."

"So we understand." Colin leaned in slightly, trying to catch the man's eye, but Captain Morgesster remained singularly focused on the out-of-doors. "You were there that night . . . ?" Colin prodded.

"You come all the way out here to be cheeky?" came the reply.

"Excuse me. . . ." Colin flopped back uncomfortably, one hand rubbing his belly as his face contorted slightly. "I must beg your indulgence," he murmured as his other hand slipped into his jacket pocket. "I've a stomach ailment that requires a bit of brandy to keep it settled. I hope you won't think me ill-mannered." He withdrew a small silver flask and unstoppered it even as I struggled to withhold my surprise. "Perhaps you would care for a spot of medicine?" He held the flask toward Captain Morgesster and for the first time the man turned and looked at him.

"Medicine . . . ," he clucked as he eyed the little container. "I prefer whiskey for my tender gut." He reached down and pulled out his own flask from the garter around his calf. "But you'd best be discreet. The staff won't tolerate self-medicating," he chortled.

Colin nodded and gave a brief salute with the flask, taking a healthy pull before burying it into the crux of his seat. "Discretion it is," he replied, chuckling.

"A stomach ailment." The captain snickered as he took a swig and ran a sleeve across his mouth. "I'll have ta remember 'at one."

"I find the word 'medicinal' to be most forgiving."

The captain wheezed out a great phlegmy guffaw, his hairless scalp momentarily resembling a plum. "You're a pip."

Colin took another quick pull from his flask before refastening the lid and stuffing the flask back into his pocket. His leisurely demeanor seemed to suggest we had all the time the day had to offer, but I was feeling fidgety. With slightly less than thirty hours remaining, I wondered why we were even here.

Captain Morgesster took several more tips of his flask before he said, "Guess my stomach is worse than yours."

"You have my sympathies." Colin smiled.

"*You* have *mine*," he shot back as he turned to the garden again. "Didja ever notice . . . ," he said after what felt an eternity, ". . . how the hummingbirds and bees visit the same flowers but never bother one another? Look at those hollyhocks. . . ." He gestured toward a small cluster of burgundy bell-shaped flowers at the opposite end of the yard. "Two creatures goin' about their business without a care as to what the other's doin'. Stands counter ta humans." He turned and peered at Colin. "Know what I mean?"

Colin nodded.

"Everybody telling everybody how ta live. Nobody's business is their own anymore. Maybe it never was. Hell if I know." He drained the last of his flask and shoved it into his pocket. "That's what happened that night at McPhee's. Irish bastards set on us and wouldn't let go. Like a pack a damn wolves. A major and three captains in Her Majesty's Life Guard and they decide they know what's what. Whoresons."

"Had you seen them before?"

"Plenty a times. They were part a the Irish Guard. Third-rate, snot-nosed, potato-farming twats. That's all they were. Guard brought 'em up on trial after Wilford died, but they couldn't prove intent, so all they got was discharged. Shoulda lynched the bastards. No intent my fat, flabby ass."

"You believe they targeted Captain Newcombe?"

"It had nothin' ta do with Wilford. That's just the kind a man he was. A fight a his friend's was a fight a his own. Not like his shite son, Avery. That tosser never earned a ruddy thing his whole life, including his rank."

"Was a Sergeant Thomas Mulrooney there that night?"

"Trevor's brother-in-law?" He scrunched up his face. "He'd already left by the time the fight started."

Colin sighed and I could sense his frustration. "How did it start?"

Captain Morgesster shook his head. "I'm done talkin'."

Colin leaned forward again, his eyes pleading. "If I'm to

bring justice for the killings of Captain Bellingham and his wife . . ."

The captain waved him off without so much as a sideways glance. "Trevor's at peace. Dashell Hampstead will take care of the rest," he answered brusquely as he heaved himself out of his chair. "My stomach's hurtin'. I think I need more medicine."

I watched him trundle from the room and felt my hopes deflate with his every step. Little of what he'd said made any sense and what did seemed meagerly parsed out. I turned to Colin and found his eyes alight. "At last," he reveled, "I believe we are finally getting somewhere. There is much to do this afternoon, but the key to this puzzle is almost certainly within our reach now."

"What? He was talking nonsense."

"He told us a great deal," Colin answered with a great grin as he swept a crown from his pocket and leapt up. "You had best reconsider his words, for I am beginning to think you will find the very heart of this case in them." He quickly spun the crown between his fingers as he headed out of the room.

CHAPTER 22

The Regiment Arms Retirement Hotel was not three miles from the Lancaster Gate house where Lady Dahlia Stuart, or Magdala Genovesse, lived. Our driver delivered us with great haste, almost as though he knew we had spent too much time with the captain. The fact of our lengthy stay was most glaringly underscored as we passed Big Ben and I noticed that the venerable timepiece was already flirting with the midday hour. I knew Colin had seen it as well when he released a frustrated sigh.

The moment Lady Stuart's houseman—or father, if Maw Heikens was right—pulled the door open to find Colin and me standing there uninvited again, he permitted a sour expression to flit across his face before curtly informing us that Her Ladyship was not presently at home.

"When is she due back?" Colin pushed. "It is urgent that we speak with her at once."

"I do not keep Madam's schedule," he sniffed.

"That's all very well, but I'm afraid you *must* be her keeper today," Colin volleyed back, "for her life may depend on it."

"What?!" The man looked stunned, his veneer of imperti-
nence cracking.

"A captain in the Queen's Guard and his wife were murdered less than a week ago, and your *daughter* may unwittingly
be involved!" Colin snapped, ending that charade.

The man blanched, gripping the doorknob like a lifeline,
though he did not immediately respond. Tiny beads of perspiration sprouted across the philtrum of his upper lip and I feared
he might be on the verge of swooning. It seemed a full minute
passed before he quite slowly stepped back and nodded for us
to enter. He brought us to the same sitting room we had been
shown to before and offered us a seat. I settled in, but Colin remained standing, casually perusing the books on the shelves.

"I am an old man," our host began as he sat down across
from me. "I did my best. I have always done my best. Plenty of
men would have left a hundred times over, but I stayed." He
sagged into the seat. "But I have been foolish. I have gotten soft
and that poisons the soul." He looked at me and I could see his
eyes rimmed with ache, yet there was also something else nestled
there, something watchful and keenly aware. "Any mistakes that
were made are mine. You must not blame my daughter."

Colin turned from the books. "Blame her for what?"

The man's gaze tightened ever so slightly as he glanced toward Colin. "You said there'd been a murder—"

"Murders. Two of them."

He shook his head. "That may be, but my daughter . . . Her
Ladyship . . . would have nothing to do with such a thing. If
anyone implicated her it was only to mislead you."

"Really?" Colin flashed a tight smile. "You didn't seem so
concerned when you were playing the houseman—"

"*Ohhhhh!*" The old man clutched his chest and grimaced.
"Water . . . ," he choked, tugging his collar open with a clawed
fist. ". . . I need some water—"

Before I could move, Colin was already headed for the small bar at the far side of the room, leaving me to go to the man's side to see what I could do. His face had already begun to turn pink as I leaned him forward and struck the middle of his back with a firm clap, though I was actually unsure whether he was choking or suffering some sort of seizure. He sputtered and yanked his collar looser even as his color deepened, making me decide not to try that again. I glanced up and was relieved to find Colin already holding out a half-filled tumbler.

The old man gripped the glass with trembling hands and began to take a long pull, but before he could even swallow he dropped the tumbler and spat the contents out in a single hissing spray. *"Damn you!"* he hollered at Colin, rising to his feet with the red-faced fury of a man twice his height and half his age. "You tryin' ta kill me?"

"Kill you?!" Colin's eyebrows lifted, a casual expression settling over his face. "I should think not. In fact, it would seem that bit of vodka has cured both your attack *and* your performance."

"V-v-vodka?!" I stammered.

"Ya right bastard!" the old man growled, dragging a sleeve across his lips as he spat into the fireplace. "If I were a younger man I'd thrash ya."

"You may be an old man," Colin sneered, "but you are keen. I would say your daughter learned from a master. However, if she is not back and receiving us within two hours' time then you will both be answering our questions through a set of bars. Do you understand?"

"Rot in hell."

"And so I may, but we *will* be back in two hours and your daughter had best be here or I can promise you a cell the size of your pockets by nightfall." Colin moved past him without a further glance and the next sound I heard was the front door slamming.

"Has it occurred to you that we may be trying to *protect* your daughter?" I bothered to point out.

"Mags doesn't need either one a you," he scoffed. "She takes care of herself. You two are just lookin' to make trouble for her, blame her for things you don't know shite about."

"In that you are sorely mistaken." I scowled at him. "Do not confuse me or Mr. Pendragon with anyone else who has crossed your questionable path during your lifetime, because you will find that we are *not* your enemy. Unless, of course, you have something to hide—" I didn't wait for his reply. I didn't need to. It would take only two hours to see whether he had understood my threat.

CHAPTER 23

True to Colin's earlier prediction, Edwina Easterbrooke looked decidedly unhappy to see us again. She was perched on an oversized armchair, all angles and gawky limbs, her dark hair swept back so harshly that it looked like her cheekbones were on the verge of rending her flesh. Her long fingers were tapping in a manner that suggested either nervousness or annoyance, I couldn't be sure which, though once the tea arrived with a plate of crustless watercress and cucumber finger sandwiches she did appear to relax. Colin kept the conversation light while we gratefully snacked, though she did not join us.

At some point during the course of our idle chatter the four-legged squire of the house, the roly-poly Buster Brown, made a cumbersome descent down the staircase to investigate us. I could tell by the glimmer in Colin's eyes that he had been waiting for the pup's arrival, and watched as he lavished the pug with a hearty greeting before casually sliding the valise containing Lady Priscilla's blanket out from under the settee with the toe of a boot.

"Did you have a good nap?" Miss Easterbrooke crowed as

she too leaned forward to scratch the pug's head. The dog plopped down at Colin's feet as if in answer, his pink tongue bobbing out of his mouth like a seizing worm. "He really does like you, Mr. Pendragon—" She beamed, but before Colin could reply, the dog abruptly shoved himself to his feet and made his way with remarkable haste to the valise. Buster Brown's single-mindedness was astonishing; as though he were heading for a plate of rib bones and with the swipe of a single meaty paw he batted the valise onto its side and began an olfactory inspection that would have staggered a chemist.

"*Buster!*" Miss Easterbrooke gasped, grabbing for her pup as though he had just marked the valise in a more rudimentary way.

"No, no," Colin said with a chuckle. "It's my fault. Your little gentleman is not to be blamed." He leaned forward and pulled open the valise to reveal its contents to the agitated beast. The dog's reaction was instantaneous. He sank into a frenzy of desperate motion as he tried to paw, wiggle, or force his way deep inside the bag. Yet the width and breadth of his anatomy would allow no such entry, leaving him no other recourse but to sink to the floor with a mournful howl of indignation.

"*Buster Brown!*" the dog's mistress cried again, her hands fluttering about her neck. "Really, I don't understand."

Colin reached in and extracted the worn pink blanket, dangling it for a moment above Buster's head. "It belongs to Lady Priscilla," he said as he let it drop to the floor. "I had completely forgotten I had it. Rather a dirty trick on the old boy."

He started laughing, as did I, but Miss Easterbrooke saw little mirth. I glanced back to find that the pug had seized one end of the blanket in his jaws and was attacking the crumpled bulk of the cloth with his hips in a manner suggestive of procreation. Unfortunately for the pug, Miss Easterbrooke saw it as well and screamed so loudly that her houseman came bounding up the stairs with a look of unbridled terror. By the time the red-faced man stood before us, gasping for breath, Colin had already extricated the blanket from the randy dog and returned it to the valise. Edwina Easterbrooke collapsed back into her chair, her ghostly pallor that of a woman on the verge of a swoon.

"Madam?!" her houseman managed to say.

"It's my fault," Colin piped up again, a hint of grayness having overtaken his features. "I cannot apologize enough. We shall see ourselves out." He looked at me and nodded in an odd way, one of his eyebrows curling up, and then started to leave. That's when I caught sight of the tail of Lady Priscilla's blanket hanging provocatively from the back of the valise. And just as I knew he'd intended, Buster Brown saw it too.

The dog charged back to his feet and scurried after Colin before I could even stand up, and it wasn't until Colin had reached the staircase that Miss Easterbrooke realized what was happening.

"Get the dog, Alvin . . . ," she hissed as I moved to beat him there.

"What?" he muttered, clearly shaken from the scream that had brought him up here in the first place.

"Get the blasted dog!" she snapped, any sense of delicacy having clearly deserted her.

I plunged down the staircase first, willing the portly beast to make it to the bottom quickly, as I gingerly picked my way down, gripping the banister on both sides, as I knew poor Alvin would never presume to push past me. Even so, I could feel him on my heels.

Buster Brown reached the first floor and crossed out of my view, and I hoped that whatever Colin was after was happening, because the instant my feet hit the foyer the houseman took advantage of the extra space to sweep past me even though neither Colin nor the dog was in sight. A swinging door off to one side was the only demarcation of their course, which was all the corpulent man needed as he flew with uncanny vigor and disappeared behind it.

I followed right on his heels, shoving the door open and finding myself in a huge kitchen resplendent with a crackling hearth fire and the scent of fresh-cut lemon and Earl Grey tea. Across the room, however, was a very peculiar scene. Colin was standing in front of a door from which the mortified houseman was dragging a highly perturbed Buster Brown. Even as Colin's feigned apologies oozed like honey I could see that he was well satisfied. Not a moment later Edwina Easterbrooke burst into the room, bellowing for her dog in a voice that was as shrill as it seemed out of character.

"*Buster Brown, you get over here this instant!*" she screeched.

The effect was instantaneous. The rebuked dog dropped low, flattening his ears against his head. The ample houseman took that moment to place himself in front of the door as though we might forget having seen it were he to remain there long enough.

"I am mortified," Colin said in a tone I found overwrought. He stalked back across the kitchen, overtaking poor Buster Brown, who had only just begun to skulk toward his mistress. "I have created an inexcusable fuss. You must forgive me." He smiled chastely, his dimples unwilling to be contained. "I appear to have gotten him riled up in search of a treat. I assume you keep his treats in the cellar?"

"Yes, of course," Miss Easterbrooke answered too quickly, sounding rather ill as she reached out and grabbed the dog by the collar the second he came within striking distance. "We cannot have him chewing those terrible things up here."

"Wouldn't be proper." Colin smiled as he glanced at me. "Shall we?"

I nodded, offering hurried good-byes with some measure of discomfort, as it felt as though we had surely caught the entire household in some sort of compromising situation. Even so, barring breaking into the basement ourselves, a possibility that had not escaped me, it seemed it would take a bit more time to see just how compromised they had been. As I followed Colin outside, watching while he casually slid an ever-ready crown out of his pocket and began flicking it across the back of his hand, I could see that he was well pleased indeed.

CHAPTER 24

The same silver crown and the promise of that much more at the end of the evening was enough to buy us the observational services of two rapacious lads. Colin wanted to be alerted if anybody arrived at or left the Easterbrooke flat and promised to pay extra for any detailed information the scrawny urchins could provide should anyone do so. He had produced the crown and sent it careening swiftly between the fingers of his right hand before palming it and making it seem to reappear from beneath the collar of the taller boy. Colin's antics earned him squeals of delight from both of them, though I was certain their interest in such sleight of hand was due to the use it could provide them in their future pickpocketing endeavors.

In the lengthening gloom of the waning day, Colin and I headed back home. It was time to cut our driver loose, as we weren't due back at Lady Stuart's for another hour yet. I had considered suggesting we fetch my things from the Devonshire, but as Colin kept absently stroking his chin, lost to some thought, I decided that task could wait.

The moment we stepped into our flat I was struck by the

florid aroma of freshly brewed jasmine tea. We poked our heads into the kitchen and saw an open biscuit tin, the bulk of its contents missing. As I scanned the meticulous little room I noticed that our silver tea set had also vanished from atop the sideboard. "It appears . . . ," Colin said before I could, "that we have company."

"I hope it's not another case. I could not tolerate a third."

He waved me off. "Stop fretting. We'll have both of these resolved tomorrow. A new one would be ideal."

I kept quiet as I followed him upstairs, hoping he had good reason for such optimism. As we reached the landing I spied a cascade of wavy black hair tucked up beneath a small, square ivory-colored hat and realized at once that it was Lady Dahlia Stuart.

"What a pleasant surprise!" Colin beamed as we entered the room. "And thank you for playing hostess in our absence, Mrs. Behmoth." He nodded at her, gesturing with his chin toward the door.

She frowned as she got up. "Was 'appy ta get off me dogs fer a minute. Ya let me know if ya need more tea." And then she turned to Lady Stuart and gave an awkward sort of bow before saying, "Was nice speakin' to ya."

"It was a pleasure." Lady Stuart smiled easily, her faultless complexion glowing in the receding sunlight filtering in through the windows.

The moment Mrs. Behmoth left, Colin refreshed Lady Stuart's tea and poured some for us, handing a cup over to me. "Your father is impressive in his protection of you," he said. "He stuck by your story with notable determination."

"My father is a selfish man who understands that as I go, so goes he." Her words were neither harsh nor accusing but spoken with the easy assurance of truth. She was continuing to prove herself an unexpected woman. "Whatever you took to be a representation of loyalty on his part was nothing more than an act of self-preservation. My mother died in childbirth, you see, and my father has never let me forget that fact. He likes me to remember that I am beholden to him." She smiled. "But I cannot imagine you want to hear my petty grievances against him. How dull we should all be to spend a lifetime castigating our parents."

"Indeed." Colin smiled tightly. "Besides, my hope is that you have come to tell the truth. I should very much like to hear that."

"Yes, I suppose you've earned it," she answered, settling back on the settee.

"Please . . ." Colin too settled back as he watched her warily. "Tell us something of the Lady Dahlia Stuart."

Her dark eyes drifted toward the ceiling. "Ah . . . ," she began after another moment, ". . . the Lady Dahlia Stuart. . . ." She could not keep another smile from curling the edges of her lips. "I suppose the truth is that she doesn't really exist. She is the concoction of a girl born in a village outside of Bucharest whose father was a swindler, disappearing off to the city for days at a time to sell tonics that were nothing more than water and bitter roots. Magdala Genovesse"—she nodded by way of introduction—"that is who the Lady Dahlia Stuart is."

"And what of her?" Colin prodded.

A deep sigh escaped as she stared back at us. "It's all so sordid."

"We all of us have something we wish to hide," he said, and I felt myself flush at the truth of his words.

"You must share one day." She grinned, but there was little pleasure behind it. "I spent most of my childhood starving to death, as my father had greater love for alcohol than me. So when I was eight, I ran off to a neighboring farm and begged the woman there to take me to my aunt in the city. She had told me stories of my mother's sister, and while she was hesitant at first, the pitiful sight of me was enough to finally get her to agree.

"She took me all the way into Bucharest that very night and delivered me to a grand building the likes of which I had never seen. The whole city was like a fairy tale, multistoried buildings of brick and mortar with façades that looked as though they had been drizzled by candy makers. Streets of stone, not dirt and mud, and walls that rose straight and true like the hand of God had set them upright. There wasn't a stick of thatch to be found anywhere." She chuckled.

I leaned forward to pour more tea and accidentally knocked the teapot to the floor in a great *screech* of shattering china. Colin leapt up as the flying pieces skittered away, but it was Lady Stuart who was the first to kneel down and begin mopping up the mess.

"Ya need more tea?" Mrs. Behmoth hollered.

"No," Colin called back as I quickly gathered the broken pieces and wiped up the mess. "We're fine. If we need anything further I shall come down and fetch it myself."

"I 'ope ta live long enough ta see *that* day," her reply drifted up.

I could see Lady Stuart suppressing a smirk as we settled in again.

"I've been to Bucharest." Colin gently guided us back to the topic. "When I was in school."

"Then you must understand something of how I felt when I arrived."

"I can only imagine, since I'm no good at divination," he tossed back.

She immediately laughed, the sound as elegant as a wind chime. "Ah, Mr. Pendragon. Apparently you have managed to ferret out much about me, including my scandalous livelihood. I wonder if you know whether I am any good at it?"

"If you didn't give the illusion of accuracy then you would never be able to woo the grande dames. For that reason I would conclude you must be good enough. What I can't fathom is how you learned such a trade."

"That is the question then, isn't it? How does one go from being an illiterate Carpathian farm girl to a London society sage?" She gave that ephemeral laugh again and I knew she could tell we were in her thrall. "It was my maternal aunt."

"So it was to your aunt's home that you were brought that night in Bucharest?" I asked.

"I'm afraid not." She glanced at me with sadness clouding her eyes. "Yours would make a better tale, but it is not mine. My aunt didn't live in that grand palace, though she stayed there from time to time at the owner's whim. He was a man well stationed in the court of King Carol, who, back then, was little more than an impatient prince.

"My aunt was an extraordinary beauty *and* clever. A powerful combination. The two of us shuttled back and forth from the palace to my aunt's tiny cottage on the outskirts of the city. She tutored me, teaching me to read and write, but when we stayed at the palace I was allowed to attend studies with the court children. It was a magnificent time, but as with all things, it could not last. By the time I was twelve my aunt had grown frail with disease and before I turned thirteen she had died.

"Thinking to do me a kindness, my aunt's patron sent for my father. He arrived in Bucharest with the clothes on his back and a demeanor soured by continuing years of drink. It didn't take long before his behavior got us exiled. We were sent to Prague with nothing but what we had arrived with: tattered clothing and a handful of coins." She shook her head. "It was a terrible time. We begged on the streets and slept in a cemetery at night. And that's when my father met Darius Stuart.

"Darius was an old man who loved his spirits every bit as much as my father. He had been born to money but had squandered most of it during a long life in which his only goal had apparently been to exist beyond a means he could afford. He called himself Lord Stuart but had earned no such title. Still, no one in Prague questioned his claim. As long as he paid his bills his façade was tolerated, and in Prague his meager funds went further than they could in England. It was the very reason he had gone to Prague." She laughed again. "Thinking him a wealthy patron, my father forced me to lie in Darius's bed to try and procure the use of his name and questionable title. But I never actually married that drunken grizzled old toad."

"You never married him?"

"I didn't need to." She smiled coyly. "While we were staying with him I met an old woman at the vegetable market on Charles Bridge. She caught my eye because, like me, she was always alone. I watched her for weeks as she went about her business, noticing that everyone either shied from her or shunned her altogether. She would go to a stall and the customers would drift away, and they would stay away until she had bought her goods and left. The first time I tried to talk to her she paid me no mind. But the next time I saw her, *she* approached *me*. She behaved with kindness, but proceeded to tell me all manner of things about myself she could not possibly have known: my name, where I lived, and the circumstances under which I lived there. She even knew that I had come from Bucharest with my father and that my mother had died during my birth. It was astonishing. And do you know how she did it, Mr. Pendragon?"

He pursed his lips and gazed up at the ceiling. "Your name and residence are simple; she either followed you or had someone else do so. The circumstances under which you lived in Darius Stuart's home could easily be garnered from your clothing and the fact that you were out shopping in the market. Your city of origin would be gleaned from your accent. But I cannot do anything but speculate as to how she learned the details of your birth."

"Please." Her smile widened as her dark eyes fastened on Colin with curiosity. "Let us hear your speculation."

"Given your father's predilection to torment you regarding your mother's unfortunate death, I would suppose he was not averse to sharing his prejudice against you with others, most particularly when he was drinking. Anyone who sought him out in a pub would surely have been able to entice him to speak freely if they plied him with drink. Am I close?"

"You are spot-on. So tell me, Mr. Pendragon, have you ever studied spiritualism?"

"Only to dismiss it. I'm afraid I find the field wholly populated by charlatans. I find nature quite diligent in upholding her laws, which leaves little room for sages and soothsayers. But"—he flashed a slim sort of grin at her—"perhaps you will prove me wrong?"

"You have no worries from me. I'll not be the one to dismantle your skepticism. As for the old woman, she taught me that I needn't rely on anyone else to take care of me. A heady bit of freedom for a girl of not quite fifteen. But most of all"—she leaned forward, an impish sparkle in her eyes—"she taught me about people."

"Of course." He nodded. "You cannot expect to dispense accurate prognostications unless you learn how to interpret the clues your quarry inadvertently reveals."

"Precisely. Not only did I learn about the tarot deck, but how every gesture, frown, smile, grimace, and sigh from a client reveals whether or not I am heading in the right direction. The spectre of a sick person would become a mother, father, lover, brother, or friend based on a tic or halting inhalation of breath. The cards could be misleading or the vibrations difficult to interpret until the moment the client, believing I was on the verge of some great truth, would suddenly prattle off a history that would blessedly provide the remainder of my prediction." She grinned mischievously. "I learned that if I kept at it—health, money, love, acrimony, deceit, revenge—there inevitably came that unconscious flick or quiver that told me I had hit the very crux of the reason I had been sought out."

"Extraordinary . . . ," I muttered.

"Hardly." She chuckled. "Haven't you ever watched someone prattle on in their own defense and noticed their eyes flicking about the room, and known they were lying?" I nodded. "Then you are every bit the seer that I am." She laughed. "It didn't take me long to become adept at it. So the night Darius died, I knew the chance had come to strike out on my own."

"A young woman on her own?" Colin said. "I should hardly think so."

"And now you sound like my father," she scolded him. "Before the dawn came my father forged a marriage certificate and last will that bequeathed all of Darius's holdings to me, and thus was born the Lady Stuart.

"We sold the house, taking a meager price from a man who asked no questions, and took what little money Darius had saved and went to England. My father was convinced that was where the bulk of Darius's estate would be. I changed my name to Dahlia during the crossing of the Channel, hoping it would give me an air of sophistication that Magdala did not, and my father agreed to play my houseman, something every decent lady would have. But when we arrived it was to discover that the only thing Darius had left here was debt."

"So why didn't you return to the Continent?"

"You think too little of me, Mr. Pendragon. I was done running. I had a title and a provenance. So I bought my little house on Lancaster Gate and set out to repay the outstanding bills of my late husband. And it was those very debts that offered my first introduction to London society. You see, I was the exotic noble widow who made good for her errant spouse.

"The noble ladies rallied around me and I began to pretend to suffer public visions about one or the other until I finally piqued their intrigue enough that I was forced to feign lightheadedness just to get them to stop peppering me with questions about their lives, husbands, children, and households. After that, establishing my business was easy, and the payment sublime." She smirked. "I was able to settle Darius's bills in little more than two years, and the fact of my having accomplished such a feat only further propelled my reputation as a just and honest woman. The woman before you."

"Was Captain Bellingham's wife one of those who sought you out?"

"Gwendolyn?" Her brow creased as she tilted her head to one side. "I thought I clarified that yesterday."

"You *were* seeing him?"

"Are you asking me or telling me?"

"I want the truth."

She said nothing for a moment, the only sound in the room the sweep hand of the mantel clock. "I am sorry to disappoint you," she finally spoke up, "but as I told you before, Trevor and I were not involved in any intimacy. He was my dearest friend. That was the extent of it."

Colin held his face steady as now *he* stayed silent for a time. It did seem unimaginable that the captain had not become intimate with a woman of Lady Stuart's beauty. There was even less sense to the possibility that he had been seeking her out for such esoteric counseling. "The captain's frequent visits would seem to suggest otherwise," Colin said after it became clear that she was not about to volunteer anything further.

"A statement that conveniently dismisses the fact that I am known as a gifted prophesier."

"A talent you have already spent some time this afternoon rebuffing."

"Do not confuse my dismissal of the craft with my ability to be persuasive."

"I see." He stood up and wandered over to the fireplace, poking at the lazy flames with a resolve that assured me he was growing weary of this game. "So Captain Bellingham came to you on a regular basis solely to discuss your intuitions about his future?"

"Is that really so hard to believe?"

He glanced back at her finely sculpted features and frame of coal-black hair and said, "Yes."

"How very flattering." She smiled.

"I don't mean to be."

"And there you are, Mr. Pendragon. Now you sound just like my dear Trevor."

He dropped the poker, sending the log he'd been poking at rolling backwards out of the grate and earning an angry rebuke from the embers below. "Do I?"

Her smile slowly faded. "Trevor was a deeply troubled man, and if you have sought me out thinking I hold the key to some love-crossed tale with him I can assure you that you are quite mistaken."

Colin nodded thoughtfully as he moved over to the windows and stared down on the street, appearing almost nonchalant as he fished out a coin and began delicately coaxing it across the back of his hand. "Are you stating a fact, then?" he asked after a moment.

A sad smile flitted across her face. "I am."

"Will ya be wantin' more tea an' biscuits?!" Mrs. Behmoth's voice suddenly blasted up the stairs.

"We're quite set, thank you," Colin called back as he tossed the coin onto the windowsill and came back to his seat. "Did you ever meet Mrs. Bellingham's brother? A sergeant in the Irish Guard by the name of Mulrooney?"

"I knew of him."

"Did you meet him?" Colin asked again.

"A time or two. I didn't care for him. I found him harsh, unapologetic, and wholly unforgiving of Trevor."

"How so?"

"He was rude and dismissive. It was appalling. I refused to have anything to do with him."

"Where exactly did you meet him?"

"Trevor and Gwen's."

"And how long ago would that have been?"

Her eyebrows knit as she looked at him. "I don't know. A couple of years, I suppose."

"I see," he muttered as he took a sip of tea. "And why do you suppose Sergeant Mulrooney was so incorrigible when it came to Captain Bellingham?"

"I'm afraid you would have to ask him, Mr. Pendragon, for while I profess to read minds, we both know it's nothing more than a parlor trick."

"Yes." And now a smile eased onto his face. "So you have said. And how did Sergeant Mulrooney treat his sister?"

"He treated her better than he did Trevor, but I found his manner toward her disapproving. As if she were his petulant child. I don't know how she abided him. Trevor said they were close at one time, but I never saw it."

"Did he tell you anything else?"

"A lady does not pry," she answered simply.

A thin sigh escaped from Colin. "And how is it that you and Captain Bellingham became such close mates?"

"It was the summer after I met him at the fox hunt. He escorted one of the Queen's granddaughters to several appointments with me. One of the late Princess Alice's daughters."

"Which one?"

"Alix."

"You consulted with Empress Alexandra?"

"Many times that summer." She smiled with pride. "A beautiful girl, but with the most peculiar melancholy streak. She did have an eager mind for my skills, however."

"I'm sure her visits were a tonic for your burgeoning business."

"Without a doubt. And not just among the aristocracy, but within the Queen's Guard as well—which included Trevor." She picked up her tea and sipped it with little enthusiasm. "We saw each other quite a bit that summer. Not just on the occasions when he was escorting the Princess, but at other times, social times. Then, about three years ago, right after Trevor had been promoted to captain, he began to come over with little excuse, wanting to talk about my readings. I thought it a ruse and wondered if he was developing feelings for me." She chuckled, but this time the sound was hollow. "It didn't take long before I realized his interests truly were around my readings."

"You were disappointed?"

"I would not break up a marriage, but I cared very much for Trevor. I won't lie about that."

I could tell Colin was pleased by this admission. "And what did he want to know about your readings?"

"He was afraid for his sanity, Mr. Pendragon. He thought he might be losing his mind."

"He confessed that to you?"

"He didn't have to. I have developed a keen sense of people, as it is the very heart of my business. For instance"—her eyes narrowed—"your Mrs. Behmoth has an unmistakable maternal streak when she speaks of you, Mr. Pendragon, that does not carry over to Mr. Pruitt. My guess is that she's been in your life since you were a child. Perhaps she filled a void for a mother who was not available when you were growing up? Am I close?"

"You've made your point," he allowed.

She smiled as she set her teacup on the table. "I loved him very much and I know he loved me in turn. We were the closest of family, he and I." She stood up and gathered the fine woolen shawl draped across the back of the settee. "I gave him hope. I told him I could see his future and that everything would sort itself out. It's what he wanted to hear."

Colin stood up and wrapped the shawl about her shoulders. "But he told you nothing more? He gave you no other indications—"

"He didn't need to, Mr. Pendragon. I already knew everything about him that I needed to know."

I could tell she was flustered as I moved to see her out, but when we got to the landing she abruptly turned and looked back at Colin. "Could I beseech you both to keep my past private? I would hope you agree that my little charade is harmless. I believe I offer a service, a bit of innocuous comfort, but I know I would be exiled back to the Continent were my peers to learn that I had been deceiving them. And I simply could not abide starting over."

Colin nodded. "We shall keep our peace," he muttered, "but should you recall anything further—"

"Of course," she answered at once. "You have well earned my loyalty, Mr. Pendragon, and I intend to yet prove my value to you."

"I am counting on that," he answered grimly. "You can be sure of that."

CHAPTER 25

Thomas Mulrooney was not pleased to see us again. Even his captain had been more reticent to give us permission to speak with Mulrooney a second time. Nevertheless, the captain had finally permitted us entry, delivering us to another small room in the Parliament building where Sergeant Mulrooney was once again displaying an appalling lack of willingness to cooperate. If Colin did not focus the thrust of his investigation against this man, I was prepared to do so for him.

"Do you have any sisters, Mr. Pendragon?" Mulrooney was asking with thick disdain.

"I fail to see what this has to do with anything!" Colin groused in return, which pleased me greatly.

"You cannot indulge me one simple question among your barrage?"

Colin heaved an exasperated sigh and I knew he was wrestling with his tongue. "I have no siblings," he finally answered.

The sergeant cracked a satisfied smile. "Then what could you possibly know about my relationship with Gwen? You're hounding me with questions and I don't see that you can understand any of it."

"Then help me understand."

Sergeant Mulrooney snorted. "And why should I have any interest in doing that?" He folded his arms across his chest and glared at Colin. "Why don't you just be honest, Mr. Pendragon? Are you here to arrest me?"

"Of course not."

"Then piss off."

Colin's eyes flashed harshly even as his voice stayed smooth. "So you have no desire to ensure your sister's killer is brought to justice?"

"Justice?" the sergeant sneered, and shook his head. "How do you know the only justice possible hasn't already been wrought?"

"Is that what you'll tell your nephew one day when he asks what happened to his parents?"

"At least Albert stands a chance now. My mum will do right by him."

"Which certainly doesn't say much for your sister and her husband."

"I don't give a bloody fig about Trevor," he fired back, pausing before adding, "Gwen made her own decisions. God have mercy on her."

"Cryptic—"

"Are we done?"

"As soon as you tell me about the fight in McPhee's between the Life Guard and your Irish mates. The one that cost Captain Newcombe his life . . . ?"

"Wilford Newcombe was every bit the blighted rubbish that Trevor was. Why aren't you asking me about the three decent men of the Irish Guard who lost their commissions because of that night? Where's your interest and compassion for them?"

"I was told those men were found culpable."

The sergeant's glare darkened. "Of course they were. They were tried in the ruddy British courts. What else would you expect? So tell me, Mr. Pendragon, where is your esteemed justice in that?"

"Tell me what you know about that night then."

"To what end? Can you reverse the courts . . . ? Give those men their commissions back . . . ? I think not."

"What started the fight?"

"Why don't you ask Dashell Hampstead that question?" He abruptly turned and headed for the door, stopping just at the threshold. "Let me be very clear, Mr. Pendragon, so you won't feel compelled to bother me again. I despised Trevor. He was a disgrace. He polluted everything he came into contact with, including my sister. He deserved what happened to him. It is the will of God. And the murder of my sister is Trevor's legacy, not mine. I'm only thankful my nephew has a chance at a decent life now." He started to turn away and then stopped once more. "Do not ask for me again, Mr. Pendragon"—he bit the words ominously—"unless you've a magistrate's warrant in your hand."

And then he was gone.

CHAPTER 26

By the time we made the short journey to Buckingham Palace the sky was as dark as I could sense Colin's mood to be. I diverted my attention to the nearly full opalescent moon peeking above the eastern horizon and hoped it might aid us in finding further illumination on our night's endeavors. I was also grateful for the clear sky, as we had stopped by the Devonshire to retrieve my things, which were relegated to the roof of our cab for fear there might be bugs in them seeking a better life elsewhere.

We swung around the courtyard in front of the palace and I was mortified at the thought of my scant possessions fastened above our heads for God and Queen to see. I climbed out while Colin conferred with the driver and slipped him the cash I had handed over during the brief ride. And then, quite suddenly, as though to further reinforce the questionable value of my belongings, the coach began pulling away. "Hey!" I shouted.

"What's the matter?!" Colin scowled at me.

"My things! He's got my things!"

He shook his head and started toward the side gate. "He is

taking them to Mrs. Behmoth to boil. He'll be back to deliver us straightaway to the Easterbrooke flat. It can't be long now before she and her houseman make their move. We have got to get that blasted case solved tonight."

My heart sank at his frustration as he beckoned one of the guards to fetch the sergeant on duty. The young man immediately snapped about and marched off. "Do you have any idea who's in charge tonight?" I asked.

"Didn't you notice the man's uniform?" Colin muttered impatiently.

"His uniform?"

"He's wearing the buttons and insignias of the Queen's Life Guard, Ethan. Haven't you been paying any attention?" I bit the inside of my cheek to keep from defending myself and watched as Sergeant McReedy came striding back across the parade ground. It seemed a lucky turn indeed until Colin finally conceded, "And Sergeant McReedy mentioned he would be on duty tonight."

"You cheat." I smirked.

"I make use of all resources at hand."

"Let them in, Private!" Sergeant McReedy barked as he approached.

The young man swung the gate wide even as he kept a firm hand on it, ready to swing it shut in case his commanding officer should abruptly countermand himself. We followed Sergeant McReedy inside and down a hall in the opposite direction from where Major Hampstead's office was, which I thought curious. The sergeant delivered us to a small meeting room and bade us sit.

"We should have some tea shortly," he announced as we settled around the table at the room's center.

"Very thoughtful." Colin managed a slight smile.

"And to what do we owe tonight's visit?" Sergeant McReedy's face betrayed nothing as he stared at us, but I could tell by the rigidity of his spine that he was tense.

Before Colin could answer, a young corporal scurried into the room with a teapot in one hand and three cups in the other. He had a creamer wedged in the crook between his chin and breastbone and an open bowl of sugar pressed against his side at one elbow. He looked like the repast version of a one-man band.

"Some things are informal," Sergeant McReedy said as he reached out and took the creamer and sugar from the man. "There is enough pomp in everything else we do, so we try to keep tea one of our simpler pleasures." The sergeant dismissed the corporal with the flick of a hand and served us himself. "I must profess to finding it a relief to know this will all be over in twenty-four hours. Less, actually."

"Thank you for reminding me," Colin said, sipping at his tea grimly.

"So you have gotten nowhere?"

"Where I've gotten is not far enough."

"I see."

Colin's exasperation continued to sour as he asked, "What do you know about the night at McPhee's Tavern when Private Newcombe's father was mortally wounded?"

Sergeant McReedy paused as though pondering the question before answering, "Nothing. I wasn't there."

"But you've heard things . . . ?"

"I've told you before that I do not trade in gossip and hearsay."

"Within every rumor lies a kernel of truth."

Sergeant McReedy set his tea down. "I really expected more of you than that sort of claptrap, Mr. Pendragon. Even the inspector could do better." Colin's face went rigid as the sergeant got up and ambled to the door. "Is there someone else you would prefer to grill for such pabulum?"

"Corporal Bramwood," I spoke into the edgy silence that had descended, even though I wasn't at all sure if that's whom

Colin had in mind. That young man, I was quite certain, could be coaxed into talking.

The sergeant scowled. "Fitting." And was out the door.

"I believe I shall fail at this case just to make sure they never enlist my aid again," Colin sneered the moment we were alone.

"Isn't there something I can do to help?"

"You have done more than your share on this case already." He flashed a meager sort of grin. We sat quietly after that until the major's young attaché, Corporal Bramwood, came striding into the room.

"Mr. Pendragon . . ." He beamed with his usual enthusiasm. "Mr. Pruitt . . ." He tossed me a quick glance with measurably less interest.

"Please . . ." Colin gestured to a chair. "I have some difficult questions to press upon you as Major Hampstead's adjunct. I shall require your full cooperation."

The young corporal furrowed his brow with what looked like artifice as he continued to stare at Colin. "Of course, Mr. Pendragon. Whatever I can do to help."

I studied the side of his face: strong chin, straight, slender nose with the faintest bob at its tip, and eager, dark eyes. Even his dusky brown hair was swept across his forehead in a rakish sort of flourish. He looked like a man yet to suffer the anguish most lives dole out, and as I watched him I knew I didn't trust him.

"Tell me . . ." Colin leaned back in his chair and gazed up at the ceiling as though operating on whimsy. "Are you solely responsible for Major Hampstead's calendar?"

"I am."

"And was it the major's habit to visit a tavern named McPhee's from time to time?"

"It was until a handful of months ago. Some malcontents from the Irish Guard set upon the major and a few other officers there one evening. A captain under Major Hampstead ended up seriously wounded and died in hospital several days later." His eyes lit up. "It was Private Newcombe's father. You've met Private Newcombe . . ."

"Indeed." Colin feigned a brief smile. "Seems a decent fellow." To my surprise Corporal Bramwood neither agreed nor disagreed. "Can you tell me what precipitated the fight?"

"Oh . . . ," he muttered as I continued to study him, watching as his face categorically shut down, ". . . I'm sure I don't know."

Colin gave an arid chuckle. "Come now, you sit right outside the major's office. I can see he doesn't make a move without you. Surely you—"

"No, sir," came the immediate reply.

"Really . . . ?" Colin was as keyed on the corporal's face as I was. "I would have bet that a bright young man like yourself would have picked up some notion—"

"You would be wrong, sir." He shifted in his chair. "Are we about finished? I've some duties to attend to—"

Colin's glare tightened, signaling that the limit of his patience was fast approaching. "You were so willing to be helpful a moment ago and now you are asking to leave? Have I done something to offend?"

"No, sir. I've . . ." His eyes flicked about the room a moment, betraying his youth. "I don't know anything and don't want to waste your time."

"Very thoughtful, but I should prefer to decide for myself what is a waste of my time. Now why is it that mention of that night at McPhee's makes you so uncomfortable?"

"What do you mean?"

"Oh, come now, Corporal, if you could see yourself in a mirror you would be appalled at your lack of cunning."

I cringed as Corporal Bramwood clenched his jaw and stared back at Colin. "Will that be all?" he asked curtly.

Colin leaned forward, talking pointedly into the younger

man's face. "Had you heard rumors that Captain Bellingham was having an affair?"

The corporal's face softened slightly as he continued to glare at Colin. "I'd heard a few things, but I didn't believe it. The captain—"

"Spare me," Colin spoke over him. "I've heard all about how wonderful the captain was, and yet there was someone who hated him enough to torture that good and kind man to death. So tell me, Corporal Bramwood, whom did you hear the captain was having it off with?"

He pursed his lips with distaste. "I don't see what this—"

"Who?!"

"The Stuart woman. The one he was always visiting."

"And is that what started the fight at McPhee's?"

"I don't know."

"Did you ever meet Captain Bellingham's brother-in-law?"

"Who?"

"Sergeant Thomas Mulrooney of the Irish Guard. Do you know him?"

"No, sir."

"Ever heard of him?"

"No."

"You have a deplorable way of helping, Corporal."

"Are we finished then?"

Colin leaned back and folded his arms across his chest. "You expound great affection for Captain Bellingham and yet offer only the barest assistance. I find that mystifying." Corporal Bramwood stood up and moved for the door without a word, but just as he stepped out into the hallway Colin asked, "Will you do me one meager service, Corporal? Will you ask Private O'Fallon to join us?" The corporal nodded wordlessly as he hurried from the room. *"Bloody hell . . ."* Colin pounded a fist on the table.

"You can't let them get to you."

He turned a deep scowl on me. "I've got twenty-two hours to solve this blasted case. Do you have a better suggestion?"

"How about a different approach? Your impatience is having little impact on these men."

He immediately dropped to the floor and knocked out two dozen push-ups before springing back to his feet just as Private O'Fallon, the tall guardsman with the porcelain complexion and wave of strawberry hair, arrived. To my amusement, when he did so Colin turned to him with a most welcoming smile that was nothing less than what I knew he could conjure. He warmly beckoned the private to the chair Corporal Bramwood had so eagerly vacated, but Private O'Fallon stayed on his feet, maintaining the same grim expression he always seemed to wear, leaving me to wonder what he had to be so cheerless about.

"I appreciate your time once again, Private, as I find myself in need of just a bit more clarification with regards to what you have already told us."

The young man gave a halfhearted shrug, keeping his eyes on the wall behind me as though preparing for a grilling by a military tribunal.

"Right. . . ." Colin shot me a perturbed glance. "Do you recollect our initial meeting at the Bellingham flat?"

"Of course." The private glanced from Colin to me as though searching for some subterfuge in so innocuous a start.

Colin sucked in a breath as he laced his hands behind his back and began pacing around the room. "You mentioned something that day that I have not been able to forget. It concerns the Lady Stuart. . . ."

Private O'Fallon's eyes narrowed. "I've already told you everything I know about her," he insisted.

"So you made clear the last time we spoke." Colin moved back around to me and sat down, trying to adopt a look of nonchalance. "But I find memories to be funny things. Sometimes the tiniest nudge can trigger a world of recollections. So let us see if perhaps we cannot stir your thoughts."

The private turned a tepid sort of pink and I feared he was on the verge of refusing to cooperate before he finally said, "If you insist."

"You mentioned you had the impression Captain Bellingham was enjoying some sort of dalliance with Lady Stuart, did you not?"

"It wasn't my impression," he answered with a thick note of condescension. "It was the truth. I was privy to his calendar. I set many of his appointments myself. Her name was repeatedly there and yet he refused even the most trivial reference to her. I found that suspect, especially for a man said to be the ideal husband and father."

"Didn't you find it odd then that he would keep a public calendar entry for a woman he was having it off with?"

"What?!" His voice increased its edge as he glared at Colin. "He was up to something with her, but I never said they were having it off."

"You alluded—"

"*Alluded?!* Is that how you investigate your cases? By allusion and distortion? And do you also manipulate the words of the people you interview to fit your own determination of how a thing should play out?"

Colin's lips stretched into a rigid line as his brow sank ominously. "Is that what I have done, Private O'Fallon? Have I misinterpreted your intent in telling us of the many visits your captain made to Lady Stuart?"

"*My* captain?" His face went as hard as the gaze still boring into Colin. "And what might *that* mean, Mr. Pendragon? What is your implication *there?*"

"Implication?!" Colin flicked his eyes to me and I could see a simmering outrage blazing within them. "I imply that you worked for him. That you answered to him. Is that offensive as well, Private?" He rose to his feet. "There seems to be a world of secrets about this case and I am beginning to find it all exceedingly tiresome. You provide nothing more than grudging cooperation, making it abundantly clear that you don't give a fig about seeing these murders solved. I would say that doesn't reflect very well on you, Private!" he snapped.

"I don't care in the least if you mean to accuse me of something, Mr. Pendragon. Have at it."

Colin lurched across the table, hovering just in front of the recalcitrant man. "Why so cavalier, Private . . . ? Perhaps you were consoling the poor captain's wife?"

"You're pathetic."

"Is that a no?"

Private O'Fallon shoved himself out of his chair, stabbing his face close to Colin's. "You can go to hell."

"Is *that* a no?"

The private clenched his fists, making it obvious he wanted to send a clout to Colin's chin, which was precisely what I knew Colin was angling for. "I'm waiting for an answer to a very simple question," he baited.

Private O'Fallon pulled himself to his full height, tugging at the collar of his blazing red tunic, and stalked from the room with all the dignity accorded one of Her Majesty's own.

"What a contemptible little shit!" Colin sputtered before the private had fully cleared the doorway.

"Do you really think he might have been involved with Captain Bellingham's wife?"

"I didn't until he started being so evasive. He professes allegiance to Captain Bellingham only to impugn the man's reputation and then deny he is doing so." Colin coaxed a crown out of his pocket and began fumbling with it. "It's obvious I've ruffled him." He sent the coin spinning between his fingers. "And where there is soreness there is inevitably a wound." He gave me a cold grin. "I do believe we are edging closer."

"Do you think?"

"I certainly hope so. Now do me a turn and see if you can fetch Corporal Blevins. That lad seems naïve enough to extort information from."

I shook my head as I started for the door. "Well, I promise not to give you any more advice on how to handle this lot. These men don't seem to have any intention of cooperating no matter how they're treated."

He gave me a malevolent grin. "I'm so pleased to hear you say that."

CHAPTER 27

"Tell me something," Colin said when I had returned with Captain Bellingham's youthful adjunct Corporal Blevins. "Did you have an honest affection for your captain or are you just another of the brainwashed sycophants more interested in confounding this case than assisting in its solution?"

I cringed as the slight young man with the coarse bristle of black hair sat down across from us, his confusion easy to read. "Pardon, sir?"

"Allow me . . . ," I piped up, hoping to get this round of questioning off to a more productive start, only to have Colin brusquely silence me with an upturned hand. It seemed the corporal was in for whatever routing Colin determined appropriate.

"You worked directly for Captain Bellingham, correct?"

"Yes, sir. I was in charge of his schedule and assisted with his correspondence and regimental duties."

"Very good. And did you consider yourself close to the captain? Did he confide in you?"

Corporal Blevins blinked several times, and while I searched his face for any hint of subterfuge, I could find none. "Only about his schedule. Is that what you mean?"

Colin looked about to reach across the table and backhand the poor naïve young man, so I shot my foot out to kick him under the table. He startled and then, to my relief, leaned back and allowed a warm smile to overtake his face. "It is precisely what I meant. You must forgive me for being so inarticulate."

"Not at all, sir." The corporal offered his own sort of smile, but it looked decidedly uneasy on his face.

"How long have you been a member of the Life Guard?"

"Just short of a year, sir."

"And how long did you work for Captain Bellingham?"

"The last five months. I was assigned to him right after training. I thought . . ." But he let his voice trail off, and for once Colin did not press him to continue.

"Did you like working for the captain? Did you find him to be fair?"

"I did, sir. Very much."

"And did you have occasion to meet his wife and son?"

"Never his son, sir, no. But I did meet Mrs. Bellingham twice. Once when she came to visit him and the second time when he asked me to deliver a small package to their flat."

"Came here, did she? Checking up on her husband?!" Colin gave a cavalier laugh, but I knew he meant to have an answer.

The young man remained stoic. "I believe she had been shopping in the area. The captain was taking her out to lunch."

"Ah." Colin nodded. "And are you familiar with Mrs. Bellingham's brother . . . ? A Sergeant Thomas Mulrooney of the Irish Guard?"

The corporal's face clouded. "I met him a few weeks ago. He came into the office to see the captain and they had a terrible row."

"Did they?" Colin tried to maintain an air of ease, but it was easy to see the information had caught his interest. "What did it concern?"

"Oh!" The corporal glanced from Colin to me. "I wouldn't know, sir. The captain had his door closed and he sent me to fetch some paperwork almost as soon as the sergeant arrived."

"What paperwork?"

"Schedules for the guardsmen from Major Hampstead's office."

"And when you returned . . . ?"

He shrugged slightly and dropped his gaze to the floor. "They were still talking. It sounded rather heated, but I didn't really hear anything. After a couple of minutes Sergeant Mulrooney came storming out. Didn't say a word to me."

"And the captain?"

He shook his head. "He was in his office the rest of the afternoon. I poked my head in before I left that night, but by then it was like nothing had happened."

"And you say you couldn't make out anything they were saying at all?"

"Well . . ." His eyes flicked about the room before he continued. "Captain Bellingham sounded quite upset about something Sergeant Mulrooney was accusing him of, but I don't know what that was. Honestly, I was trying not to listen. . . ." His voice trailed off, accentuating his acute discomfort.

Colin flashed a brief smile as he eyed the young man. "How old are you, Corporal?"

"Twenty, sir. In a couple of weeks."

"Still living at home?"

"In the barracks, sir, with the other new recruits."

"Your parents must be very proud of you."

He nodded with a hint of embarrassment. "They are. My mum makes a fuss. Comes round once a week with something she's baked. The others look forward to her shortbreads and tarts, but I really wish she wouldn't."

"Save your wishes for better things. I take it you're the only son?"

"Yes, sir. How did you know?"

"Such a doting mother could only have time for one boy."
He grinned. "How long have your parents been married?"

"Twenty-seven years," he said with pride.

Again Colin smiled before continuing. "When Mrs. Bellingham came to her husband's office, did you sense the same sort
of marriage your parents have?"

"The Bellinghams . . . ?" His brow furrowed as he seemed to
consider the question. "They weren't married even half the
time of my mum and dad. I'm sure that made a difference."

"Of course. But what did you think when you saw them together?"

"She was very kind to me and the captain was always a gentleman. He set a fine example. It was a privilege to work for him."

"Yes, yes, a regular candidate for canonization . . ."

"Pardon, sir?"

"The thing is"—Colin hopped up and began yet another
slow arc around the periphery of the room—"somebody obviously didn't feel that way. Are you certain you don't remember
any other details of his argument with Sergeant Mulrooney?"

Corporal Blevins shook his head.

"Did you mention it to anyone? A friend in the barracks
perhaps?"

"No, sir."

"What about Lady Dahlia Stuart? What do you make of
your captain's visits to her?"

He looked momentarily taken aback but managed to hold
Colin's gaze. "It was business, sir. He saw her a couple of times
a month. There was always a log of it in his calendar."

"What sort of business would a captain of the Queen's Life
Guard have with a known seer?"

"I'm sure I don't know," he mumbled.

"You sat right outside the captain's door for forty . . . fifty hours a week for five months, Corporal. Tell me what you *do* know."

A pall came over the young man's face as he struggled with Colin's words. "I've told you—" he started to say, but then stopped, his brow knitting as though he suddenly recognized a falsehood.

"Corporal Blevins . . . ?"

"I'm sure it's nothing." He shook his head self-consciously. "About a month ago the captain gave me a letter that he had sealed with his insignia and asked that I personally deliver it were anything ever to happen to him."

"Deliver it to whom?"

"I don't remember. But I gave him my word that I would do it. I've forgotten all about it until just now."

"Where did you put it?"

"In his safe."

"Would it still be there?"

"Yes, of course."

"Would you fetch it then? I should very much like to see it."

The corporal shifted in his chair uncomfortably. "It's sealed," he repeated. "You can't open it. I gave him my word I would deliver it. I should have done so already."

"I understand, Corporal, and I think all the more of you for your loyalty. So let me give you *my* word: Allow me to see the addressee on the outside of that letter and if the person in question lives anywhere within the city's limits I will hand deliver the missive myself, *this very night,* in precisely the same sealed state you present it to me. And if it belongs to someone outside of London, then you may return it to the safe without my ever touching it. Would that be fair?"

Corporal Blevins gazed at Colin and I could tell he was trying to determine whether such an agreement might violate the promise he had made to Captain Bellingham.

"I can vouch for Mr. Pendragon's character," I spoke up.

"You must be aware that he is a man of impeccable integrity and reputation."

"Of course."

Colin smiled warmly. "I find it quite admirable that you seek to uphold your promise with such resolve."

"Thank you, sir," the corporal said gravely. "We'll have it as you say then. Shall I get it now?"

"That would be ideal."

Corporal Blevins nodded grimly and took his leave, looking as though he was off to perform a far more repugnant task than the retrieval of a letter.

"How can we possibly have time to deliver that tonight?" I asked, unable to imagine what Colin was thinking beyond a determination to see whom the letter was written to.

"Because if it's written to someone in the city it will likely be *worth* our efforts to deliver it, and should it be addressed to someone beyond we may have just stumbled upon another cog in this case."

"What do you suppose it will say?"

"I haven't the slightest notion, but it is our first indication that perhaps he was feeling threatened." Colin abruptly cocked his head to one side and held a hand up.

"What is it?"

"Someone's coming and it is definitely *not* Corporal Blevins."

"What?" I strained to listen and just barely caught the far-off sound of boots clacking on marble. As he suggested, these footfalls were heavier and more methodical than the light, scurrying sounds Corporal Blevins had made.

"It would seem," Colin muttered as he took the seat next to mine, "that we have ruffled some plumes. It is undoubtedly the major." He had no sooner said the word when Major Hampstead came through the door, a thin smile flickering across his face.

"Nice to see you both again," he said hollowly.

"I'm glad you've joined us." Colin smiled. "There are ever more questions to pepper you with."

"Really?" The major leaned back against the doorjamb, gazing in upon us. "And what might they be?"

"Are you familiar with Captain Bellingham's brother-in-law?"

"Sergeant Mulrooney? I know who he is."

"I'm told he was quite disparaging of Captain Bellingham."

Major Hampstead dismissed Colin with the wave of a hand. "They had little use for one another. It's hardly the stuff of murder."

"What was their point of disagreement?"

"Who can say, Mr. Pendragon?" He offered an indifferent shrug. "Families can be such complex creatures."

"I see." Colin's smile grew thinner. "Then let me ask you about something you *will* know. What precipitated the fight at McPhee's the night Sergeant Newcombe's father was mortally wounded?"

"McPhee's?" His brow caved in on itself. "What the bloody hell does that have to do with the murders of Captain Bellingham and his wife?"

"That is what I am trying to determine," Colin fired back.

"I really don't think you need to concern yourself with—"

"I'd prefer to judge that for myself."

A grin slowly eased across Major Hampstead's face. "You know what I think, Mr. Pendragon . . . ? I think you haven't the slimmest notion about who committed these murders. Which means that"—he pulled out his watch—"in about twenty hours you will be addressing the newsmen with the conclusion I shall have laid out for you."

"You're evading my question, Major."

"Your question?"

"What precipitated the brawl at McPhee's?"

He pursed his lips a moment and then said, "Too much liquor, I suppose."

"And what, precisely, was the liquor saying?"

Major Hampstead chuckled. "That's rich, Mr. Pendragon. I shall see you tomorrow. Shall we say four thirty so you'll have time to prepare? I am already putting the finishing touches on your speech."

"There is no point in writing a speech for a story that has yet to be finished. And make no mistake, Major, I *will* resolve this case in time."

The major's grin did not waver in the least. "You mean to tell me you're here harassing my young officers because you are so close to a resolution?" He let out a guffaw.

Colin's face went rigid, grimness etching his features. Then something happened that, at first, brought me relief—only to be followed immediately by the realization that it was not at all a good thing: Corporal Blevins returned with Captain Bellingham's sealed letter.

With Major Hampstead filling the doorway, Corporal Blevins was forced to hover just outside, a dusky cream-colored envelope clutched in his hand. He seemed to be trying to decide what to do when he caught Colin's eye, and in that same moment I saw Colin flinch as he too realized what was about to happen. "You've made your opinion very clear, Major," he blustered as he moved to usher him out. "But if you will excuse me, I should like to complete my work."

Major Hampstead turned with a smirk, giving a perfunctory nod to Corporal Blevins. "Certainly. You can spend the whole of the night here if you wish, but tomorrow at five we have an appointment with the press that you *will not miss*."

Colin flashed a stifled smile as Major Hampstead passed through the doorway. Corporal Blevins stepped smartly aside, snapping his hand up to salute his commanding officer, and to my horror it was the hand clutching the letter, which waved like an unfurled sail from his brow.

"What's that you've got?" The major frowned.

"A letter from Captain Bellingham, sir."

"A letter? What letter?"

The young corporal held it out as though the mere sight of it might answer his superior officer's enquiry. "He gave it to me a while back, sir. Asked me to deliver it should anything happen to him."

I saw the slightest stitch fleet across the major's brow as he asked, "Deliver it to whom?"

Corporal Blevins tilted the letter and read, "*Lady Dahlia Stuart.* I was to deliver it to her. . . ." His arm slowly lowered. "But I'd forgotten until just now. I'm terribly sorry, sir."

"You've nothing to be sorry about, Corporal," Major Hampstead demurred with a grace that sounded unnatural. "These are trying times for all of us. The point is that you've remembered now. I shall see that it gets noted in your record." And with that, the major snatched the letter from Corporal Blevins's hand and turned back to Colin. "Is this what you mean to turn your attentions to, Mr. Pendragon?"

"I have offered to deliver it tonight on behalf of the corporal."

"Oh, come now." He flapped it toward Colin like the broken wing of a bird. "Are you telling me you're not the least bit interested in what it says?"

"It's not addressed to me."

"Really, Mr. Pendragon. Do let me guess. I'll bet you're acquainted with the lady in question, is that it? You're going to have her read it to you?" His face went dark as he abruptly tore the back of the envelope open. "Well, let me save you the bother."

"*Sir!*" Corporal Blevins jumped but made no move toward his officer. "I gave my word."

"Don't be insolent, Corporal!" he roared back. "This is the property of Her Majesty's Life Guard. You're dismissed."

The young man sagged. "Yes, sir," he said, then backed up and disappeared without another word.

"You're incorrigible, Mr. Pendragon." Major Hampstead yanked the letter free and unfolded it. "Tricking that neophyte toady to get a look at something you have no business seeing."

"You made it my business when you hired me to solve this case."

But the major was no longer listening. He had turned his full attentions to the letter, his eyes skimming the lines even as his face remained indecipherable. I wondered how long Colin would stand here, allowing himself to be baited, but more than that, I feared the case was edging away with every second that passed.

"Well, Mr. Pendragon"—the major finally looked up—"it would seem you are right about one thing." The tic of a grin scratched at one corner of his mouth. "This letter is indeed valuable. It would seem to bear evidence as to what happened." And now a mirthless smile overtook his face. "And in the spirit of the cooperation I promised, I shall read it to you."

"I would rather see it for myself."

Major Hampstead's eyebrows arched. "Not a trusting man? Here—" He swung the letter to me. "Why don't *you* do us the honor then, Mr. Pruitt? Read it aloud. Read it twice if you would like, but then I shall keep it. It is the property of the Guard, after all."

I seized it from him with a scowl and gazed down at it. It was a brief letter, barely filling half the page. Given its brevity, it was clear Major Hampstead had studied it quite intently before deciding on the nature of its meaning. That he was sharing it ensured that it either reiterated some belief he had been peddling all along or amounted to much of nothing.

I sucked in a quick breath before describing the script of the letter to Colin: scratchy and haphazardly slanted, clearly that of a man's hand. It looked to have been written in haste with little attention paid to spacing or punctuation. And then I began to read:

"How heavy is my heart that I should find myself putting these words to paper. I loved you with everything I had and know you loved me back. I could see it in your eyes. I could feel it in your touch. And yet you betrayed me. You have thrown back what I have so freely given and deny that which we both know to be true. It shall not be. I will not be cast aside like the fool nor dismissed as one who does not matter. You will acknowledge me, you will embrace me once again, or the price will be complete and you will know that you alone were to blame. Of this I give my solemn vow. Once more will I offer all that is in my heart and trust that you will return the same. For if you do not, then you shall receive this letter and know that it is done."

I looked at Colin and was relieved when he did not ask that I read it again. I carefully slid it back into its envelope, the red waxen seal rent like a bleeding gash upon otherwise flawless flesh, and tried to comprehend its meaning. That Captain Bellingham had implicated himself in something untoward was irrefutable. His declaration for Lady Stuart was as disturbing as it was unexpected. But what I could not understand was what it said of her. Had she misconstrued his intentions . . . ? Or had she been lying to us all along?

"I should think this concludes your investigation, Mr. Pendragon," Major Hampstead announced as he grabbed the letter from me. "It seems clear he was obsessed with this woman. Terrible tragedy. Atrocious how the deviant mind works."

"And what of his own end?" Colin scoffed. "That he may have murdered his wife to exact some sort of revenge on Lady Stuart is possible, but then what happened to *him* in that attic?"

"Suicide, Mr. Pendragon. The ultimate sacrifice. Have you never read Shakespeare?"

"An extraordinary conceit considering he was bound to a chair. Difficult to put a bullet in your own head while tethered. Even more so given that the gun has yet to be found. Imagine the poor man stumbling about with half his face ruptured, trying to hide the weapon. Remarkable. And then there are the three hundred and seventy-one match burns to his body. Such dramatics are most surely worthy of the Bard."

Major Hampstead's face betrayed little emotion. "I am finding your sarcasm tiresome, Mr. Pendragon. Nevertheless, it does not change the fact of our deal. Twenty hours until you present the conclusion I give you to the press." His expression soured. "I must say I find it disturbing that you admit to a preference for making a public spectacle of this family's tragedy rather than allowing us to take care of it in private. The Queen's business is not for the rabble. I should think a man like you would understand."

"The Queen's business?" Colin snorted. "I'm sure Her Majesty would be appalled at your antics in her name."

Major Hampstead allowed a tight smile as he tugged out his watch and glanced at it again. "You must excuse me, as I'm afraid I am out of time, much as you almost are, Mr. Pendragon. I shall have this letter put safely away. You have heard its contents. I have fulfilled my end of our bargain." His smile took on an air of derision. "You will fulfill yours tomorrow." He glanced at me with a curt nod but offered no such pleasantry to Colin as he stalked from the room, Captain Bellingham's letter clutched firmly in his hand.

CHAPTER 28

Neither of us said a word until we were well away from Buckingham. Night had completed its descent over the city, which served as a reminder of how little time was left. The first tendrils of daylight would begin stretching across the city's horizon in little more than eight hours and here we were heading back to Edwina Easterbrooke's flat yet again. As I could have predicted, we'd had no word from the lads we had hired to keep an eye on her place. When I was their age I would never have stayed and I doubted they had, either.

As we wound closer to the Easterbrooke flat on the north side of Regent's Park, I struggled to hold my tongue. Colin's brow had not released so much as a notch of its furrowed intensity, yet I was finding it increasingly hard to keep from peppering him with questions. I was desperate to hear what he had made of Captain Bellingham's letter. It was obvious Lady Stuart was implicated in some fashion, as she had undoubtedly been aware of his obsession with her. Perhaps she had even resorted to hiring someone with the intent of frosting his passion.

We had seen the remains of such intent too many times in the past.

"That was a bloody rout for Hampstead to have come in when he did," I finally tossed out.

Colin gave something of a snort as he yanked the cab's blanket higher across our laps and began absently rolling a coin between his fingers. His gaze drifted aimlessly over the flickering gas lamps as we clattered past and I could tell I wasn't going to get any further. "There must be something I can do to help . . . ," I said somewhat meagerly.

"Isn't there always?" He turned to me at once, seizing the coin in midair, and I realized he had been waiting for me to make just such a statement. "I need you to find Major Hampstead's corporal—Bramwood, isn't it?" I nodded. "You have to convince him to give you that letter from Captain Bellingham. I'm sure he'll have put it in the major's safe."

"The letter?"

"Yes. We need to bring it to Lady Stuart. Tonight."

"Tonight?" I parroted, fighting to keep my jaw from unhinging. I understood why he wanted to see it and could even comprehend his desire to confront Lady Stuart with it, but I could not *fathom* how I was supposed to convince Corporal Bramwood to release it to me.

"Will you do it, my love?" Colin asked as he nudged the coin effortlessly through his fingers again.

"I can't imagine how . . . ," I mumbled, my mind reeling at the very idea.

"You'll think of something. You always do."

"So you say . . . ," I answered with far less faith than he had.

No response was forthcoming as our cab came to a halt just down the road from the Easterbrooke flat per Colin's instructions. To my astonishment, a slim black shadow came hurtling down the street toward us almost at once. As it passed beneath a street lamp I spotted a mop of curly black hair atop a pale, angular face, one of our lads.

"I *knew* it was you," the scruffy boy chirped. "Things is 'appenin'. You'll be right glad you 'ad us 'ere tonight."

"Excellent." Colin grinned. "And where is your cohort?"

" 'Oo?"

"Your friend. The sandy-haired bloke."

"That's me point. 'E's gone after the great carriage that pulled out 'bout twenty minutes ago. 'E 'opped on the back bumper and went ridin' off. I been waitin' 'ere for ya ever since."

"Outstanding work." Colin grinned, gently cuffing the youngster's bony shoulder. "You have most definitely earned your second crown." He tossed the one he'd been rolling over his hand to the lad and said, "I've a suspicion you may earn another before this night is over."

The boy's eyes about burst from their sockets. "Ya can't get better 'elp than me an' me mate." He puffed out his chest as he cast a sideways glance at me. " 'Cept maybe 'im, a course," he bothered to add.

"Speaking of which." Colin called up to the driver, "I need you to take Mr. Pruitt back to Buckingham."

"Ay."

Colin turned to me and by the light of the brilliant moon I caught a mixture of resolve and apprehension. "You *have* to get that letter."

"I'll do my best."

"No." He grabbed my arm before I could climb back into the cab. "You have *got* to get it."

I looked at him and felt a knot settle deep in my gut. It twisted about as I sensed the weight of the case descending upon my shoulders, leaving me almost without voice as I muttered, "Of course."

Only then did Colin release my arm and step back. "Come back here as soon as you get it. This lad will know where to find me." He shifted his eyes to the boy. "Will you do that for another crown?"

"Yes, sir!" he answered with unbridled vigor.

Colin watched as I eased back into the cab, the disquiet in my belly now thundering up through my chest. "Godspeed," he said with the faintest of smiles.

CHAPTER 29

I found myself returned to Buckingham Palace long before I was ready. I had been racking my brain to think what I might say to Corporal Bramwood, with little success. Between his obvious disinterest in me and the afternoon's confrontation with Colin, I was certain the corporal would be unlikely to allow me to plead my case. The one thing I *had* decided was to ask to speak with Corporal Blevins rather than Corporal Bramwood. At least that way I could be sure of gaining entry. I knew *he* would agree to see me again if only to lament the major's seizing of the letter.

The guardsman who'd gone to announce me took no more than a handful of minutes before he hurried back and ushered me to Corporal Blevins's tiny office.

"Oh, goodness," I feigned exasperation the moment my escort left, "I'm afraid I have made a foolish error."

"You have?" As always, Corporal Blevins gave me a pleasant smile.

"I have confused you with the major's adjunct . . . Corporal Bramwood, isn't it? How terribly embarrassing."

"Not at all." He grinned. "He's just down the hall. Follow me then," he said as he headed for the door.

"No, no." I waved him off with a chuckle, eager to be on my own when I confronted his colleague. "I know where he is. You mustn't bother yourself."

"It's no bother."

"I have been dim enough already," I insisted. "If you lead me down the hall like I'm starkers I shall be quite mortified." I backed toward the door, smiling with all the humility I could muster. "I shall see you tomorrow, Corporal. You have been most kind."

"It's my pleasure, sir," he said, following me to the door but thankfully going no farther. "I do hope you and Mr. Pendragon will get this behind us soon. It is such a terrible thing."

"You can be certain we will." I nodded fervently, as much to convince myself as him. I gestured toward the vicinity of Corporal Bramwood's office. "I remember now." I chuckled.

He waved but did not go back inside his office until I had reached Corporal Bramwood's door. I signaled to him and drew a quick breath, waiting for the instant when Corporal Bramwood would catch sight of me, but as I stepped inside all remained silent. I looked around to find the small anteroom empty. "Hello?!" I called out in an alarmingly feeble voice. No answer came. There were no lamps lit in Major Hampstead's interior office, although several were still on in Corporal Bramwood's area.

I wandered around to the far side of the corporal's tidy desk, trying to discern whether he might have left for the night. Everything was in impeccable order and I could see at once that the letter had not been carelessly left out. With a sinking disappointment, my eyes drifted over to the large metal safe in the far corner of the room. It was a foreboding piece, jet-black and nearly six feet in height, without the slightest hint of scrollwork or decoration that might suggest it was anything other than

226 / Gregory Harris

what it was—an impregnable fortress, immovable and unyielding in its secrets. Why had I never learned to pick a lock?

"Forget something?" A hard, sarcastic voice startled me. I turned around to find Corporal Bramwood standing in the doorway, a chagrined expression on his face.

I tried to smile, but fear caught the best of me, constraining my throat and seizing my face as though with rictus. What had lulled me into thinking that wandering over to this side of his desk was a good thing? "I've been waiting for you," I managed to say, trying to casually sidle out from where I was. "I owe you an apology, Corporal. Mr. Pendragon's behavior was inexcusable this evening. It's the reason I came back." I hoped I sounded plausible.

Corporal Bramwood stared at me, his face dour, and I feared he was on the verge of telling me to bugger off. He pursed his lips and stepped all the way into the office, taking great pains to cross behind his desk from the opposite side I had been trying to extract myself from. Still, he said nothing.

"I was looking for paper and something to write with," I offered belatedly. "I thought perhaps you had already left. I wanted to leave you a note. To apologize—" I bit my tongue and told myself to shut up.

The corporal brusquely sorted an already-meticulous pile of papers on the near corner of his desk before finally raising his gaze to me. "Well then"—his eyes were hooded and dark, his mouth a thin line—"you have accomplished your goal."

"No," I said at once, a pained smile coming easily to my face, "I don't see that I have. I can tell you're angry and my apology is ringing untrue. You have taken offense with Mr. Pendragon's methods and I can hardly blame you." I was desperate to get him talking, or commiserating, or yelling . . . anything to get him to engage. "I know he can be infuriating at times, but I assure you it is only out of passion for the case at hand. I don't mean to offer an excuse, only to state a fact. Even so, there *are* times when he does go too far."

"He's pompous"—the young corporal seized the bait—"and he's accusatory. I don't like being accused. I haven't *done* anything."

I nodded agreeably. "Well understood, Corporal Bramwood, but you must realize that everyone is a suspect until the case is solved. While that may seem harsh, it has proven to be effective over the years. It has allowed Mr. Pendragon to see past the rhetoric of those who are most deceptive."

"Nevertheless," the corporal grumbled, "it might do him good to learn to be more discerning."

"And there is no denying that."

"I don't know how you work with him."

"There are days . . . ," I chuckled, but the young man did not join me. With nothing else coming to mind, I gestured to one of the chairs and asked, "May I?"

He nodded and sat down himself.

"Is Major Hampstead still here?"

"No."

I feigned disappointment, though it was what I had been counting on. Even as the young man continued to absently rearrange papers on his desk I knew my time to try for that letter had come. There would be no other. "I am sure you must be aware of the deadline imposed on us to solve these murders," I started, desperate to find the right words.

"Of course."

"Yes." I nodded again while he continued to fuss about his desk. I let a minute pass before pressing on. I would like to say I was playing a calculated game, but in truth I was only stumbling haphazardly forward. "Most of your regiment wishes to dispense its own judgment outside the public's scrutiny, but there is a chance that an error could be made, or worse, that no conclusion might be reached at all. Murders like these can be a mire. Even Scotland Yard struggles to wring justice from such cases. Just look at the Ripper killings a few years back."

Another group of papers moved from one corner of his desk to another, followed by a thorough reshuffling. "And what's your point?"

"We *can* solve this case properly, Corporal, and have an end to it by five o'clock tomorrow. We will bring justice where it is due and make certain that the murderer of Captain Bellingham and his wife pays the price at the end of a rope."

"And why are you telling me this?"

"Because you could make the difference." I leaned forward and locked eyes with him. "Corporal Bramwood, you could make *all* the difference."

"I don't have any idea what you're getting at." His voice was clipped and strained, but he did not drop his gaze.

"It's the letter, Corporal. The one Captain Bellingham wrote to Lady Stuart. I should very much like to get my hands on that letter for just this one night. I can have it back in your hands with the dawn, delivered whenever and wherever you tell me."

"Out of the question!" he snapped, turning back to his desk.

I was glad he had looked away, as I'm certain despair was etched all across my face. While it was certainly the answer I had expected, it was distressing to hear just the same. I leaned back and watched as he shoved an appointment book into a top drawer. This was it. He was clearly ready to go home. "I'm sorry," I blustered out of nowhere. "I just assumed you had access to the safe."

"I have access." He turned on me as though I had questioned the very state of his virility. "Who do you think put the wretched thing in there?"

"Then I don't understand. I know you admired Captain Bellingham. You told us so yourself. This case can be finished tomorrow. The Bellinghams avenged—"

The corporal scowled. "You can do all that with one letter?"

"The letter is critical."

"I read it. I didn't see anything so important there."

"To be honest, Corporal Bramwood"—I offered a crooked

smile as though we were in league—"neither did I. But Mr. Pendragon insists differently, and in all the years I've watched him work, I have never seen his instincts fail him."

"You have great faith in your Mr. Pendragon," he said with a noticeable measure of animosity.

"It's not faith." I smiled. "I have been at his side for almost a dozen years now. Time and again I have been witness to the depth of his abilities, and while his methods and demeanor can be unorthodox"—I gave an uneasy shrug—"even abrasive . . . his skill is without equal. And tonight, Corporal, I am telling you that there is no one here who can have a greater impact on this case than you. That letter, something you and I have both dismissed, may well hold the key to the solution of this case and I am beseeching you to allow me to take it for just a few hours." I held his eyes and endured the discomfort of him studying me, gauging, I am sure, my sincerity.

"I'm not sure I like your Mr. Pendragon," he said after a moment. "I don't know why I should help him."

"It's not for him," I scoffed. "You misunderstand me, Corporal. This has nothing to do with him. It is about Captain Bellingham and his wife, Gwendolyn." And even though I felt as if I had just wielded a sledgehammer, I thought I detected a crack in his façade.

"I have no desire to cooperate with your Mr. Pendragon," he said again, only this time with an odd gruffness. "And I am not all that interested in helping you, either," he added, "but Captain Bellingham was good to me, kind to me, at a time when many others were not. I owe him a great deal and never had the chance to tell him." He glanced down and I watched as his body sagged the tiniest bit. "I won't be the reason some bastard gets away with what was done to him."

I nodded but kept silent, my heart ramping up with hope that maybe . . . just maybe . . .

"However"—he leaned across the desk and his eyes flashed

angrily—"I will not take a fall for you or Mr. Pendragon. When I walk through that door at five forty-five tomorrow morning the first thing I will do is open that safe to get Major Hampstead's ledger, same as I do every day, and if you haven't already handed that letter back to me I shall send up an alarm that the safe's been breached. And you can be sure I will tell them how you were poking around asking to see it tonight. The two of you won't see the arrival of six o'clock before a contingent of Life Guards will be raging at your door."

"I would expect no less," I immediately agreed.

Without another word, he stood up and went to the safe, tumbling the dial with the assurance of someone who did it routinely. At the sound of a loud *click!* he yanked one of the horizontal handles and swung the massive door wide. He reached in and extracted the familiar envelope with its hastily torn flap sticking up and then slammed it shut again, tossing the envelope into my lap. "There," he said with finality.

I stared at it like some sort of feral thing, fearful that I was about to find myself the brunt of a terrible hoax. That as soon as I picked it up a phalanx of the Queen's Regiment would come tumbling out from the blackened inner office to arrest me for what I had attempted to do. "I will be outside by five fifteen tomorrow morning waiting for you," I said, my heart thundering as I stood up. "I shall not let you down."

He shrugged. "Makes little difference to me."

I slid the letter into my coat. "You have done a noble thing."

"If you don't mind . . . ," he muttered as he crossed back behind his desk, otherwise ignoring me.

"Of course. Thank you, Corporal Bramwood." He did not respond as I moved to the door, and I took his silence as a warning to get out quickly lest he should change his mind. With my heart pounding in my ears, I hurried off, hoping I would be able to dissolve into the night long before he could do so.

CHAPTER 30

———❖———

" 'E said ya gotta put this on." The skinny little black-haired urchin we had hired to watch the Easterbrooke flat shook a long, dark cloak and cap at me. " 'E don't want ya ta be seen when I take ya to 'im."

"He said that, did he?" I scowled as I plucked the wrinkled, threadbare cloak out of his hand. "And where did you get this?"

"Me da," he answered. "And I gotta get it back to 'im afore 'e 'eads out ta get guttered. So I 'ope ya don't plan on keepin' it all bloomin' night."

A strong pungency of sour ale and infrequent hygiene assaulted my nose as I settled it on my shoulders. "Perish the thought," I muttered.

I accepted the cap from the boy, taking care not to inspect it too closely before slipping it on my head. I had only just arrived from Buckingham and he had me smelling like one of the bilge rats that lurked about the shores of the Thames. If Edwina Easterbrooke or one of her neighbors had peeked out their window they would surely have summoned a bobby posthaste, and I wouldn't have blamed them. "So where exactly *is* Mr. Pendragon?"

"I already told ya—'e went off with me mate. Tol' me ta stay 'ere and bring ya to 'im when ya showed up." He was staring at me with a critical eye and I had the distinct impression I was failing his assessment. "Wants ya ta be dark as the night. Don't want no one ta see ya comin'.'"

"So you have said."

My young accomplice shook his head. "It ain't right. Yer bloomin' face is shinin' like the bleedin' moon."

"Well, I suppose that's because I haven't had the time to collect the detritus covering your face," I shot back.

"You got a funny way a talkin'." He snickered.

"Why don't you just take me to Mr. Pendragon and let me worry about the glow of my face," I said, struggling to maintain some civility.

"Not till we get it right. 'Ere—" He reached over and splashed a fistful of mud onto my cheeks. I jerked back, but it didn't stop him from quickly transferring a portion to my nose, forehead, and chin. "Quit yer squirmin'." He scowled before stepping back with a huge grin. "There now. You're good as the night. Should be worth a tuppence at least."

"Get me to Mr. Pendragon or you will get nothing!" I groused.

"We 'ave ta take the Tube part a the way unless ya wanna snag a ride on the back of a carriage?"

"How about we get a ride *in* one. Assuming we can get someone to pick us up now that you have slathered me in muck."

"Ya look good! 'E'll be right pleased ta see ya like that."

"Just get us a ruddy cab already," I grumbled.

The boy was successful almost at once, hailing a cab as it came bounding out of the park. I tugged the cap down over my face before stepping out of the shadows, keeping my chin low as I climbed into the seat.

"Take us ta Wappin'," the boy ordered. "And don't bugger about, either."

"Piss off," the driver called back.

"So we're headed to Wapping?" I asked as we got under way.

" 'At's what I said." He looked at me with a sly smile, brash and jaded. I had been so less sure of myself at this boy's age but no less determined.

It was a relief when the cab finally came to a halt a few minutes later just around the corner from Wapping High Street. The boy was very particular about where we should be dropped off: along the brick ramparts walling off the Thames, just behind a row of warehouses lined up like silent black monoliths.

I handed cash to the driver, who didn't even bother to take a second look at the mud caked on my face, and then waited with my young escort until the carriage had disappeared from sight. Only then did he whisper, "Let's go."

He pulled his jacket around himself and hunched his shoulders against the wind that had kicked up near the water, starting down the High Street in the opposite direction from where the cab had just disappeared. We walked along the Thames for about a block and a half before abruptly cutting back behind a massive warehouse that hulked in the reflected moonlight. In spite of the extra light, I couldn't make out a sign or scrawled name anywhere along the length of the building. It had few distinguishing features at all as it stretched off far beyond my ability to discern it. Lanky weeds licked its sides and I could see some measure of disrepair: bits of crumbling mortar, curls of dark rotting paint that had drifted down from the eaves, and occasional shards of broken glass twinkling in the glow of the moon. It appeared that the warehouse had long ago outlived its usefulness.

Just as I began to gird myself for the possibility that this ruddy little scoundrel might be about to toss me, a dark form came flying down from somewhere overhead, landing nimbly in the shadows just to my left.

"That you, mate?" my companion hissed.

" 'Oo else?" The sandy-haired boy stepped into a swath of light. While probably a year older and almost a handful of inches taller, he was every bit as slight. " 'Bout bloody time ya got back," he said.

"It were 'is fault—"

"We're here now!" I snapped. "Now where's Mr. Pendragon?"

"Up there." The older boy, clearly the leader of this duo, gestured toward the roof. "I'll take ya up, but it'll cost ya another crown."

"I do not need to be taken up," I informed him, aware that neither of these boys could conceive that I had once been as they were. "Just show me where he is and the both of you can be off."

The taller boy tilted his head and smiled at me before raising a hand and pointing toward the roof. " 'Bout there."

I stared up the thirty or so feet and realized I had seen no steps, ladders, or even trash bins upon which I could leverage myself. There was only the Cheshire grin of the rascal confirming that I was indeed being tossed.

" 'Cause I like ya, I'll take ya up fer 'alf a crown," he added, well pleased with himself.

"Fine!" I gritted my teeth, angry at having been bested by these two.

"And ya owe me a crown fer gettin' ya 'ere," the smaller boy piped in.

I paid them both, grudgingly and without the dexterity Colin would have used, and in less time than it took to extract the coins from my pocket the older boy moved into the darkness across from where we were standing and seized a thin, flimsy ladder that had been hidden in the scrubby undergrowth.

It took the full depth and breadth of my character to keep from throttling him, and I suppose a modicum of begrudging respect.

"Up ya go, now." The cunning lad smirked at me.

I grabbed hold of the rickety frame and carefully worked my way to the top. The older boy held the bottom of it, but the fact of its fragility worked considerably against him, allowing it to sway and wobble with every step I took. It was a relief when my fingers finally grasped the lip of the flat roof and I was able to boost myself the rest of the way up.

The first thing I spotted was Colin squatting a short distance away peering through a roof access door. I leaned over and waved at the two boys to let them know I had made it safely, but neither seemed much interested. I figured I would have to pay them for a better response.

I glanced back at Colin and was startled to find him staring in my direction. I had thought my arrival appropriately furtive but had apparently overestimated myself. He gestured down with his open palm and I knew he meant for me to stay low. Keeping my legs bent and my hands on the roof, I moved rather like an ape who has yet to master walking upright.

"What's all over your face?" Colin asked the moment I reached him.

"Mud," I grumbled. "Courtesy of your urchins."

He chuckled. "They're good lads. And how'd you do with the corporal?"

"I got it."

"Excellent!" He cuffed me before turning and glancing back through the doorway he'd been holding open with the toe of a boot.

"What are we doing here?"

"We're allowing the Nesbitt-Normand case to solve itself." He grinned. "A carriage driven by Edwina Easterbrooke's houseman and bearing both Miss Easterbrooke and a package the diameter of an oversized hatbox left the Easterbrooke flat little more than an hour ago. It made its way inside this warehouse, where it has been waiting patiently ever since."

"Waiting for what?"

"Not what." He looked back at me with a smirk. "Who."

"It's just as you said then—they mean to get rid of their hostage."

"Precisely. Now listen closely, because we're only going to get one chance at this. There is a catwalk running along the perimeter of the ceiling just a few steps below us. I'm going to wedge this old whore of a door open just enough for us to get inside. We need to witness everything that happens here tonight."

I nodded as he set to work easing the door open one millimeter at a time. It was painstaking work, with the door giving grudgingly, but at least it wasn't screeching under his duress. I looked at the hinges, amazed at their continued silence, and was surprised to find them glistening as though after a recent rain. "Did you put oil on those?" I whispered, wondering where he would have found any.

"No. Piss."

"*What?!*"

"The acid makes a passable lubricant for rust." He shrugged. "And I had to go anyway." He worked the door to just about the halfway point before quietly sidling inside. "Not a word," he mouthed under his breath.

I shook my head as I stepped in behind him, making sure not to brush against the door or its frame. We left it like that, gaping like a toothless rummy, and I knew it would stay that way until someone else came along and recoaxed those hinges back to life—one way or another.

Colin pulled me down beside him and I caught my first glimpse at the catwalk itself. It was wrought iron and not even four feet high, which meant we would have to move about on our hands and knees. A notion my joints were already loathing.

I gazed down and saw a single carriage on the warehouse floor amid a sea of stacked crates and boxes. Rows of skylights glowed with the moon's frosty brilliance, bathing the great space below in diffused light. A small lantern flickered near the carriage, seemingly serving no other purpose than to further banish the darkness. I couldn't see anyone nor could I detect any movement within the carriage itself, as its curtains were drawn, without even the faintest sliver of light peeking from within.

Colin beckoned me with a wave and we began to make our way through the silent darkness high above the warehouse floor. My knees objected almost at once, but I determined to pay them no heed as I worked to keep Colin from disappearing from sight.

A sudden clatter on our left startled me, but Colin took advantage of it to move quicker. I had to redouble my efforts to keep up with him and was relieved when he finally slowed and came to a halt. He pointed a short distance ahead to a metal ladder attached to the wall that descended to the floor. Given the steadily increasing clamor coming out of the darkness, it seemed that now was as good a time as any to make our move. It took another minute before I recognized that the thunderous racket was the sound of one of the warehouse doors grinding open. I only hoped it was to allow someone entry rather than for Miss Easterbrooke to leave. The thought of accomplishing nothing after all this effort felt intolerable.

Colin grabbed hold of the ladder and swung himself onto it, quickly dropping from sight. I followed suit, clinging to those cold metal rungs as I made my way down, all the while hoping the ladder was well attached to the wall passing inches from my face.

My feet found the floor faster than I had anticipated and I arrived at Colin's side just in time to hear another carriage clatter past on the other side of the crates we were hiding behind. A low, deep voice urged the horse to slow and then stop, and before the animal even settled Colin started creeping forward on the balls of his feet. I stayed right behind him, though he had yet to signal me forward.

Hurried footsteps rushed toward us from the direction of the grinding door as we plastered ourselves against the tower of crates. I cautiously leaned into a crevice of light cast between the gap along two rows of boxes and caught sight of Edwina Easterbrooke's man, Alvin, rushing past. I was certain he had gone by too quickly to have spied us, yet my heartbeat ratcheted just the same.

Colin moved off in the same direction and I trailed him, trying to keep my footsteps in a steady rhythm with his. Even so, I had to slow down, as it seemed the *tap, tap, tap* of my shoes echoing against the wood floor would surely give us away. I was considering removing my shoes entirely when I glanced up and realized I had lost Colin. Stacks of crates stretching more than fifteen feet above me formed so complete a maze that I could no longer even be sure if I was heading in the right direction. The cascading moonlight did little to dispel my confusion as it struck the tops of the towering containers, diffusing itself at oblique angles but never quite reaching where I was stumbling about.

My heart thundered in my ears as I stopped for a moment and struggled to get my bearings. I couldn't spot the warehouse walls through the jumble of boxes and began to fear that I was moving in an ever-increasing circle. I cursed myself for being so careless as I pulled the foul-smelling cloak tighter around myself and began slowly creeping along, all the while listening for anything that would help me decipher my whereabouts. Drawing my breath with methodical precision, I strained to catch a murmuring voice, the snort of a horse, or even a carriage wheel clicking idly against the floor. Something . . . anything . . .

I snuck across an intersection of boxes and was on the verge of hazarding another breath when a hand clamped over my mouth at the same instant an arm seized my chest, yanking me backwards and nearly arresting my heart. "Ssshhh," Colin hissed, his lips raking my ear. He released me and pointed to the left through a tiny space between two enormous crates. I could just make out a bit of Edwina Easterbrooke standing in a small circle of light by her carriage. She was not more than twenty feet from where we were, wearing a most grim expression.

"This has become a torment," she suddenly spoke up. "I have had enough."

Colin edged forward between the two spires of crates, sliding his boots across the floor with exquisite slowness to keep from making so much as a whisper of sound. I followed him, moving in tandem to ensure I was equally stealthy. As I peered over his shoulder I saw that Alvin was standing next to Miss Easterbrooke with an oversized package cradled in his arms. It was indeed the size of a large hatbox, only there was a furious commotion coming from inside: low whining and the occasional pop against its side, none of which was lost on Miss Easterbrooke. With militaristic precision, she spun on Alvin and jerked an arm toward his face as though about to backhand him.

"Mum?" he said.

"Let her out."

"No!" came a familiar voice from somewhere to our left, but Alvin paid it no heed. He set the box on the floor and wrenched the lid open, and immediately a small cream and black muzzle popped up to sniff the stale air. The compact face looked to be wearing a smile and appeared quite unperturbed at having suffered such ignominy. In an instant the pup reared back and leapt free of the case, revealing a sweet little feminine form, trim and stylish, with a perfect corkscrew tail at her nether end. Lady Priscilla Elizabeth Windsor Hanover Nesbitt-Normand was in our presence.

I started to smile until the little dog abruptly turned and

240 / Gregory Harris

came charging toward us, her tongue lolling to one side as her tiny tail beat a happy rhythm only she could hear. It was as if the pug knew we had come to rescue her.

Before Alvin could start after Lady Priscilla, Colin stepped from our hiding place and scooped the little pug into his arms, slipping the small bit of dried pig hide that he'd been holding into her mouth. "Well, well," he purred. "Aren't you just the most beautiful little girl."

Edwina Easterbrooke swooned, sagging backwards against her carriage as Alvin scuttled over to attend her. I moved out of the shadows behind Colin just as I heard a voice say, "You schtupid woman. You let dem follow you here. Dummkopf." A look of unbridled disgust was evident on Elsa's face.

"This was *her* idea!" Edwina Easterbrooke howled. "*It was her!*"

"Shut up," Elsa warned.

"I won't . . . ," Edwina gasped, a hand fluttering to her throat as though to protect herself from attack. "She came to us. She knew I wanted to breed my little boy. He *is* a former champion—" Her eyes looked desperate. "You know that, Mr. Pendragon. You've met him." Colin just stared at her. "She said Lady Nesbitt-Normand would never agree to it. That she disparaged my Buster Brown." Miss Easterbrooke sagged even farther against Alvin, who held her emaciated frame without the slightest show of effort. "I am simply destroyed."

"You're a fool!" Elsa snapped.

"That horrible woman said she would deliver Lady Priscilla to us in exchange for the pick of the litter. I swear it." Miss Easterbrooke, on the one hand, looked so frail that I feared if Alvin released her she might simply tumble apart. Elsa, on the other hand, appeared to be suffering from no such attack of feebleness. With the low-slung stance of a bulldog and the ferocity of a sow bear defending her cub, she made me begin to fear for us all.

"Der is nussing wrong vit da little lady. I have seen to dat. No harm done."

"And yet," Colin finally spoke, "I suspect Lady Nesbitt-Normand would view it differently."

"Oh, please, Mr. Pendragon"—and now Edwina Easterbrooke began to shake, her face turning a blotchy pink even as her eyes grew heavy with tears—"you mustn't turn me in. You simply mustn't. I know I've done a terrible thing, but I was a pawn! This would ruin me, Mr. Pendragon. I am a woman of years. I beseech you."

"Miss Easterbrooke has spoken nothing but the truth, sir," Alvin muttered, raising his broad face and staring directly at Colin.

"*How dare you!*" Elsa roared.

"That's quite enough." Colin turned and handed Lady Priscilla to me.

Elsa sized him up a moment, as though measuring her options, before finally letting out a labored sigh. I exhaled in tandem and nearly jumped when I felt something soft and wet brush the back of my hand. Lady Priscilla was licking the salt and fear from my skin and I wondered if the little pug understood the trouble she had caused.

"The way I see it," Colin said easily, "there are two choices. Either we all take a trip to Scotland Yard and let a magistrate sort this out, or you can agree to abide by my determination right here and now. I shall leave the lot of you to decide."

"Whatever you say, Mr. Pendragon," Edwina Easterbrooke chirped at once. "I'll do whatever you say."

Elsa did not respond, holding her ground, though it was clear she was doing so with much less force.

"Very well then." Colin looked to Miss Easterbrooke. "You and yours shall be tasked with looking out for the health and well-being of Lady Priscilla for the rest of her life." He playfully cuffed the dog's ears. "If she should ever disappear again,

242 / *Gregory Harris*

or become inexplicably ill, or develop an unexplained limp, or hiccup, or even fart before she reaches a ripe old age, it shall be upon your head. Am I clear?"

"Yes, of course," she said, fresh tears softening the great angles of her face. "But however shall I do such a thing? I hardly know Lady Nesbitt-Normand."

"Then I would suggest you become her closest confidante," Colin sniffed.

She blanched at his tone, shrinking back against Alvin again. "Yes." Her eyes dropped to the warehouse floor. "Of course."

"As for you"—Colin shifted his gaze to Elsa—"it will be simple. You will go back to the Nesbitt-Normand estate tonight, pack your things, write a lovely, maudlin note explaining how responsible you feel for Lady Priscilla's disappearance, and be gone from the whole of England before anyone in the household rises. And should I ever spot your sour face in our charmed city again I shall have you permanently shipped back to Prussia before the Kaiser can get word to his beloved grandmother. Is *that* clear?"

"*Gehen bumsen sich, Du bombastisches Arschloch!*" she blasted back.

"*Reizende Methode, damit eine Dame spricht,*" he shot back.

"Please . . ." Edwina Easterbrooke pulled herself free of Alvin's supporting grip. "Please do as he says. I shall pay you to go. I shall give you a hundred pounds."

Elsa's face slowly shed its look of revulsion as she considered the offer. "You vill pay me von hundred *und* fifty or I vill not go."

"Y-y-yes," Miss Easterbrooke stuttered. "Fine. Come with us now."

"Von hundred fifty pounds," Elsa reiterated.

"Yes, yes," Miss Easterbrooke repeated as Alvin helped her back into her carriage.

Elsa turned on Colin. *"Ich hoffe du fäule in der Hölle,"* she seethed.

"If I do"—he offered a tepid smile—"you're sure to be right there with me."

The Easterbrooke carriage lurched forward, heading for the door of the warehouse before Elsa had the chance to hoist herself back up onto her own. She reared back and whipped her tethered horse, and I wondered why I hadn't noticed that cruel streak in her before. If she had any propensity toward animals I had yet to see evidence of it.

"We shall return the prodigal daughter to Lady Nesbitt-Normand first thing tomorrow morning," Colin called after Elsa, "and will look forward to noting your absence."

Elsa hollered something back, but there was far too much clattering of hooves and wheels to hear what it was.

"Extraordinary," I muttered as we started out.

"That woman is as delicate as an ox," he said. "She'd do better to train bulls than small dogs." He turned to me and his nose curled. "Let's do get that vile cloak back to the lads and have them take dear Lady Priscilla to Mrs. Behmoth. She can coddle the pup 'til morning. It's time for Lady Stuart to make good on her promise of value for us."

"At this hour?" I yanked out a handkerchief and wiped at my face, cleaning the mud off as best as I could.

"This hour"—he frowned at me—"is perfect. The lady is bound to be at home."

I stuffed the cloth into a pocket of the cloak and glanced at my watch. We had little more than sixteen hours left. He *had* to be right about Lady Stuart.

CHAPTER 31

—⟫◦⟪—

Getting a carriage out of Wapping proved harder than we'd expected, which forced us to walk some distance down Fleet Street before Colin finally managed to hail a decrepit coach to take us back to Lancaster Gate. We said little as we clattered past Saint Paul's before taking a hard right and passing through Covent Garden and Oxford Circus. While Colin absently teased a half crown around his hand, I worried that no one would even answer the door at Lady Stuart's house. Given that the moon had already crossed the center point of the sky, I knew midnight was near.

By the time we reached Lancaster Gate it was to find the street entirely empty. Rows of street lamps flickered from within their glass cocoons, their gentle hiss the only sound beyond the hollow echo of our horse and carriage. Even the wind seemed to be holding its tongue, without so much as a leaf rustling.

Our driver stopped in front of Lady Stuart's, her dahlias awash in moonlight, revealing a display in variant shades of gray. There was a distinct order to the house and grounds that seemed to reflect a certain willfulness. I hadn't noticed it before, but as we arrived at this inconceivable hour to confront her with the captain's letter I was struck by the force of it. Had she been playing us for fools all along?

Colin handed the fare to the driver and I watched as the coach pulled away, the clacking of the horse's hooves gradually receding down the street. The moment was abruptly ruptured by the sound of Colin pounding on the door, sending me hurrying up the walk after him. On such a quiet night I was convinced he would wake the whole of the neighborhood.

"Colin . . . ," I hissed before realizing the dearth of alternatives open to us.

He wisely ignored my brief reproof, remaining focused on the door, and before another moment could pass he raised a fist again and applied the whole of his considerable determination against it. "If we don't get an answer in one minute," he growled, "then we shall bang on every window until someone in this blasted house responds!"

I nodded, knowing he meant it. Once again the thought occurred to me that perhaps no one was *in* the house, stirring a cold discomfort in my belly. Had this clever woman known we would come back? My nerves began to fray as the sweep hand on my watch soldiered on. Even when Colin let loose with both fists in a barrage of frustration and outrage I feared we had been defeated. We had simply run out of time.

"Cut that bloody bangin' before I blast your buggered head off!" an outraged male voice bellowed. "Who in the bleedin' hell is out there?"

"Colin Pendragon and Ethan Pruitt, and I will thank you to open this door at once."

"The hell I will. Sod off, ya shite."

"Not until I speak with your daughter!" Colin hollered back. "Now open this ruddy door or I *will* do it for you."

"How dare you!" he yelled, and then, quite unexpectedly, fell silent.

Not another sound emanated from within for several minutes, although a reflective glow from several lamps could now
be seen through the prism of glass set high in the door. I fully
expected Colin to launch himself into another attack, but he held
himself still, and after longer than even my patience could bear
the door finally swung open to reveal Lady Stuart wrapped in a
burgundy night coat, her thick black hair tied back with a ribbon
of the same color. In spite of our appalling intrusion and the ferocity with which her father had tried to repel us, she managed
to offer a generous smile that looked as inviting as it did genuine.

"Come in," she said, stepping back, a candelabra held aloft.
"I must apologize for the ill-mannered greeting, but we are not
used to visitors at this hour."

"It ain't right!" her father snapped from somewhere in the
darkness behind her.

"That will do," she said without pretense as she led us back
to the study. "Why don't you go and fetch us some tea."

"You mustn't make a fuss," Colin insisted. "It is enough that
we are here at such an hour."

"Nonsense." She waved her father off, garnering a sneer before he turned and strode from the room, swinging his lamp angrily. "It will give him something to do besides glare at us."

We settled ourselves for a moment while Lady Stuart lit several more lamps, but before she could turn the room into any
sort of blazing normalcy Colin could contain himself no longer
and started in. "You mustn't go to any more trouble. We won't
stay but the time it takes to show you what we have brought.
And then . . ." He let his voice trail off, but she did not seem to
hear the threat lingering there.

"It is simple enough to make a guest feel welcome," she said
easily. "It doesn't matter the hour of the day." She laid a couple
logs atop the embers in the fireplace and poked them back to
life, instantly releasing a bit of warmth into the chilled space. I

was grateful for the heat and found myself relaxing in spite of my inherent tension at being here. "I am certain . . . ," she said as she slid the fireplace screen back into place and sat down, ". . . that the two of you wouldn't be here if it was not urgent."

"I appreciate your faith," Colin answered simply. "And you are correct." He nodded toward me and I pulled Captain Bellingham's letter from my jacket pocket. "We were shown a letter this evening that was written to you by Captain Bellingham. He composed it three or four months ago and gave it to his attaché with explicit instructions that the lad deliver it to you should anything happen to him. While it was meant for your eyes only, I am sorry to tell you that a major in Her Majesty's Life Guard took it upon himself to open it this evening once its existence became known. The letter"—he nodded to me again and I handed it to her—"would seem to discount some of your previous statements."

Her brow pinched as she glanced down at the missive and read it, her eyes flicking across its few lines rapidly. Once finished, she went back to the top and read it again, poring more carefully over it the second time. Only then did she finally look over at Colin and say, "This letter may have been intended for me, but it was not written by Trevor."

"No?" Colin's face revealed nothing.

"It is not his handwriting." She stood up and went over to a desk on the far side of the room, pulling it open to reveal several small drawers and a host of cubbies too numerous to count. She reached in and seized a thick packet of folded papers tied together with a ribbon. With the letter in one hand and the folded notes in her other, she came back and handed it all to Colin.

"See for yourself," she said. "These are all from Trevor. There"—she pointed to the bottom of the one Colin had flipped open—"you can see his signature."

He turned the note toward me and I could indeed see

Trevor's name scribbled across the bottom in a smooth, fluid hand. His writing appeared languid and unhurried, strikingly different from that in the letter he had given to Corporal Blevins. But while the card was nothing more than an enquiry for an invite, the letter had clearly been written in a state of immense agitation. I couldn't help but think the hand of any person would change under such circumstances.

I suspected Colin was mulling the same possibility as I watched him flip through the handful of notes Lady Stuart had given him. He kept glancing back and forth as he sorted through them, and when he reached the bottom of the stack he slid the whole of the writings to me before standing up and wandering over to the fireplace.

I studied the handwriting on the letter as I peered from one note to the next, all innocuous blather about visiting, or thanks, or the impending inclement weather. None of it compared to the desperate wrath contained in the note Corporal Blevins had been entrusted with. Yet even so, I could find no similarities. There were stark differences in the capital letters and subtler divergences in much of the rest. By the time I looked up again I understood what Colin had seen. It was exactly as Lady Stuart had said—the vitriolic letter had not been written by Captain Bellingham at all.

"Then who wrote this?" I asked.

Colin turned from the fireplace and leveled his gaze on Lady Stuart. "Do you know?"

"I give you my word that I haven't the faintest notion."

His eyes remained fixed on her. "Then why did he want this brought to you?"

"Surely I've made that clear by now. Trevor and I were like family. He knew he could count on me if something were to happen to him. To see that his honor would be upheld or his family taken care of—" Her voice faltered as she looked away, her eyes momentarily reflecting the firelight. "If I knew *any-thing . . .*"

Colin stood there, staring at her, the two of them looking as though engaged in a contest of wills before he quietly asked, "This letter is written *to* Captain Bellingham, isn't it?"

She glanced away and released a burdened sigh before finally answering, "Yes."

"Was it someone in his regiment?"

"I don't know. He would never tell me."

"Did his wife know?"

Her gaze softened as she looked back at the fireplace and I thought she might be on the verge of tears, but when she spoke her voice remained strong and clear. "In the end, she must have suspected."

Lady Stuart's father abruptly shuffled in with a rattling tray of cups, saucers, spoons, creamer, sugar, and a pot with an ill-fitting lid. He seemed oblivious to the tension in the room as he set the things with a heavy thud onto the table and began pouring. "Do ya take cream and sugar?" he mumbled without looking up.

"We have imposed enough already," Colin said, catching Lady Stuart's eye. "I apologize for having interrupted the middle of your night this way. You have been most gracious."

"I only wish I knew more," she said.

Her father looked up with irritation. "You're not staying for tea?"

"We cannot." And with that, Colin nodded to Lady Stuart and headed for the door. "Sorry about your efforts," he added without conviction. "We shall see ourselves out." Lady Stuart looked stricken as I walked past her, the toll of what she had told us evident on her ashen face.

As soon as we passed beneath the nearest street lamp I took a moment to yank out my watch and was disheartened to discover it nearly one o'clock. I had little more than four hours before I was to meet Corporal Bramwood outside of Buckingham to return the captain's letter to him. "Shouldn't we get a cab?" I sighed heavily.

"Yes," Colin muttered under his breath. "We're certainly not walking all the way to the Irish barracks."

"Where?"

"We must pay another visit to Sergeant Mulrooney. The extent of his distaste for his brother-in-law seems quite clear now. He owes us some answers."

With exhaustion weighing heavily upon my brain, I longed to protest, but the incessant ticking of the watch stowed deep within my pocket assured me that there would be no rest tonight.

CHAPTER 32

Sergeant Mulrooney was furious. We had presented ourselves at the Chelsea Barracks, not far from Parliament on Chelsea Bridge Road, and made our presence known to the officer in charge. While he had been quite disturbed by our reprehensibly late intrusion, reminding us repeatedly that it was after one in the morning, he had agreed to allow us access to Sergeant Mulrooney after Colin mentioned the Bellingham murders, Scotland Yard, and our sovereign herself, referring to her vaguely as the increasingly alarmed Mrs. Saxe-Coburg and Gotha. That had finally forced the man to jump to the obvious conclusion without Colin having to completely perjure himself. Nevertheless, Sergeant Mulrooney was another matter entirely.

"This is bloody well insufferable!" he bellowed at us, his face ferocious with rage. "Who the hell do you think you are, wheedling your way in here and disturbing me with this rot in the middle of the night?! This is unconscionable. This is—"

"Oh, come now, Sergeant," Colin interrupted, his tone soft and smooth. "Doesn't our arrival at this ungodly hour stir the least curiosity in you?"

The man's frown deepened. "And why would it? Do you think I don't know why you're here?"

"Then do you care so little about your sister?"

"To hell with you!" he growled. "You rouse me in the middle of the night to judge my character?! I'll not stand for this." And with that, he strode to the door with the clear intent to be done with us.

"Is it shame for your sister's husband that drives such vehemence from you?" Colin asked, his voice tightening appreciably. "Is that what you would have me understand, sir?"

Sergeant Mulrooney came to a halt just inside the small room, his posture ramrod straight as he glared out into the hallway, wondering, I presumed, whether he shouldn't just keep walking. "What would you know of any of that?" he said after a moment, his tone as rigid as his manner.

"More than you can imagine," Colin shot back, before adding, "I am an investigator, Sergeant. I am paid quite handsomely to find things out. Now may we have this discussion so our intrusion is not without reason?"

"I have nothing to add to what you already seem to have learned!" he snapped, his back still toward us.

"And I should like to judge that for myself. Will you not sit down for even a minute? We have already done the damage to your night."

"I shall not," he seethed.

Colin glared at me and I tried to encourage him to remain calm with the look in my eyes. As the man had yet to step from the room, I considered that progress. "Very well then," Colin said brusquely as he stood up. "When did you discover that your brother-in-law had proclivities outside of his marriage?"

The sergeant didn't answer for a moment and I thought perhaps he had no intention of doing so, but just as it seemed his silence was the only answer we would get, he slowly turned and leveled a most hateful gaze on Colin. "Is that what it's to be then, Mr. Pendragon? Euphemisms?" He took a step back into the room, his body hulking in the doorway. "Trevor was an abomination and I have nothing but pity for my sister for shielding him."

"Pity, is it?"

"Her misguided affections made her a casualty in this war."

"And was it your war, Sergeant?"

"It is the war of every God-fearing man, woman, and child. Does that include you, Mr. Pendragon?" His eyes flipped between Colin and me, but I refused to allow even the slightest reaction.

"Then I don't believe we share the same God, Sergeant," Colin fired back. "For mine would never condone such ignorance."

Sergeant Mulrooney scoffed at him before, quite suddenly, taking a step back and spitting on the floor. Before either of us could react, he stalked out.

CHAPTER 33

For reasons I have never understood, the hour before dawn is always the coldest. Even though I was well insulated in a thick woolen coat that ended well below my knees with a cashmere scarf around my neck and a cap on my head, I could still feel the bracing chill of the predawn air fingering at my bones. I stomped my feet and rocked from side to side as though such antics might truly warm me, but they were of little use. At least the cold was keeping me awake after my woefully brief two-hour nap.

I was stationed at the fountain outside Buckingham's main gate scanning for signs of Corporal Bramwood. The only company I had was a bent street cleaner laboring over horse droppings with a shovel and cart. I had begun to suspect that perhaps Corporal Bramwood had chosen this reprehensible time simply because he knew I wouldn't dare refuse him, that he would show up in an hour or more with a jolly smirk upon his face. Even so, I had given my word and would wait until noon if I had to, god forbid.

The street cleaner gradually moved farther down the promenade and I braced myself for a protracted wait just as a carriage entered the parade grounds from out of Green Park. I prayed it was Corporal Bramwood. I had thought the young man would arrive on foot, but the carriage was old and well worn, and I decided an enterprising young corporal could commandeer such a benefit for himself. He would likely send it right back out to collect his major.

I began walking toward the approaching carriage, and just as I guessed it would, it veered in my direction as I reached the cobbled path by the palace gates. I wondered if the young man was surprised that I had kept my word and whether he might, in some small fashion, be disappointed. I pulled Captain Bellingham's letter from my pocket as the driver brought the carriage to a stop directly beside me. Nothing less would be expected from one of the Queen's horsemen.

The door swung wide, and before my eyes could adjust to the darkness within I sensed that something was terribly wrong. Corporal Bramwood's face was ashen and drawn, his eyes as red as a wound, and for a moment I thought perhaps he had suffered the same sort of sleepless night I had, and that was when Major Hampstead leaned forward with a grand smile upon his face. "What a pleasure to see you so early this morning, Mr. Pruitt." He leered. "Get the letter, Corporal."

Corporal Bramwood's desperate gaze did not leave my face as he reached out and pulled the letter from my fingers. He looked stricken and neither of us said a word as he leaned back in his seat, looking as though he wished it would swallow him outright.

"And where is Mr. Pendragon?" the major asked. "Sends you to do the shite errands, eh?"

"He's working," I answered, but it sounded hollow even to me.

"Well, do me a favor and give him a message, will you?" I nodded mutely. "Given that he has seen fit to coerce one of the more impressionable members of my staff, not to mention denigrating himself by pilfering state property, I have decided it is time to end this charade—"

"We have stolen nothing," I interrupted, holding out my empty hands as though that were proof even as the hair on the back of my neck bristled with dread.

Major Hampstead waved me off with a grunt. "Please don't demean yourself, Mr. Pruitt. Your willingness to manipulate this young man into disobeying a direct order is venal, and yet I shall overlook it." He glowered at Corporal Bramwood before sliding his eyes back to me. "But in return for my generosity your Mr. Pendragon will address the newspapermen as quickly as I can assemble them. I will expect him at my office at eleven o'clock. Five hours from now. Do let him know, won't you?"

I nodded again, certain my voice would not work.

"You're lucky I don't throw you both in the brig!" the major growled, pounding his fist on the carriage ceiling and setting it in motion at once.

The door slammed shut as it glided away, leaving me standing there as the first pink tendrils of the rising sun stretched across the sky in an effort to abate the cold. My brain and insides took turns revolting as I made way down the central parade route toward Trafalgar. Time was even a more precious commodity now, yet I could not stop myself from walking back to our flat until a lumbering carriage crossed my path, making it impossible to ignore. Only then did I halfheartedly hail it and allow myself to be delivered home with some haste. I paused on the steps of our flat and pulled out my watch: four and a half hours left.

I let myself in and gently swung the door shut. My head ached and I don't believe my stomach could have been more sour if I had licked the floor. I poked my head into the kitchen and caught Mrs. Behmoth stirring a pot. She glared at me with a knit brow and said, "Wot?"

"Something smells good," I lied.

"Porridge," she tsked. "Same as yesterday, same as tomorrow."

"Yes, of course. Colin still home?"

" 'E's in the bath."

"Good," I said for no reason, and got a scowl for my efforts. "And Lady Priscilla?"

"Asleep in me room, so don't go disturbin' 'er. She's 'ad enough without you pawin' 'er. Now go on."

I moved back to the foyer and looked at the stairs. There was nothing else to do but go up.

By the time I reached the bathroom door I had already considered a half-dozen ways to break the news to Colin. Even so, as I raised my fist to knock I had yet to settle on the best.

"What is it?" his voice drifted out.

"It's me," I answered, poking my head inside.

"Hurry up. Don't let the cold air in." He was reclining in the tub with a wet cloth draped across his face. "How did everything go?"

I closed the door and leaned against it, glad his face was covered. "W-w-well . . . ," I stammered.

"He didn't show up?" Colin mumbled through the cloth.

"He showed up." I sucked in a ragged breath. "And Major Hampstead was with him."

"Hampstead? What the hell was he doing there?"

"Looking for me. He knew I had coerced Corporal Bramwood into giving me the letter. The poor young man looked terrified."

"Pity."

"But that isn't the worst of it—" My voice cracked and I clumsily cleared my throat. "Because of my manipulation of Corporal Bramwood, the major is demanding that you be at his office at eleven to address the newsmen. I'm so sorry, Colin."

He reached up and dragged the cloth from his face to reveal an expression of grim determination. "You have nothing to be sorry for. I have been an utter fool about this case. Hand me a towel, would you?" he said as he bolted up, sending water everywhere.

"What?" I asked, unsure I'd really heard him correctly.

"Eleven will be fine, though there is much to be done by then. What time is it now?"

"Half past six."

"Four and a half hours . . . ," he muttered, hopping out of the tub and tying the towel about his waist. "We will do this," he vowed as he flung the door open and burst from the room. I stood there a moment, fully startled, unable to think of anything better to do than lean over and yank the plug from the drain. *"Come on!"* I heard him holler. And that was all I needed to go rushing after him.

CHAPTER 34

I was tasked with two errands to be accomplished in just a hair less than two hours. It seemed a credible request, yet I was keenly aware that the slightest event unaccounted for would be enough to delay me past the nine forty-five deadline Colin had set for us to meet back at Buckingham. What concerned me, however, was that his timing determination hadn't taken into account the human factor, the very thing we had the least control over.

As my cab slowed among the row of houses lining Regent's Park, I leaned over and peered inside the small canvas bag nestled beside me. Lady Priscilla lay inside, curled up on a swirl of the pink blanket. The pug's fatigue was evident in that she didn't stir, her cream-colored chest rising and falling with the gentle rhythm of deep sleep. Lady Nesbitt-Normand would be ecstatic. Nevertheless, it was imperative for me to make a quick exit so I could get to Lancaster Gate as well. If the streets became impassable I would have little choice but to sprint or retreat into the Underground, two options wholly unappealing.

My furry companion and I were deposited outside the

Nesbitt-Normand home and quickly made our way up the circular drive. It was evident my young charge knew precisely where she was, as she suddenly woke up and began jostling about inside the bag the closer we got to the door. By the time I stood on the portico, the bag cradled in both arms, the pup's whimpering anticipation was incontestable. I couldn't help but laugh as I grabbed the bronze knocker and slammed it firmly.

Mrs. Holloway opened the door so quickly that I wondered if she hadn't been waiting right there. "Oh," she said with curiosity, "it's you, Mr. Pruitt."

"It is." I smiled. "Is Her Ladyship at home? I think she will be most pleased to receive me."

Mrs. Holloway's eyes dropped to the squirming bag in my arms and her breath caught. "Oh my," she gasped. "*Oh my!*" I grinned as she ushered me to the study. "Don't move," she gushed. "I shall have Lady Nesbitt-Normand here before you can even sit down." She ran from the study like a giggling schoolgirl, bounding up the stairs two at a time as though they were less than standard size.

I put the satchel containing Lady Priscilla onto the floor near the fireplace. The sides of the bag bulged and flattened randomly over the course of a minute and I knew the little pup was shuffling her blanket in anticipation of lying down again. She had no sooner settled when a blast of commotion drifted in from the foyer.

"Mrs. Holloway tells me you've brought some sort of parcel?!" Lady Nesbitt-Normand squealed as she burst into the study, Mrs. Holloway on her heels. "Tell me it's what I think . . . ," she begged, her face as full of hope as a youngster's on Christmas morning.

"Mrs. Holloway has not steered you wrong." I grinned, stepping back to reveal the little carrier now quite alive with motion and whining.

"Oh!" Lady Nesbitt-Normand nearly swooned at the sight,

a hand racing up to her chest as though her heart were on the verge of seizing. *"Oh my lord!"* she gasped as she rocketed forward like a tidal wave. *"My baby!"* she cried, scooping the frenzied dog out of the bag and into her arms. "It's a miracle. How did you find her? *Where* did you find her?"

"A dognapping ring," I answered as Colin had instructed. "Very bad business, but I think you will find your little lady all the same for it." It was as close to the truth as we could offer, given Colin's deal with Edwina Easterbrooke. "Mr. Pendragon disbanded the entire operation. I believe you will find your dear girl much safer now." And that, at least, was fully true.

"I am simply overcome!" Lady Nesbitt-Normand beamed as she pressed the little pup to her chest.

"There now," Mrs. Holloway piped up. "The day has gotten better already."

"It has . . . it has . . ." Lady Nesbitt-Normand agreed, plying Lady Priscilla with a bathing of kisses. "And to think how distraught I was just a short time ago."

"Had you lost faith in Mr. Pendragon?" I chided.

"Heavens no!" she squealed as the little pug batted at her face with an errant paw. "Not at all, Mr. Pruitt. It's Elsa. She left us during the night. Put some terrible note on her door and spirited away. Mrs. Holloway found it. What did it say?"

"That she felt responsible for Lady Priscilla's disappearance and had no option but to resign."

"Just dreadful," Lady Nesbitt-Normand muttered, putting the dog on the couch as she settled in beside her. "I suppose it *is* the noble thing to do, but I hardly relish finding a new trainer."

I shook my head with a smile even as I sidled toward the door. "Any trainer would be honored to work with such a beautiful ward. But you must excuse me, as I have business to attend to for Mr. Pendragon. May I give him your good wishes?"

"You may give him more than that!" Lady Nesbitt-Normand

heaved herself off the couch and went round to a desk on the far side of the room. "I had a bank draft prepared for him. I knew he would succeed." She tossed me a coquettish smile as she reached into one of the drawers and yanked out a check. "You shall give this to him with my deepest gratitude."

I glanced down at the draft as she handed it over and saw a number many times larger than what we had agreed upon. "Oh, madam," I almost choked, "you are too generous. We cannot possibly accept this amount for only three days' work."

"Fie." She waved me off. "You can and you will. I'll not hear another word about it. And you must give Mr. Pendragon one more thing."

"Of course." I nodded, now prepared to do whatever she asked. Even so, I was quite taken by surprise when she suddenly stepped forward and seized me in a great, plastering hug. The air heaved from my lungs as she squeezed me, and then just as abruptly she released me again and stepped back with a beatific smile.

"I am a fortunate woman," she said, "but you and Mr. Pendragon have returned the one blessing that means more to me than anything else in this world. I could never thank you enough."

The sincerity of her words struck me as much as the glistening tears that sprang to the corners of her eyes. "It has been our privilege," I said, my own emotion catching in my throat. I looked at Mrs. Holloway and found her grinning happily and could not help the smile that spread across my face. As I let my eyes drift over her shoulder to a clock on the far wall, however, my pleasure came to an immediate end: eight thirty-five. My smile curdled as I realized I had just over an hour to get all the way to Lady Stuart's and back to Buckingham, an assuredly impossible feat. I glanced back at the radiant face of Lady Nesbitt-Normand and in that instant was struck by the ideal solution.

CHAPTER 35

The small coach picked up speed as we turned the corner off Lancaster Gate and headed away from Lady Stuart's home toward Green Park by way of Bond Street. Lady Nesbitt-Normand's driver, Fletcher, was proving more than adept at guiding us around clogged streets and impassable alleyways, just as I had known he would be, which assuaged my guilt for having taken advantage of her gratitude to enlist his aid.

We rocketed through the turn into Green Park, the uneven cobbles rattling furiously beneath our wheels, as I pulled out my watch to discover that it was just past nine thirty; I would make it on time. Fletcher guided us around a steep corner and through a pocket of trees before, at last, we careened across the final leg to Buckingham Palace.

"Shall I wait for you?" he asked as we drew up to the massive bronze gates.

"No. You have done me a world of service. I cannot thank you enough." He tipped his hat and threw me a small smile as he pulled away.

The guard stationed at the gate seemed aware of my immi-

nent arrival and gestured to a younger guardsman who immediately ushered me inside the grounds. That young man handed
me off to yet another gentleman at the side portico who once
again led me down the same austere hallway I had traversed so
many times over the past three days. At last I was delivered to
the same meeting room Colin and I had been using from the
start.

Colin was already there, tilted back in a seat on the far side
of the table, his agitation evident by the speed with which a silver coin was being rotated between his fingers. I thanked my
escort and went inside, catching sight of a burlap sack tucked
under the table by Colin's feet. I was about to ask what he had
collected when he spoke up. "Thank heavens you've arrived
first."

"First?"

"We are about to be joined by three of the Life Guards, one
of whom I am certain is the killer. I'm afraid this is a most sad
and regrettable case made doubly so by our own circumstances.
Was Lady Stuart cooperative?"

"Without hesitation," I responded as I sat down beside him.
"But what are you talking about? You know who the killer is?
And what circumstances of ours?"

But he only waved me off. "I haven't time to tell you all I've
come to believe, but you must brace yourself for a most disturbing revelation," he said, his brow furrowing and his lips
drawing tight. "And there is one last thing I will need from
you. One last lie you must sell." My heart began to gallop again
as he quickly started to lay out my part. Before he could finish,
however, a clamor arose from the hallway and I knew the men
he had summoned were coming. "Follow my lead," he charged.
"You'll just have to figure out the rest as we go." My stomach
flopped as he pushed himself up, setting his feet firmly on the
floor with his hands folded neatly atop the table.

I glanced over to the door just as Major Hampstead came

bustling in with the dour rusty-headed Private O'Fallon and thin, loping Private Newcombe. That these were the three Colin had summoned did not surprise me, and yet, had I been forced to pick the guilty man, I knew I could not.

Major Hampstead, his oval face a vision of pinched angles and displeasure, spoke up first. "I find your beckoning us here an hour before you are to address the newsmen most disagreeable, Mr. Pendragon. If this is some sort of game then I shall thank you to not waste my time."

"I assure you it is no such thing," he answered, remaining stiffly upright in his chair. "There are some crucial aspects to this case that I have only just become aware of in the last several hours, and I feel I must outline them for you. I only ask your indulgence for a brief time before I face your cadre of newsmen, six hours earlier than we had originally agreed, I might add."

"That's not my fault," he shot back, his eyes shifting to me.

Colin raised a hand. "It hardly matters."

"I should think your time would be better spent memorizing the announcement I've had prepared for you."

"You have asked me to lie, Major. There is little preparation needed for that."

"I have asked you to make them believe it!" he snapped, his face as dark as the room's shadowed corners.

"Yes, yes." Colin waved him off. "Now if you don't mind, I do have a spot of time left. . . ."

For an instant I thought Major Hampstead might refuse to cooperate, but until Colin addressed the newsmen he retained the upper hand. With a tight nod, all three of the men reluctantly took a seat.

"Private Newcombe," Colin said smoothly, addressing the normally affable young man. "You will permit me to once again address the evening that cost your father his life?"

He shrugged, though I could tell he was already on edge. "If you must."

"Who did you tell me was with your father that night?"

He frowned and I noticed his eyes flick to the major. "Major Hampstead, Captain Bellingham, and Captain Morgesster. Same as the last time you asked me."

"Of course. And who told you what happened that night? That your father had been injured?"

"I don't remember."

"It was I, Mr. Pendragon." Major Hampstead spoke in a voice as chilled as frost. "I relayed the story to Private Newcombe. I was there, after all."

"Yes . . . so you were," Colin muttered. "So tell me, Major, will it surprise you then to discover that there was someone else with you that night?"

Private Newcombe frowned. "What?"

"Captain Morgesster—"

"—is an old flummoxed fool!" Major Hampstead growled.

"That old sot was always seeing double." Private Newcombe laughed. "It's why they retired him. You're making a mistake if you're paying heed to any of *his* stories."

"What about Captain Brady of the Irish Guard? He mentioned that *almost* all of the men from the Life Guard were officers that night. Funny word, 'almost.' " Colin shifted his gaze back to Major Hampstead.

"Either you are insinuating that my memory is at fault . . . ," he answered with rigid composure, ". . . or you are calling me a liar."

"I only mean to arrive at the truth," Colin said, forcing a smile that I'm sure we all recognized as hollow. "What that means with respect to your memory or reputation is beyond my control."

"Do not piss on me. I'm warning you."

"You're warning me of what?"

The major held his tongue but took that moment to glance at his watch.

"I don't understand." It was Private Newcombe who spoke up again. "What does that wretched night have to do with Captain Bellingham's murder anyway?"

"Everything," Colin answered as he shifted his eyes to Major Hampstead again. "Wouldn't you agree?"

The major calmly drew a breath and announced, "We are done here." He dangled his watch by its fob, spinning it around like a priceless gem. "I'm certain the majority of the newsmen have already arrived, and as you have failed to solve this case as we agreed, it is time for you to prepare." He pushed himself up from the table.

"If you are ignorant as to who committed these murders," Colin said with equal aplomb, "then how can you be so certain I have failed?"

"So now you mean to accuse me?!" he roared.

Colin shrugged as his eyebrows eased skyward.

Major Hampstead leaned forward with a sneer, locking his gaze on to Colin. "If you have an issue with me, Mr. Pendragon, then you shall take it up with me alone. I will not have you bandying about my reputation in front of my men." He spun on his two young privates. "You are both dismissed."

"Not just yet." Colin's grin was tight and threatening. "I still have some time left, Major, and if you don't live up to your part of our agreement then I shall have no choice but to present my case to your newsmen as I believe it to be true. You must understand, Major, that I am certain I have solved this crime."

"What?!" Private Newcombe's blasé countenance abruptly fell away. "What are you saying?"

No one spoke for a moment as Major Hampstead continued to glare at Colin. My heart was racing and I could not so much as draw a breath until after the major slowly lowered himself back into his seat.

"All right, Mr. Pendragon," he tersely allowed, "I will hear you out. But not with these men here."

"No concessions, Major. These men stay."

Major Hampstead's fury at Colin's unwillingness to be cowed was evident in both the deep furrow of his brow and the tight set of his mouth. "Have your say then," he growled through clenched teeth, "but unless you have a tintype of the deed being done you shall find my hand up your ass moving your lips to the words I decide in exactly thirty minutes!"

Colin's gaze did not waver. "We shall see. So let us begin with one simple question for you, Major: Who was the fifth person with you the night you were set upon by those Irish blokes?"

"Why do you keep bringing that blasted night up?" Private Newcombe stared from Colin to Major Hampstead, outright fury now flushing his cheeks.

Colin glanced at me and I knew it was time to spin the tale he had fed me. "There were three Irish lads," I spoke up, "all of whom were court-martialed and discharged from their guard as a result of your father's death." Having repeated what little truth we had, I began spinning the folly Colin had instructed me in. "We found one of those boys, Private. A scrawny lad who has yet to afford passage back to Ireland. It has left him right foul and he remembers the fifth person with the officers that night. A ginger, he said. And he remembers what started it all."

"I won't listen to this." Private Newcombe jumped up. "What my father was—killed my mum. I'm glad he's dead. He got what he deserved." And before any of us could react, he turned and fled, leaving a steely silence in his wake.

"Well"—Colin spoke gravely—"I suppose Private Newcombe has made the point all of us fear the most. Besides which, he's not a ginger anyway. But you, Private O'Fallon"—he turned to the pale young man seated next to Major Hampstead—"you rather fit that description."

"So what?"

"Come now, Mr. Pendragon," Major Hampstead scoffed. "What sort of drivel is this?"

"Will you still think it drivel when I ask Mr. Pruitt to bring the young Irish rogue in here to identify Private O'Fallon?"

"Bollocks!" the major barked too harshly. "You haven't the time for such a thing. You're out of tricks, Mr. Pendragon."

Colin nodded to me and I stood up, just as he had warned that I would need to, and began heading for the door. "I believe Mr. Pruitt mentioned that the Irish bloke is right foul," Colin reminded with utter calm. "Which has made him most eager to be of assistance. Came right over this morning—"

"So what?" Private O'Fallon glared at Colin, ignoring me as I passed behind him. "So what if I was there that night?"

"Shut the hell up!" the major snapped.

The faintest smirk edged onto Colin's face as I stopped. "So what indeed?" he said, leaning back in his chair. "There's certainly no law that states a private cannot be seen in public with his ranking officers. And yet, until this very moment with the threat of an eyewitness, neither of you has ever mentioned that you were there that night. I cannot help but wonder why."

"It would seem there has been some misunderstanding, Mr. Pendragon." The major spoke in a condescending tone as I quietly returned to my seat. "You weren't asked to enquire into the death of Captain Newcombe. That travesty has already been dealt with."

"Ah!" Colin said as he held a finger up. "Now you see, Major, there's the thing. I'm quite convinced that the genesis of Captain Bellingham's murder was born that same night. But then I would wager you have suspected that all along."

"I have no idea what you're insinuating."

"Oh, come now. The ramifications of that night were swift and severe. Captain Newcombe died within days and the three Irish blokes were instantly discharged without honor. Nevertheless, no formal charges of murder were ever brought against them for the simple reason that no one knew who actually delivered the fatal blow to Captain Newcombe. There appeared to be fault all around—even among the five of you."

"That is absolute rubbish," Major Hampstead sneered. "You are flailing about like a fool."

"Am I? Then let us consider the other repercussions of that night: Captain Morgesster forcibly retired within the month, rumors of your promotion to lieutenant colonel silenced, and the once jovial Captain Bellingham left inexplicably sullen and secretive. Why?"

"You have no idea what you're talking about!" the major roared.

"Oh, but I do," Colin said grimly. "Private Newcombe made that clear just now."

"*He said nothing!*" But in spite of his indignation Major Hampstead did not move.

"It was the very thing that bound the five of you together," Colin continued. "The truth that leaves Captain Morgesster perpetually besotted and blathering on about hummingbirds and bees leaving each other in peace. It's why Private Newcombe abhorred his father."

"You're playing a treacherous game, Mr. Pendragon."

"It is far from a game," he answered at once. "I certainly have no right to judge the determinations a man comes to understand about his own life. If you are the least bit clever, Major, you have long since figured that out. But you denigrate the uniform you wear when you seek to muddy the facts of these terrible murders to cover your own self-loathing."

"How dare you—"

Colin's hand shot up. "Don't. You sully the best of what any of us can hope for with your continual lying. Now I'm almost out of time and you *will* want to hear me out before you set me in front of your newsmen." He pushed himself to his feet and walked around to the far side of the room. "I must admit, at first I didn't see the correlation between the brawl at McPhee's and the murder of Captain Bellingham, but that was before I realized how dire the outcome of that night had proven to be for him. I only realized it after I saw the letter he had given to Corporal Blevins for Lady Stuart. Where I made my mistake was in thinking that Captain Bellingham had *written* it. Something you were happy to have me believe." He flashed a tight grin.

"So let me tell you what I believe happened that night," he went on. "The argument with the Irish lads started as a direct consequence of Private O'Fallon's being in attendance. I'm guessing it was one of the first times he ever joined the four of you. The Irish blokes recognized you, Private, as having once been with their regiment. Yet there you were sitting at a table with four older men from the British detail, men who had a whispered reputation for being different. While there may not have been any proof to those inferences, I think we can all agree that gossip is more insidious than truth anyway.

"You were there at the behest of Captain Bellingham. In fact, you were very much *with* him that night. A heady feeling, wasn't it?" He did not wait for a response. "But as the drink flowed and you allowed it to steal your restraint, you never noticed that your Irish brethren did not like what they were seeing. Eventually, someone said something; it hardly matters who. With honor at stake and inhibitions well drowned, things got out of hand. We all know the end result."

Major Hampstead glanced at his watch, only this time I saw that his hand was noticeably unsteady. "That's a rich story," he muttered with feigned indifference. "Perhaps you will regale us with the rest when there is more time."

"I will finish it now, thank you," Colin said as he continued to slowly circle the room. "At first I thought Captain Bellingham had escaped any consequences from that night, but he hadn't at all. Given that he had a wife and young child, it was made clear to him that a stable family life would spare him permanent sanctions. Which, no matter what lay in his heart, meant that he had to be rid of you, Private O'Fallon.

"And so he determined to be." Colin moved back to our side of the table and sat down. "He ended your liaison only to discover that you had no intention of letting go. You remained enamored with someone who could not"—he shook his head—"would not feel the same."

The private shifted in his chair and Major Hampstead reached over and gripped his arm, effectively holding him in his seat.

"It was Lady Stuart who corrected me," Colin pointed out. "Captain Bellingham didn't write that letter threatening some unutterable outcome if she didn't return his affections; *you* wrote that letter." He settled his gaze on Private O'Fallon. "And when you didn't get your way, you wrested your revenge."

Private O'Fallon said nothing, but his hands had balled into fists and his face looked as ferocious as the malignancy I now realized him to be. Major Hampstead slowly released his hold on the young man's arm and let his gaze drift over to a far corner of the room, his expression stony.

"Shall I go on?"

Major Hampstead made no move to acknowledge the question that precipitated Private O'Fallon to growl, "I don't give a bloody fig what you do. You've no proof!"

Colin leaned over and fished out a pair of shiny boots from the sack by his feet and set them on the table. "Are these yours, Private?"

The young man glared at them but did not answer.

"Let me help you," Colin said, reaching out to reveal Private O'Fallon's name etched on the inside of both boots. "I do believe that's you."

"Where did you get those?" he seethed.

"From your flat. I admit to having made up a bit of a story for your flatmates, but it was worth it when I discovered the most astonishing thing." He flipped the boots over to reveal one sole hastily cleaned while the other was as pristine as the day it had been cobbled. "They're obviously not new. You can see the heels are worn a bit toward the outside on both of them." He glanced up. "You might watch your posture, Private. These would indicate you have a tendency to lean back when you walk with your hips rotated forward. That's what's causing the uneven wear."

"Piss off."

Colin flashed a deadly grin. "Look at the bottom of your left boot—" He shoved it forward. "It looks like it's just been taken from its box. Not so much as a speck of dirt stuck between the crevices of its corrugated tread. An amazing feat, Private O'Fallon, and one that must have taken days and many tiny utensils to accomplish. All of which makes sense when I consider the single boot print left behind in the blood beneath the chair where you tortured and killed Captain Bellingham. A print from a left boot. I would guess you noticed it too."

"A clean boot," Private O'Fallon scoffed. "That's what you've got?"

"I've got the letter you wrote to Captain Bellingham."

I don't know who was more startled, me or Major Hampstead, as Colin reached back into the sack at his feet and pulled out what looked to be the same folded letter I had handed to the major hours before. "You will forgive me the hurried copy I made last night, Major, but this is the original." He laid it on the table before reaching down and pulling out a few sheets of blank paper, a pen, and a small inkwell and shoving them across at Private O'Fallon. "Why don't you do me the favor of penning a copy of this note? I believe we will find a convincing match." He gestured to the boots. "Of course, just looking at how you've written your name inside your boots one can see the similarities. Look how you make your *Os*. . . ."

Private O'Fallon made no move to take the pen, his eyes filled with contempt.

"Come, come." Colin grabbed the pen and shook it at him. "Let me get you started." He set one of the blank pages down, dipped the pen into the small bottle of ink, and began to write, reading aloud as he did, *"How heavy is my heart that I should find myself putting these words to paper."* He glared at the private as he flipped the sheet around. "You see"—his voice was heavy and dark—"nothing like the original."

Major Hampstead glanced at the paper, but Private O'Fallon kept his eyes riveted to Colin.

"Next line, Private . . . ," Colin prodded. "It says, *I loved you with everything I had . . .* That might have been touching if you hadn't murdered him. Tell me, did you torture Captain Bellingham to try and coax some equally profound sentiment from him? Didn't anyone ever tell you that only love freely given has any real value? You cannot burn affection and devotion out of another person!" he snarled, and I could not help but recoil at the cruelty of it.

"Go to hell," Private O'Fallon's voice rumbled from somewhere deep. "He was a bloody coward. You're all bloody cowards. Not me. I'll not be cowed by anyone."

A cold look settled onto Colin's face as he studied the young man. "I am afraid, Private O'Fallon, that you have seriously misjudged yourself. For you are the *worst* sort of coward. Love is not a demand, it is a gift. That is what makes it so valuable. But you have left the carnage of innocents in your wake. You have robbed it of any value whatsoever and will have the rest of your pitiable life to think about that."

To my utter amazement, Private O'Fallon cracked a crooked smile in response. "And that is where *you* are wrong,

Mr. Pendragon." And before I could even begin to guess at what he meant, he jumped up and pulled a small derringer from beneath his vivid red coat and in a single fluid motion shoved it into his mouth and fired, spraying the back of his head against the wall behind him.

CHAPTER 36

My mouth felt as though I had been sucking on a wad of cotton and my stomach was worse. I was certain I wouldn't be able to eat again for some time to come. Yet all of it paled in comparison to the throbbing of my head. Even though I was sitting completely still in Major Hampstead's office, it was all I could do to keep from crying out from the pain. The major looked little better. We had fled there as soon as the coroner had been summoned.

It was evident by the major's every movement that he was as stunned as I, but it didn't appear the same could be said for Colin. His composure had returned with the arrival of the first guardsman who had come running at the sound of a shot being fired in the palace. Colin was also the first to remind the major that we had to focus on what should be told to the newspapermen, for it was too late to back out now. So we had moved to his office and struck a fast agreement. Colin had laid it out, but then there had been few options. And only after that was done did Colin finally ask, "Am I right about what happened at McPhee's that night, Major?"

His answer took a moment to come, but as he spoke it was easy to see he was well rid of the weight of it. "It is a terribly difficult thing to be a man who does not fit right in his world. It forever needles."

"I can assure you that Mr. Pruitt and I understand only too well. Nevertheless, there are choices people make—"

"Choices thrust upon us," the major corrected.

"Only if you let them be."

Major Hampstead tsked. "You're being naïve, Mr. Pendragon. I'm certain you know better than that. For in the end, if a man does not fit in, then he is forever exiled from society."

"Which is hardly a terrible thing, if you ask me," Colin said, arching an eyebrow. "I'll not be boxed in by anyone else's ideals."

"And yet"—the major's eyes dimmed—"the fact of your discretion would seem to state otherwise."

"What I do is no one else's business," he answered.

The major chuckled. "You are a public figure, Mr. Pendragon; it is everyone else's business. Suffice to say that those of us not fortunate enough to dwell on the outskirts of convention do our best to fulfill what is expected of us. Some with more success than others." He shook his head. "Would it surprise you to learn that I am married and have a daughter? My family lives in Oxfordshire, but our poor girl isn't right. Prances about like a four-year-old even though she's nearly twenty. Requires constant attention. My wife blames me, of course." He sagged. "I wonder if she isn't right." He brushed a hand through his thinning hair and exhaled, his body crumpling further.

"I met Edmund Morgesster first. He was a proud man who devoted his entire life to the Queen's Guard. The only one of us who can claim that. He introduced me to Wilford Newcombe. Extraordinary men, the both of them, and honorable friends. It made it easier for a while, having someone to share such thoughts with, but mostly we just drank to forget." He fell silent a moment.

"Trevor Bellingham joined our rank about six years ago. He and Gwendolyn were enduring difficult times; Trevor was suffering doubts, terrified that he was losing his mind. . . ." He shook his head again. "Always the same things. Edmund, Wilford, and I offered what solace we could, but we all urged him to make another go of it with Gwendolyn. It was his only chance at a normal life. But things between them were never right again.

"Trevor went through terrible periods of melancholy after that. It made me fear for him at times. At some point Gwendolyn confided her own anguish to her brother, Sergeant Mulrooney. He took it upon himself to begin taunting Trevor, spreading gossip. . . ." He closed his eyes a moment. "The sergeant never stopped menacing Trevor after that. It was just the way of it. . . ." He rubbed his forehead and I wondered if he wasn't suffering the same headache I was.

"It is a devastating burden you men have carried all these years," I spoke up. "It contributed to my own undoing once."

He glanced down at the floor. "Thank you, Mr. Pruitt."

Colin sat forward in his chair, a look of pain and determination fleeting past his eyes. "I'm afraid we have a roomful of newsmen waiting for us, Major, and I should very much like to hear about that night at McPhee's before I speak with them. . . ."

"Yes. . . ." He pushed himself up and sucked in a deep breath. "Of course. About a year ago Private O'Fallon moved from the Irish Guard to the Life Guard. He had been having trouble getting along with his mates, fighting, mouthing off. . . . We were his last chance before a discharge." He glanced at Colin. "How cruel fate can be."

"You had no way of knowing—" I started to say before realizing the ignorance in my words.

Colin filled in my abrupt silence by asking, "Is that when

the relationship between Captain Bellingham and Private O'Fallon began?"

"It was. And like old fools Edmund, Wilford, and I were happy for them. We thought perhaps the two of them could achieve what none of us had ever been able to do." He looked up and his eyes were hollow, his expression filled with regret. "Private O'Fallon was like a fawn, hanging on Trevor's every word and movement. And Trevor allowed it. He liked it. Anyone could see that. Mulrooney and those Irish lads saw it. It was Mulrooney who got them incited that night. Only he was smart enough to take off before the violence started. After that . . ." He let his voice trail off.

"And no one was tried for the murder of Captain Newcombe because none of you could admit why the fight had started and the Irish lads dared not say."

He nodded. "It was classified as just another tavern brawl, though this time it ended in a man's death. Those Irish bastards were happy to get away with their lives. Mulrooney wasn't even implicated. The rest of us were sanctioned for gross misconduct: Edmund shunted out to pasture, my career capped on the eve of the promotion I'd been steering the whole of my life toward, and Trevor was warned that one more misstep would mean the end of his service."

"And Private O'Fallon?"

He looked away a minute before speaking. "We made a pact to cover for him. We thought him nothing more than a foolish boy at the beginning of his career." He shut his eyes, clearly pained at the memory. "Trevor swore he'd end their affair and I knew he meant it."

"After he was killed, did you suspect . . . ?"

He snapped his eyes back to Colin. "I am not such a monster."

"And yet you hired me for no other reason than to avert a meddlesome press. Surely you had some notion . . ."

"I . . ." He started to say something, but did not continue.

There was a reticent knock on the door as Corporal Bramwood peered in, his face as ashen as his major's. "The newsmen are impatient, sir."

"Yes." Colin stood up and tugged on his jacket. "Let's get this done with."

I took a seat at the back of the great hall, a sea of heads in front of me, coughing, whispering, nodding, and fairly aching for a chance to shout questions. Colin moved directly to the dais, looking every bit the man in charge, the major appearing stooped and drawn as he followed in his wake.

". . . the perpetrator was apprehended . . . ," Colin was already saying as I struggled to pay attention, ". . . but through no fault of Her Majesty's illustrious Guard, he was able to get his hands on a pistol and take his own life."

"*Mr. Pendragon!*" A man in a dark suit jumped to his feet. "Did the man know Captain Bellingham and his family?"

"It is evident he took great pains to watch the comings and goings of the Bellingham family before deciding to wreak this terrible brutality. This was the act of an infected mind. We can be grateful that the captain and his wife did not suffer at the end." It was the only story that allowed both Captain Bellingham and Her Majesty's Life Guard to emerge with their honor and reputations intact.

A scuffling of feet to my left caught my attention and I turned to see Inspector Varcoe entering with a contingent of his men. I knew he would be outraged at Colin's having laid to rest another case the Yard had been unable to solve, though they had hardly been given the opportunity.

I pressed my eyes closed to try to soothe the skirmish raging in my brain even as indictments for further information on the perpetrator were being shouted at Colin and the major. This assemblage of men were not about to be shunted aside for inanities when there was a front-page story to be ferreted out.

"Isn't he full of himself?" The grating voice erupted so close to my ear that I snapped my eyes open, immediately renewing the excruciating din inside my head. I stared into the inspector's sneering gaze. "How do you stomach that pompous ass?"

Relieved to find the conference already breaking up, I forced myself to my feet without answering and ambled to the front, where Colin and Major Hampstead were making a hasty exit out a rear door. I had no idea the inspector was following me until I heard Colin say, "Always a pleasure, Emmett."

"Sod off, Pendragon!" he snapped as we all pushed through to the back hallway. "And a hell of a display from you, Major. Yard not good enough to take care of your business?"

"Protocol!" he snapped.

"*Protocol my ass!* It was a cold-blooded murder and I will *not* be shut out again. What sort of message do you think that sends to the people of this city?"

"I'm sure they assume you are still working the Ripper case," Colin parried.

"That is *not* my case!" Varcoe blasted. "And isn't it fitting you should solve this case so rapidly, Pendragon. Takes an aberrant to spot an aberration."

I could sense Colin on the verge of clouting him, so I discreetly reached out and touched his upper arm, not at all surprised to find his muscles coiled and ready to strike. He relaxed beneath my fingertips and a moment later turned to exchange a quiet word with Major Hampstead. After that, the two of us made our leave of Buckingham for the last time.

CHAPTER 37

Mrs. Behmoth came pounding up the stairs with our afternoon tea just as Colin finished another round of exercises with his dumbbells. He leapt up and swooped over to her, taking the tray and spiriting it to the table near where I was writing.

"You still on 'bout that last case?" she asked as she dropped onto the settee.

"I am." I looked up from the sea of papers piled around me and wondered what else she thought I might be doing.

"It's been two weeks already," she muttered as she slapped Colin's hands away and began fixing the tea. "Yer usin' too many words. Ya always use too many words."

I scowled as she handed our cups to Colin. "Ethan knows what he's doing," he defended, plunking my teacup onto the desk with enough force to cause a bit of it to splatter across several pages.

"Hey!"

"Watch yerself." Mrs. Behmoth chuckled. "That's yer legacy you're buggerin' with. You make a mess outta that and you'll be tellin' yer own story."

"That case won't see a printer's press for a good many years to come," he said. "I'm afraid few would find the truth palatable, and besides, I've just told a very different tale to the men of the press."

"You types keep shootin' each other and you blokes'll always be on the outside," Mrs. Behmoth said as she chewed on a biscuit.

"We are not shooting each other." Colin scowled. "In fact, most of us are quite invisible, so what harm can there be in any of it?"

"Tell that to your Mr. Wilde." She snickered.

I frowned at her as I picked up a page near the end of my chronicle. "What I still don't understand is what made you go to Private O'Fallon's flat to look at his boots in the first place?"

"It was a hunch." Colin shrugged, sauntering over to the fireplace with his tea. "When Major Hampstead demanded I meet with the newsmen six hours earlier I knew I had to be close to the truth. And getting our hands on that letter had precipitated his sudden demand. A letter we had just learned had *not* been written by Captain Bellingham, a fact I am certain the major knew the moment he saw it. It made me reconsider all of the men in the regiment we had met, and Private O'Fallon struck me the most. For three reasons, actually—"

I snatched up one of my earlier pages and piped up, "He was the first to suggest that something untoward had been going on between Captain Bellingham and Lady Stuart."

"Indeed." Colin gave me a sly grin. "And he was an Irish lad not serving with the Irish Guard. I found that most peculiar, and when I made some enquiries I learned that he'd once been mates with the Irish blokes responsible for the death of Private Newcombe's father. It was too coincidental to be easily dismissed. However, the most important thing of all"—his brow knit fiercely—"was the last night we spoke to him, when I referred to Captain Bellingham in the possessive: *your captain*. I had done it many times before when speaking with Sergeant McReedy, Private Newcombe, and Corporal Blevins, yet only Private O'Fallon became incensed at my perceived inference, demanding to know what I was implying."

"I remember that," I said, setting my pen aside.

"It's just tragic," Mrs. Behmoth muttered. "Me and my mister had quite the fire in our day too, but it weren't worth killin' over. When he died . . ." She heaved a sigh. "Thirty-five years ago. Can that be?" She glanced at Colin. "You was just four. Ya 'ave any memory of 'im?" He shook his head. "Just as well. He'd a spoilt ya fer the rest of 'em."

"I very much doubt anyone could have kept me from Ethan."

"There's a lot coulda kept you two apart." She glared over the rim of her cup at him. "You don't know half—" But a sudden pounding at our door kept her from continuing that thought. "We expectin' anyone?" she asked as she pushed herself off the settee. We were not.

As she trudged down the stairs, her heavy footfalls marking her progress, I decided that whoever it was had real business with us, since their pounding had grown in both rapidity and timber. My curiosity was assuaged in due course as she appeared back at the top of the stairs with a slight, lovely woman of middle years beside her. But while Mrs. Behmoth's face was flush from her exertions, the woman next to her was ghostly white.

"Mrs. Annabelle Connicle," Mrs. Behmoth announced. "Go on in, me dear. I'll get ya a cup fer some tea."

"Thank you," she answered in a delicate, almost toneless voice as Mrs. Behmoth took to the stairs again.

"Do come in, Mrs. Connicle." Colin smiled and gestured to her. "Make yourself at home and tell us what we can do for you."

She stepped inside, her skirts rustling as she stopped just behind the settee, gripping its back tightly. "Mr. Pendragon—"

Her voice caught and she looked down at the floor a moment, taking a deep breath before slowly starting again. "It's my husband. Something awful has happened. There's no trace of him"—her eyes began to well with tears—"only splatters of blood—" Her voice hitched as her fingers tightened on the back of the settee. "It is everywhere—" And before she could finish the sentence her eyes abruptly rolled up and she collapsed to the floor.

I rushed over and seized her hand, finding it cold and clammy, though her breathing was steady. As I yanked the coverlet off the back of the couch and laid it over her, I made a cursory check of her head and face to see if she had injured herself. Thankfully, she had not.

"Is she all right?" Colin asked.

"She's just fainted."

He nodded and went over to the stairs and called down, "Mrs. Behmoth, we've a fainter up here."

"I'm comin'."

"Get her on the settee," I ordered.

"Right." He swept her into his arms and delicately placed her on the sofa. "Now wake her up, Ethan, so we can find out what she was on about," he pestered. I turned to level a scowl at him only to find that I could not when I saw the spark of thrall in his eyes. He had already taken the case.

ACKNOWLEDGMENTS

There are many people to whom I owe a debt of gratitude for their efforts on this book. The staff at Kensington have been so enthusiastic and encouraging that I simply cannot thank them enough. In particular I have received thoughtful guidance and support from John Scognamiglio every step of the way. Vida Engstrand has been tireless, and Kristine Mills has continued to thrill me with her creative and eye-catching covers.

Once again I owe heaps of thanks to Diane Salzberg, Karen Clemens, and Melissa Gelineau, who all read multiple drafts and never hesitated to ask great questions and press me to reach higher. My agent, Kathy Green, had a particular impact on this story, and I am grateful to her for that. John Paine also gave me solid encouragement and direction very early on and helped me find my way.

I must also call out the extraordinary support I have received from family and friends. It has been truly humbling.

In writing a story set in the past, many hazards abound. People much smarter than I may detect errors in the history I have unfurled, and I take full responsibility for the liberties I took. Some were allowed for the sake of the tale while others, I fear, are the result of too much daydreaming when I was in school. Either way, those belong to me alone.

The only other person I must acknowledge is Russ Hoffman, for his impact upon these stories is as vast as the hole he left behind.

Thank you everyone!

Please turn the page for an exciting sneak peek of
Gregory Harris's next Colin Pendragon Mystery

THE CONNICLE CURSE

coming in March 2015!

CHAPTER 1

Annabelle Connicle was right: The blood was everywhere.

We had accompanied her back to her home in West Hampton, Colin as eager to see the scene of what sounded like a ghastly attack as I was to make certain she reached her home safely. The poor woman had already fainted once in our study and remained as pallid as milk glass, her lips tinged blue and her eyes so drawn and red that she looked not to have slept in days.

Several Scotland Yard carriages were on site by the time we arrived at the Connicle estate. Mrs. Connicle had sent for them even as she herself had rushed to our Kensington flat to implore Colin's help. While it was the right thing to do, it was bound to prove problematic for Colin and me given that the Yard's senior inspector, Emmett Varcoe, was eternally envious of Colin's flawless record for solving the crimes we were brought in on. The one thing I was happy to note, however, was that the coroner's wagon was nowhere to be found. A positive sign that not only was there no body to collect, but also that the reprehensible coroner, Denton Ross, would not be here. That suited me just fine.

Mrs. Connicle had insisted we come inside despite the fact that I knew Colin to be far more interested in the gaggle of bobbies circling the gardener's shed in the side yard. The house was a hush of shadows and unease as we entered, the shades drawn, presumably to block any view of the work being done by the Yard. It took a moment for my eyes to adjust before I noticed the black-suited, heavyset man with a balding pate sitting in the drawing room and the girl in maid's attire pacing the floor behind him. The instant the door swung back with a resounding *click*, the girl twirled about and bolted toward us.

"Oh, Mrs. Connicle," she gasped. "Thank heavens you're back."

"That's enough now, Letty," Mrs. Connicle said heavily as she steered the girl—for she didn't look older than her middle teens—to the young housekeeper who had presented herself upon our entrance. "Go with Miss Porter now. I simply haven't the heart to deal with your fretting." Miss Porter, a pretty, slight, brown-haired woman meticulous in her deportment and dress, stepped up right on cue, ushering the quavering girl out of the room with a finesse that suggested she had done it before. "You must forgive me." Mrs. Connicle sagged into the nearest chair, her tiny, winsome frame nearly swallowed by its generous dimensions. "I'm afraid I am quite done in."

"Annabelle . . ." The portly man stood up and moved to us, adjusting a pair of glasses clinging to the bridge of his nose. I could tell at once, both by the suit he wore and the leather satchel he carried, that he was a doctor. "You have suffered a tremendous shock, and I am certain these men understand that." He glanced at me before quickly flicking his eyes to Colin. "I take it Annabelle has retained your services to look into this . . . this business, Mr. Pendragon?"

Colin gave him a stiff smile. "And you would be?"

"Doctor Benjamin Renholme." He stuck out his hand, but

did not offer a smile. "I've seen to Annabelle for years. Edmond less so. He could be quite dismissive of the medical arts."

"Past tense?" Colin fished idly.

A disapproving frown settled onto the doctor's face. "I take it you have yet to see the shed?"

Mrs. Connicle groaned, and Colin gave her a gentle smile before turning back to the doctor. "Sometimes people say things they do not mean, and other times they spill what they did not intend. It can be a razor's edge."

The doctor took a moment before he gave a stiff nod. "No doubt. I'll take no umbrage. All that matters is that you discern what has become of Edmond." His words elicited another moan from Mrs. Connicle that finally stole his full attentions as he swooped over to her. "Come now, Annabelle. I have prepared a tincture of laudanum to help you relax. There is nothing more for you to do but let these men have a look about. I must insist you go upstairs and get some rest."

"I cannot rest until I know what has happened," she mewled in the most pitiful voice.

"We will let you know the moment there is anything to report," Colin said. "The doctor is right: You must attend to yourself just now."

She gazed at him, her thin, drawn face a mask of pain. "All right," she muttered. "All right . . ."

Dr. Renholme shoved his glasses up onto his forehead as he bent forward to help her to her feet. She leaned against him, and he guided her from the room with the gentle assurance of a man of his profession. Even so, the moment they disappeared, Colin turned to me with a frown. "It seems to me that man is awfully full of himself."

I couldn't help chuckling. "You know . . . ," I said as we were finally able to head out of the house for the side yard, ". . . there are those who would say the same about you."

He shot me an unamused scowl. "Little, pesky, small-minded people, I should think." And this time, I did not try to suppress my laughter.

The moment we cleared the corner of the house the phalanx of bobbies milling about became instantly apparent; so many that the little gardener's shed was almost inconspicuous amongst the quantity of navy blue uniforms. Oddly, it appeared that nothing more was happening than idle conversation and the general passage of time. If a crime had been committed, it seemed lost on this leisurely band.

"Do you see Varcoe?" Colin asked.

"No. But you know he's here somewhere."

He pursed his lips. "Pity," he bothered to say as we reached the nearest cluster of men. "Excuse me . . ."

The young officer we were nearest to turned from his companions with a frown. "Excuse yourself," he snapped. "You can't be here. This is official Scotland Yard business."

His companions broke into laughter. "Don't you know whom you're talking to, Lanchester?" clucked one of the older men.

He glared at Colin. "Should I?"

"You're a tosser," the older man snickered. "You're telling me you've never seen a picture of Colin Pendragon?" He turned to Colin with a mocking scoff. "These young buggers don't have a lick of class. Don't let him bruise your ego. Not that he could," he added as he and his buddies brayed laughter.

"Pithy," Colin answered with a spectacularly forced smile. "But tell me, what have you good men of the Yard determined thus far?"

Unfortunately young Constable Lanchester found his tongue first. "I don't think that's any concern of yours, Mr. Pendragon," he shot back, punching Colin's name as though it tasted bitter on his tongue.

"Lighten up," another of the more seasoned men cajoled, a sergeant I recognized by the name of Maurice Evans. "There's